The
DOOM BRAE
Witch

Colin Youngman

The Works of Colin Youngman:

The Doom Brae Witch

Alley Rat

DEAD Heat

Twists*

*Incorporates:

DEAD Lines
Brittle Justice
The Refugee
A Fall Before Prid
Vicious Circle

All the above are also available separately

Colin Youngman

A SprintS Publication

Copyright 2019 © Colin Youngman

ISBN: 978-1-7942-4161-9

DEDICATION

For Chris

Table of Contents

The blackest chapter in the history of witchcraft lies not in the malevolence of witches but in the deliberate gloating of their prosecutors

Thelda Kenyon

CHAPTER ONE

The dawn sun cast gilded shadows over a patchwork quilt of golden corn and lush fallow land. Swallow and swift darted overhead, horses whinnied in a stable bank, and dormice clung to ears of corn like sailors in the rigging.

Louisa Goodchild remained oblivious to the idyll around her. She sprinted over the fields, at once breathless and adrenalin-fuelled. She hopped twice on one foot while she removed a shoe, then pulled off the other. Louisa hoisted her skirts and set off once more, glancing behind at her pursuer.

Lord Edwin Pendlebury, youngest son of the Earl of Doom Brae, ran after her. He, too, gasped for breath in the thin air. Neither his tight leather boots nor his long-tailed jacket helped his cause but, ever-so-slowly, he closed the distance between them. He stumbled as he ran, clawed ape-like at the ground as he continued uphill, before he regained his footing.

Louisa glanced back once more, golden hair streaming behind her like maypole ribbons. Far below, Doom Brae manor was little more than an ornate doll's house amidst neglected gardens as she increased her stride and veered right towards Bluebell Wood.

Before she knew it, Edwin had reached her. His hand touched her back, enough to send her tumbling, and she felt his weight upon her.

Louisa's breath came in sharp bursts. Her bosom heaved and quivered above her corset. But she found the energy to giggle. Lord Pendlebury laughed, too. They lay next to each other, panting in unison, unable to speak from the exertion.

Gradually, their breathing subsided. Louisa's hair fanned over the grass like a cluster of buttercups. Eyes the colour of sky searched Edwin Pendlebury's face as it hovered inches above hers. She felt his breath, warm and welcoming as a summer breeze, as he lowered his face to hers.

Abruptly, she turned her head to one side. "Edwin," she paused. It still seemed strange to call his Lordship by name, even after three weeks of togetherness. "You know no good can come of this. Your father will never give his blessing."

Lord Pendlebury rolled onto his back. Gazed up at cotton-bud clouds. He released a sigh. "Does he need to know? Is it of such importance?"

She pushed herself onto her elbows. "Of course, it is."

"Why? If it's what we desire…"

"Because he's your father. He's the Earl. You have so much to lose."

Edwin closed his eyes. "I have nothing to lose but you. All this," he made a circular motion with his hand, "All this shall belong to Felix when father passes. He is father's heir, not I."

"Then, we should tell him."

"I wish it could be so."

A heavy silence hung over the couple. Louisa spoke first. "Tell him, Edwin."

He shook his head. "You don't know father as I do. You see him as the Laird of Doom Brae, he sees you as a maid. And I see him for what he is."

"You talk in riddles, Edwin."

"It's better that way, believe me."

"So, what now?"

His eyes sparkled. "Now, I kiss you."

"My good Sir, you wouldn't be taking advantage of a kitchen-maid, would you?" she teased.

Lord Pendlebury laughed. The sound reminded Louisa of warm treacle. "I am the master of the house, Miss Goodchild, and a huntsman by nature. You must do as I ask."

She recognised the jest in his voice. "Then, pray, allow this maiden time to compose herself. And you to enjoy the chase of the hunt." She glanced towards the woods, not thirty yards away. "Allow your quarry to secrete itself in a hiding place. Your pleasure will be all the greater for it, I assure you."

Edwin felt himself stir. "Then a hunt it shall be. You have until I count to one hundred. Now, go. Before I change my mind."

She feathered her lips against his cheek. "A mere taste of things to come," she breathed, before dashing off towards the shade of trees.

Once inside the wood, she turned sharply left, followed the line of trees, before she took a right turn and hopped over a brook.

"…seventy-three, seventy-two, seventy-one."

It was dark inside the wood; darker than she'd expected. Louisa ducked under a bramble bush, stepped over a fallen tree.

The earth felt moist where the sun had yet to penetrate, the ground slick beneath her stockinged feet. Wet leaves licked her arm like serpent's tongues, knotted bark formed dozens of eyes watching her progress, and wispy fingers of mist sought out her ankles as the forest floor warmed. The dankness absorbed most sound. She barely heard Edwin count down.

"Forty-six, forty-five, forty-four…"

A squirrel startled her as it bolted up a tree-trunk. She headed deeper into the woodland. Another fallen tree, larger heavier and thicker than the one before, barred her path. She circumnavigated it, hunkered down behind it amidst a mushroom patch, and waited.

"…three, two, one. Ready or not, here I come."

Louisa couldn't hear him from her hiding place. She was deep in the woods. She wondered if she was too deep, if he'd ever find her.

Her lips curled and her nostrils flared at a carrion smell behind her. She looked at the fungi sprouting from the floor of Bluebell Wood. For a moment, her memories took her back to her childhood; to a time when her mother would send her into the woods to gather material for her effacations. Louisa knew what these were.

Stinkhorn.

Phallus Impudicus.

She sniggered and hoped Edwin would find her.

Time passed slowly. Louisa's ears strained for any sign of Edwin, but she heard nothing. Flies buzzed around the stinkhorn. She flapped them away, wishing she had a tail with which to perform the task. Irritated, she chose to move location.

Perhaps Edwin would hear her, even if she couldn't hear him. She opted to move towards the fringes of Bluebell Wood; to a place where she'd be found more easily. She smoothed her skirts, looked around - and realised she didn't know which-way-was-which.

She was lost.

Louisa gazed upwards, tried to gauge the position of the sun in relation to her own. She thought about crying out but resisted. He'd think her foolish, helpless and child-like. That's what she was, but she couldn't show it. Why would he want her, a mere kitchen-maid, if he knew the truth?

She heard a rustle in the trees ahead of her. Twigs snapped. Branches moved. And a full-grown doe and her fawn emerged feet from her. Girl and beast stared into each other's eyes, a magical moment, and then the deer turned and bolted back from where they had appeared.

With an enlightened heart, Louisa spun around as a figure stepped from the trees. "Edwin, at last. You'll never believe…"

She cut the sentence short.

It wasn't Edwin.

The man's riding crop flayed the side of her face twice. Her vision blurred, everything within it turned red and, mercifully, she was only vaguely aware of what happened next.

CHAPTER TWO

The air-brakes spat out a wheeze and a hiss as the coach crunched to a halt at the end of the winding gravel drive. The tour company representative stood, slightly hunched, at the front of the coach and blew into the microphone twice.

"Welcome to Doom Brae Manor and Gardens, the historic home of the Pendlebury family." She turned to gaze at the turreted home. "We are currently outside the main entrance of the manor. As you will see, the building left and right of the centre portico are a mirror image. As we look at the manor, the west wing is to our right. Once ruined by fire, the wing stood dormant for two-hundred years. It was restored to its former glory in 1976 using timber from a nearby forest and stone hewn from the very same quarry as the original material. Quite splendid, I'm sure you'll agree."

A murmur of agreement ran through the party of tourists as they craned their necks to take in the majesty of the building. The entrance to the manor was reached by a flight of thirteen stone stairs, worn smooth in places by three-hundred years of footfall. From either side, a ramp sloped gently to ground level. A small convoy of shire horses, carriages and liverymen lined one ramp, readying themselves to ferry the elderly and infirm around the grounds.

An ornate semi-circular portico, help upright by intricately carved pillars, sheltered the entrance from the elements. Marble statues guarded the door, one portraying a Roman handmaiden carrying a jug of wine, the other a Grecian Olympian. He was missing a hand and the discus it once held.

Once the initial hubbub subsided, the guide continued the speech she'd delivered dozens of times. "Doom Brae Manor is unique amongst the stately homes and castles of the United Kingdom in that it provides a hands-on, interactive experience of life in the 18th and early 19th century. Not only do you get to see what life was like, you get to live it."

The rep paused whilst her words registered with the party. She held the mic away from her and whispered to the driver, "Quiet lot we've got today. Need to milk them for all we've got to get a tip out of 'em."

The guide returned the microphone to her lips and painted a smile on her face. "Please bear with me whilst I collect your tickets and passes. I'll be with you as quickly as I can."

She hopped down the stairs and walked towards a posse of reception staff gathered around the manor's entrance. They all wore Georgian costume, authentic in every detail.

"Gee, honey. Look at the costumery. We got the real deal going on here," an excited client said.

"Uh-huh." His wife sounded bored already. "Must we go into the house, Hank? It's a real fine day and I'd like to explore the grounds. Weather been as wet as Ol' Man River all the time we been over here. Seems wrong to spend a day like today indoors when we could be outside enjoyin' it."

"Relax, Mae. We got plenty a' time for both. Look, here they come." He pointed towards the rep and the manor staff making their way towards the coach.

A chap in a long purple tunic and lime-green leggings clambered into the coach. He wore a voluminous white wig, almost triangular in shape, curled in on itself at the edges.

"What devilment do we have here?" he asked as he took the mic. He shook it. Sniffed it. The tour party laughed as he licked it as if it were an ice-cream. The coach's speakers echoed with a rasping sound as the man's tongue rubbed against it. He feigned surprise at the noise and stumbled backwards, hand on heart. The party sniggered again, Hank and Mae laughing louder than their fellow-passengers.

"Good morning, my friends, and welcome to Doom Brae Manor."

A muttered chorus of 'thank yous' and 'mornings' came back at him.

The man cupped a hand to his ear. "Hark - did I hear a mouse squeak? I said, 'Good Morning'."

"Good morning," the tour party responded with forced enthusiasm.

"Aha. Our guests awake. My good lords, ladies, and little ones. Welcome to Doom Brae. My name is Wilberforce Long and I'm a footman on this glorious estate. Today, you shall meet the lords and ladies of the manor, all the while in the company of the good folk who work their fingers to the bone to keep them in their accustomed manner. I believe you would refer to it as life Upstairs and Downstairs."

The man turned towards the entrance of the building. "In honour of your visit today, our courtiers have arranged a special welcome for you."

The tourists craned their necks, some half stood to see, as the manor doors swung open and a group of instrumentalists stepped out. Flautists led the way, followed by a stooped gentleman in dark wig plucking a lyre. A mandolin player somehow succeeded in doffing his top hat to the coach without interrupting his tune. At the end of the procession, three maidens shook and rattled timbral in accompaniment.

The minstrels wandered to where a line of stiff-backed, bewigged men stood, one hand tucked behind their backs. Facing them, a row of women wore voluminous skirts in various shades of blue, scarlet and primrose.

Mae took Hank's hand. "I think they're gonna' dance for us."

The band struck up a new tune. The women curtsied, demure smiles hid behind colourful fans, as their menfolk stepped towards them. The men bowed, took their partners fingertips at shoulder-height, and proceeded to perform an elegant processional dance.

"Waddya know. It's a line-dance. Hee-haw," Hank brayed, waving an imaginary Stetson.

The man who had introduced himself as Wilberforce Long spoke into the microphone again. "Today, we shall split you into three groups. Families: please alight your carriage now. You shall be travelling with Megan and her band who will teach you the music, dance and song of our age."

A blonde-haired lady waved towards the coach, waggling her timbrel above her head. The children aboard waved back.

"Once finished with Megan, a member of our kitchen staff will help you prepare your own picnic from the foods of our day, before you complete your time with us by playing the games our children play, while learning the origins of some of the nursery rhymes you know so well."

Megan stood by the coach door as Wilberforce Long concluded his mantra. "So, young ones, are you ready?"

Excited shouts deafened the coach's occupants as the children scrambled out, their parents trailing behind.

Once left with only adults, Wilberforce Long's tone changed. "Now, we shall send some of you to explore the grounds and the woods first. Mr Fairbody will accompany you." A young man in a gamekeeper's costume stepped forward. "For the rest, you shall go indoors with Miss Lambert." A woman in a cook's pinafore curtsied.

The man in the peculiar wig addressed the group again. "If I can be of service to you, or if you wish to ask me any questions, please do so before I leave you to your travels."

The company put their heads down, turned to look out the window, none prepared to speak first.

None but Hank. "Hey, bud," he asked. "Why you got a slice of stuffed crust pizza on your head?" He guffawed loudly. The others tutted. Even Mae looked away.

"I know not of what you speak," the Wilberforce Long character shot back. "Nor the strange tongue in which you express it." The others smiled at the gentle putdown. Hank flushed.

Long's voice took on a serious timbre. "There is a reason your young ones have been sent afore you. My lords and ladies; be warned that not all in Doom Brae is as it seems. Darkness lurks within our grounds and halls. Sinister goings-on fill our history, a history of despots and wickedness, witches and curses."

Wilberforce Long moved to the steps of the coach. Turned back to face the passengers for a final time. "As I take my leave, I beseech you to take great care, my friends, for you are about to discover what puts the Doom into Doom Brae."

Strident organ tones belted out from speakers hidden around the manor's entrance, accompanied by an amplified wicked laugh straight out of a Christopher Lee B-movie.

Hank's eyes lightened. "This is gonna be sweet, Mae. I feel it."

Mae looked less than convinced.

CHAPTER THREE

By the manor's entrance, a liveryman tended to a handsome horse and the black carriage to which it was attached. The horse pawed the ground, breath snorting from nostrils like steam from a dragon.

A dark-haired man in frilled collar strode by, taking the stone steps two at a time. A footman gave the well-heeled gent a deferential bow as he pulled open the manor doors and allowed the man to march into the hall.

The gent's clogs echoed around the stone hall. He ignored the tapestries on the walls, the stag's head set above the ornate fireplace, and the portraits lining the high-ceilinged corridor as he hurried to his destination.

He paused outside a solid oak door and waited for the flush to subside from his cheeks. He regulated his breathing and brushed loose grass from his leggings before inhaling deeply.

A footman stood further along the corridor. He gesticulated towards the dark-haired man. Viscount Felix Pendlebury gave him a disdainful look, ignored him, and rapped on the drawing room door. Without waiting for a response, he heaved it open.

Inside, a huge dog, Great Dane with a hint of Wolfhound, lay in front of a marble fireplace. Lupo raised his head, looked the intruder over, and plopped it back on his paws.

Behind the hound, two men sat at an oblong table, facing each other. One, a round-faced, chinless man with snub nose and powdered wig, used a compass pointer to indicate features on a technical drawing spread across the desk. The other, Mortimer Pendlebury, the third Earl of Doom Brae, was a hawk-faced man with bushy eyebrows which expressed annoyance at the interruption.

"My lord," Felix Pendlebury bowed, "May I speak with you?"

The man glared at him from beneath his bushy eyebrows. "I expressly declared I was not to be interrupted. I shall have words with Maltby. He should not have let you enter."

"Sir, it is important. I would not have interrupted were it not."

The man sighed. "Mr Brown," the Earl said to his seated guest, "This is my eldest son, the Viscount Pendlebury. He takes after his mother. He has no manners."

The other man laughed. "I have no wish to come between a man and his son. I shall leave you with my drawings. My carriage and driver have waited long enough. May I suggest we reconvene next month and agree on my fee? I assure you, I am more than capable of delivering you the finest Pleasure Gardens in the county, your grace."

"That suggests your services shall not come cheap. We shall discuss it next month." The men stood and shook hands. "Thank you for your time, Mr Brown. It's been most rewarding."

The chinless man nodded, straightened his coat tails and swept out of the room, giving Viscount Pendlebury a faint nod as he swept past.

"Felix, my boy. Your timing is impeccable. That Lancelot Brown is a truly insufferable gabster." Mortimer laughed. "Please, take a seat."

Felix Pendlebury fanned his jacket tails behind him as he lowered himself onto the high-backed chair. He gripped the heads of the gargoyles carved on the arms with such force his knuckles turned white.

The mannerism didn't escape the Earl's attention. "Felix, my boy. What have those poor griffins done to deserve such harsh handling? Come, relax. Let's share a brandy."

"Father, I have grave news."

The older man regarded his son, chin resting on steepled fingers. "Spit it out, man."

"I'm afraid I must tell you there is a witch abroad. Here, in this very house."

Mortimer Pendlebury spat out a laugh. "Nonsense, my boy. There hasn't been a witch in these parts for nigh on two-score years. The year 1720, I believe. Your tale is too smoky by half."

"If I hadn't witnessed it myself, I would ne'er believe it, too. But I'm afraid I did more than witness it. I, myself, have fallen foul of her spells and witchcraft."

A beam of sunlight from a high window fell across the younger man's eyes, rendering them unreadable. The rest of his face lay in shadow.

The Earl of Doom Brae studied his son for a long time from beneath his furrowed eyebrows. "Pray tell."

Felix lowered his head. "I dare not, father, for it brings great shame upon me and this household."

"You came here for a reason so spit it out, man."

Felix swallowed. "Sir, I was walking in the woods when I came across her. She had bewitched a doe and foal from the estate. They stood at her side, as if in communication. I disturbed her before she could cast her malevolence on them but, alas, in her spite she turned herself on me."

"Really? You expect me to believe this bag of moonshine? Tell me, what evil did she cast upon you?"

Felix looked around the room, at its high ceilings and the portraits lining the wall. The eyes of his forefathers appeared to train themselves on him. He cast his eyes downwards. "I failed to see her runes or hear her words, but I lost track of time and space. When I awoke, she lay beneath me."

He paused. Ensured his words registered. "Of course, I tried to fight her off once I came to. I raised my horsewhip to her. I fought a brave battle and eventually I beat her off. But I fear it was too late. She had taken my honour."

Mortimer Pendlebury remained silent, his mouth a thin line. "And the creature was of this household, you say?"

"Yes, sir. I'm afraid she is. She works in the very kitchens where our food is prepared. I believe the name she goes by is Louisa Goodchild."

"Goodchild? Is that the tempting armful who dallies with Edwin?"

Felix met his father's gaze, struggled to suppress a smile. "Yes, sir. It is she."

"Then the succubus must pay. Come, we must find her at once. Put her to the test."

The Earl stood. Felix followed suit, head bowed not in deference but to disguise the smirk on his face.

"One thing, Felix."

"Yes, sire?"

"Next time you wish to have your way with one of the household, don't come to me with your damned hum and poppycock. Keep your member in your breeches, where it belongs."

CHAPTER FOUR

The young man who went by the name of Erasmus Fairbody led the party up a meandering country-stream of a path. He brought the group to a halt here and there, indicating wild flowers and singling out the tracks of deer, cattle and smaller creatures which, he explained, roamed free throughout the estate.

At the top of the hill, the Fairbody character asked his audience to turn and look back to the manor house. An audible gasp of admiration escaped the group. They looked over gently rolling land which led down to twenty-five acres of formal gardens.

A couple of Canadians joined Hank and Mae. They muttered their admiration at colourful flower beds, rockeries transformed into shapely inkblots by lavender and heather, and orangeries which reflected sunlight like diamond ear-rings.

Fountains sent a glittering cascade of silver water high into the clear air from a pair of kidney-shaped lakes either side of the manor house. Immaculately tended lawns, a cluster of privets and hedges moulded into elaborate creatures, and a large aviary to the south of the manor completed the chocolate-box picture.

Hank raised a camera the size of a bazooka and began clicking away. Others with more modest equipment joined him while still more simply committed the scene to memory, during which time Fairbody outlined the history of the gardens in eloquent terms.

After a few moments, the gamekeeper herded his party together. He marched them to the periphery of the estate. "Ladies and gentlemen, we are now overlooking public land; land owned by the parish of Doom Brae and not the Pendlebury family. Yet, it is here where the Earl of Doom Brae spent much of his time with his two sons. It is in the land beyond the estate where he taught his sons the skills of huntsmanship."

Erasmus Fairbody halted his speech and invited a question from a man in waxed jacket and tartan cap. "Excuse me, I was wondering why the Earl hunted off-estate when he has so much land available?"

"You ask a good question, sir. The Earl, despite his wealth, is a prudent man. He has no desire to damage his own land or deplete his stock of deer."

An elderly woman raised her hand. "You mention the Earl and his sons. Did the womenfolk join the hunt?"

The gamekeeper looked unhappy. "Alas, madam, they did not. Sadly, by the time the Viscount and Lord Edwin were of an age to hunt, the Countess, Lady Elizabeth, had fallen foul of smallpox. The Earl and his boys hunted alone."

Mae piped up. "Did the Earl remarry?" she asked.

"No, madam. His father, the second Earl, raised his son to believe a wife's role was to provide a man with son and heir. The Earl never did remarry. He had no need. In the eyes of his Lordship, Lady Elizabeth had fulfilled the requirement of any woman."

Mae and the other women shook their heads at the stark reminder of their gender's history.

As they'd been talking, Fairbody had led the tourists back into the estate. They reached the fringe of Bluebell Woods where they rested from the heat under the shade of an oak tree.

Fairbody's mood changed, evident by the tone of his voice. "My good folk, we are now about to enter Bluebell Wood. Stay close to me, I beseech you, lest our woods reveal their secrets to you; secrets best kept hidden."

The party closed ranks as Fairbody led them into the woods. He stopped at various junctures. Conveniently, a pair of red squirrels scaled a sycamore tree in front of their eyes. In his haste to snap them, Hank clattered his elongated camera lens into the head of the lady alongside him. She rubbed the side of her face and moved away with a scowl.

At the next stop, by a bubbling brook, Fairbody pointed out flora and fauna. In a clearing, they came across a wild hog snuffling for fungi. A majestic stag emerged from a patch of brambles and turned to watch them, its movement almost robotic. It was only when a badger crossed their path in dappled sunlight, and Fairbody explained the nocturnal nature of the long-snouted creature, the party realised the truth.

The woodland creatures were animatronic.

"Gee, and we thought Disneyland had it good. I hate to say it, Mae, but the Brits have gotten one over us here." For once, Mae had to agree with her husband. The effects were stunning.

Fairbody gave a furtive glance around. Beckoned the tourists to him. He lowered his voice. "I ask you to be on your guard. Some of you may have heard of the witches of Pendle." Some nodded, others shook their heads. Hank nodded but didn't have a clue. "What is less well known," Fairbody continued, "Is that we have our own tale to tell, the tale of the Pendlebury witch." The party laughed at the obvious play on words. "And I urge caution, for she is oft seen around these parts when she senses strangers about."

Fairbody led them deeper into the woods. Stopped suddenly. "What is that I smell?" A device secreted in the roots of an oak tree puffed out a foul aroma, much the way a bakery circulates the smell of warm bread to entice customers.

The party began to gag. Pulled their jackets up over their face. Fairbody explained, "Aha. The scent of the stinkhorn mushroom. I fear the witch may be close. We must hurry. Come, this way."

He ducked under a bush. The tourists followed, but there was no sign of him. The Fairbody character had slipped into a hide disguised as a grassy mound. They looked around them, puzzled.

Suddenly, a speaker crackled to life. It emitted a cackling laugh at the same time as a hologram appeared in front of the party. A couple of women closest to the projected image jumped in fright, shying from it and clutching hands to their hearts before they dissolved into fits of nervous and embarrassed laughter, much to the amusement of their fellow tourists.

The hologram wasn't particularly convincing. The wart-faced, sharp-chinned image could've been lifted from the Wizard of Oz, but that only added to the humour.

Fairbody leapt from the hide, startling the company once more. "'Tis the Pendlebury witch; or the witch of Doom Brae as she is better known," he cried. "We shall hear more of her anon but, for now, we must hasten from her before she casts an evil curse upon us. Quickly, this way. Through the hedgerow and far away from the ugly crone."

The party followed Erasmus Fairbody onto the next stage of the adventure. All, that is, except Hank. He hung back, staring avidly at the hologram.

"Ugly?" he said in reverential tones. "You're the most beautiful creature I've ever seen."

The witch turned directly towards him and fixed him with a smile. Sky-blue eyes glowed from a flawless face fringed by long flaxen hair.

"Beautiful," Hank whispered again.

CHAPTER FIVE

The air in the kitchen was thick with the stench of boiling vegetables. Steam belched from monstrous pots and pans. Maids stirred the contents with heavy metal spoons. Others turned a hog roasting above the range whilst still more polished silverware or inspected delicate china for chips and flaws.

The appropriately-named Kitty Cook stood aside from the chaos, mopped her brow with a cloth pulled from her waistband, and puffed out her rose-red cheeks. She raised her head towards the window high above her but could see nothing through the misted-over glass. It was like looking through cataracts.

Kitty felt a tug at her skirts. She smiled benevolently. "Not now, Henry. I'm full of busy." She ruffled the eight-year old urchin's hair.

Henry didn't have a surname. He didn't have a mother or a father, either. Henry was an eight-year old orphan taken in by the kitchen staff. Henry was also persistent.

He pulled at Kitty's skirts again, this time with the urgency of a dog dragging a branch. The mute child made a guttural sound, his eyes wide and pleading.

"Whatever's the matter with you, child?"

Henry made the noise again in response. He raised an arm and seemed to point at the wall. Kitty followed the line of his outstretched arm towards a rack of saucepans.

"You want to help, is that it? The kitchen's no place for you." Kitty made as if to touch a hot pan, let out an 'ouch' sound, and shook her hand. "Hot. Too dangerous for one as small as you."

The boy shook his head. Exasperation showed in his face. He repeated the stabbing motion towards the wall. Pulled on Kitty's apron once more. Made the sound for a third time.

Kitty tried to understand. She stood, arms akimbo, and watched the urchin tilt his head to one side and rest it against clasped hands.

"Sleep? Is that what you want? Are you knocked-up tired?"

The boy shook his head. Then, he made a slashing motion and held a finger against his cheek.

The cook's brow furrowed in bewilderment. "I don't know what you want."

The boy heaved at her with even greater urgency. Mind made up, Kitty glanced around to ensure no-one watched, wiped her hands on her apron, and took the boy's hand. "Show me."

He dragged her out the kitchen into the cool of a stone corridor, pushed her out a side door, and led her up towards Bluebell Wood.

Kitty doubled over, breathless from the uphill scurry. "Henry. Slow down. I'm fagged to death. Let's wait a while." The boy refused to wait. Beckoned her to follow. With a look of resignation, the cook did so. She wheezed and coughed but trudged after the boy until she saw him clamber over a dry-stone wall.

"Wait. I can't climb like you young whipper-snapper. I go by the gate." Henry took no heed. He was already inside the stable block.

Five minutes later, Kitty Cook entered the stables. When her rasping breath eased, she was struck by the silence. The horses were eerily quiet. Some would be out working the fields, others tethered to carriages, a few perhaps mounted for the hunt. But there should be horses here. Indeed, she knew there were; she'd seen their heads as she entered, and she could smell them. Yet, there was scarcely a sound.

"Henry? Henry? Where are you, boy?" She knew he wouldn't answer – couldn't answer – but Kitty needed to fill the silent void.

Mottled sunlight filtered through glassless windows, golden fingers scrabbling at the cobbled floor. The rest of the interior was dark and forbidding.

"Henry?" Kitty's voice was hushed now, caution in her tones. She looked into one pen. It was empty. She moved to the next. Empty, too, save for a mass of soiled straw, and brasses and harnesses hanging from the wall.

Kitty moved on. A grey mare met her gaze. The old horse didn't whinny or flick her tail. She just stood, fixing Kitty with her big brown eyes.

She moved to the next, and the next; one empty, one with another occupant, silent and still as the mare.

"What's happened here?" she asked it. "I wish you could tell me."

Kitty reached the end of the row of pens. She did a hairpin turn and began searching the eastern side of the stables. She found nothing but vacant paddocks or stock-still, silent horses.

Until she reached the penultimate stable.

Louisa Goodchild lay bent and broken, her head lolled to one side. Her bodice was ripped, skirts filthy and unkempt. Henry sat by her, Louisa's hand in his, while a young foal tenderly nuzzled her.

Kitty hand shot to her mouth. "Oh, my poor child."

At the sound of Kitty's voice, the foal moved in front of the stricken girl as if to protect her. It snorted and pawed the stable floor, eyes flared, the whites exposed, as Kitty stepped towards Louisa.

Kitty backed off. Henry left Louisa's side. He brushed the foal's mane and made his guttural croak. The foal immediately backed away, allowing Kitty space to enter.

The cook looked between boy, horse, and Louisa. Not for long, but long enough for something to register. She offered a faint smile and nod of deference to the foal and rushed to Louisa's side.

She ripped off a piece of her apron, doused it in a trough of pea-green water, and held it to Louisa's brow. She brushed a wisp of the girl's hair aside. "My dear, dear child. What have you done to yourself? Let's get you back to the house."

Kitty heard a terrified Henry make a noise. She glanced towards him. He shook his head so fast she thought it would spin off his shoulders.

"Henry, we must help her." She bent to hoist the girl to her feet. Louisa's head rolled aside, exposing a cruel, deep wound across the right-hand side of her face.

And an eye resting on her cheek beneath an empty socket.

Kitty Cook stumbled backwards into a pile of steaming dung, gagged by bile in her throat. Before she passed out, she heard Henry make his unearthly cough again, a double-barrelled explosion of air.

She could have sworn it sounded like "Viscount."

CHAPTER SIX

The party stood in a meadow part-way back to the manor waiting for Hank to catch up. The guide gave him a harsh look for his tardiness. Hank raised his hands and nodded an apology in response.

Erasmus Fairbody acknowledged Hank's regret with a curt nod and was soon regaling the party with vivid descriptions of the flora of the period, and how it changed and evolved over the millennia.

Hank quickly recovered his breath after his exertions but just as quickly lost interest in Fairbody's words. Not for him lectures and talks. He responded to visual stimuli, to mechanics and motion, not speech. He turned his back on the group and found himself staring uphill, back towards Bluebell Wood.

Raised as a country boy, Hank was always at home outdoors. But there was something special about those woods, something mesmeric, which pulled at his heartstrings. He set aside the special effects and the electronic wizardry which brought to life the woodland creatures: he just knew he'd felt at home in its sunlit glades and shaded bowers.

It reminded him of his childhood. He'd been lonely as a child yet, paradoxically, felt comfortable in the wildernesses of his home State. The grounds of the Doom Brae Estate bore little resemblance to the territories he explored in his youth, yet he'd found instant peace here.

Hank was aware Erasmus Fairbody continued his well-versed presentation, but the words drifted by him.

"…and we see today how much a visionary Capability Brown was. The immature saplings he planted at irregular intervals on the approach to the manor have blossomed into the splendid orchards we see spreading all the way to the main highway."

The company murmured in appreciation as a girl in a maid's costume began doling out fruit from a handcart wheeled up to them. Behind her, a trailer with built-in brazier offered roasted chestnuts.

"Sir," Erasmus said. "Sir?" He had to raise his voice for the man to hear him. "Would you return to the party, please?"

The man kept walking away from him, slowly, methodically, almost like a sleep-walker.

Mae looked around. Hank wasn't at her side. "Hank. Where you goin'? Get your ass back here, honey. We're all done up there. You holdin' everyone up. Again."

Hank took another couple of paces. Stopped. Turned 180-degrees to face the party, a blank expression in his eyes, face a mask. He completed the circle and set off once more, back towards the dark mass of Bluebell Wood.

After a few shuffling steps, Hank stopped abruptly. He hung his head, fell to his knees, and sobbed.

Mae broke from the party at a trot. She called his name. Once. Twice. Three times. Hank didn't respond. Not to her, he didn't. Instead, he responded to something else; something unseen. He raised his hands above his head, fingers extended skywards, and muttered something unintelligible.

Three other tourists broke rank and hurried towards Hank. Erasmus shouted to him. "Sir, are you all right? Do you need help?"

Hank let out a deep moan, an otherworldly sound which raised gooseflesh on those close enough to hear. Slowly, he raised his head.

"Hmm? You guys talking to me? Yeah, sure, I'm fine. Guess I'm a little tired, that's all."

The guide and Mae exchanged glances. "Has this happened before?" Erasmus asked, all pretence of Georgian-speak gone.

Mae shook her head.

"No history of epilepsy or seizures? Perhaps the hologram triggered something?"

Mae's head moved left and right again. "No. Nothing."

Erasmus handed Hank a bottle of water. "Here, take a drink. A few sips." Fellow-tourists took an arm each and helped him to his feet. "Steady, now," Erasmus urged. "Take your time. You've a long day ahead if you wish to carry on. Or we could leave you to rest in the coach if you prefer, after our nurse has checked you over."

Something shifted behind Hank's eyes before he fixed Erasmus with a cold stare. "No quack's gonna' be cupping and blood-lettin' me, boy."

Erasmus breathed a sigh of relief. The man was compos mentis enough to recognise the day's theme. "Good. That's better. We could get a wheelchair for you if it helps, though."

"You kiddin' me, man. I'm fine. Real fine. Let's get this show on the road." He straightened himself as if nothing had happened.

As they set off towards Doom Brae manor, Mae raised an eyebrow. She took Hank's arm in the crook of hers. "What was all that about?" she whispered. "You sure you're ok?"

"What was all what about? Nuthin' happened, cutie. Just real taken aback by the forest and the animatronics and the hologram. Don't know how they did it, that's all"

"But that's your thing, Hank. You love stuff like that. You sure never acted that way on the Tower of Terror."

Hank expelled air, horse-like. "Tower of Terror ain't nothing like the purdy witch girl."

Mae opened her mouth to correct him, but her response was drowned out by Hank's voice calling across to another group of tourists heading towards the wood guided by their own 'Erasmus Fairbody' character.

"Hey, buddies," Hank shouted. "You got a real treat lined up for you up there."

The original Erasmus asked him to remain quiet. "Please, don't spoil the surprise for them. Keep it to yourself, if you would."

Hank put his finger to his lips. "Sorry, sorry. Not another word, I promise."

"Good. Thank you."

As they returned to the rest of their party, Hank broke into a strident song directed towards the other party.

"Marie, Marie La Voodoo-Veah, She's the Witch-Queen Of…Of New Orleans"

"You know," Mae said to Erasmus, "I think I preferred him when he was odd."

CHAPTER SEVEN

Outside a stone annex to the stable block, a man watched two horses and their riders approach over the brow of the hill. The man wore a course brown shirt which struggled to contain his stomach. A tan leather apron reached down to his knees, covering battered and worn breeches.

The man was bare headed and, though most of his face was hidden behind a mask of white whiskers, the flesh that showed through revealed a brandy-faced complexion born from years in front of the forge and nights nursing flagons of ale.

George 'Piggy' Trotter studied the horses as they beat their way towards the stables. Fine, strong beasts; beasts he'd shod only that morning. The riders handled their mounts with aplomb. There again, Piggy thought, they'd had plenty of practice. They had precious little else to do.

As he watched, one of the horses pulled-up abruptly. Felix Pendlebury, astride the stallion, dug his heels into the horse's flanks. The spurs made no impact. The horse didn't budge.

Felix snapped his crop against its shoulders, and again higher-up, against its withers. His mount stayed still, no movement other than the steam of its breath.

The other rider circled his horse and pulled-up alongside the first. "Felix, you'd think you were atop a queer prancer not the finest steed," the Earl laughed. "Come on man, get your beast moving. Dig your heels in; get those bleeders working on him."

"Father, I swear this pile of backward-breeze is good for nothing but glue."

The elder man chortled again. He dismounted his horse and landed in the turf with a thud and a tinkle of spurs. He took his son's mount by the bridle. Patted the white blaze on its nose. The beast watched him suspiciously, eyes flared.

"Get a haste on. We need to find this Goodchild girl, this 'witch' as you call her, afore anyone else finds her in a mood for a-hexing."

Felix stopped beating his horse. He sat still. "Listen. Do you hear it?" The Earl strained to hear. "You imagine it. I hear nothing."

"Precisely, my Lord. Nothing. No birdsong. No insects. No farmhands or stable-lads toiling in the field. There's nothing."

Mortimer cocked his head as he listened again, waiting for something, anything. And then he heard it. Little more than a breeze, it whispered across open fields.

Ears of corn rubbed together, the sound of a pensive man scratching his beard, before the wind reached the trees. It strengthened within the forest. Conifers swayed to Mother Nature's overture and pine needles seemed to sing a sweet melody.

Piggy Trotter heard it, too. He gave a knowing smile, pushed himself off the smithy wall, and stepped inside; making sure the door was closed behind him.

Out of nowhere, the skies darkened, purple and indigo clouds blanketed the sun like a bruise spread over flesh. The wind whipped to a frenzy. Branches, ripped from trees, flung themselves at the gentry and their steeds.

Crows, dozens of them, rose from where they nested in Bluebell Wood until the flock formed a shield which blocked out all remaining light. Their cacophony of caws drowned out even the howl of the wind.

The men's horses broke from their trance. Stripes of chalky white sweat flecked their flanks, their lips curled back, froth foamed their gums. They pawed at the earth, ears flat, eyes wide.

The Earl sensed it first. "Felix. Dismount. You won't hold him." He shouted to make himself heard above the gale. He made a frantic grab for his hat as the wind tore it from him and tossed it to the field's border.

"No. You doubted my horsemanship. I'll show you my worth."

The steed tossed its head. Cantered backwards. Then, as a crack of thunder filled the air like musket-fire, it reared up on itself, fetlocks clawing at the sky.

"Get down, Felix. Now!" the Earl urged.

Too late. The stallion had passed the point of no return. Its balance had shifted. It reared beyond the vertical plane and whinnied as it tipped over backwards with Viscount Felix Pendlebury still in the saddle.

Felix felt it happen. Knew he had nowhere to go. He launched himself free at the last moment, but his left ankle caught in a stirrup. He dangled from it, head downwards, as the weight of the horse bore down upon his neck. Felix closed his eyes, waited for the impact, hoped it would be quick.

As if in slow motion, Felix felt the air expel from his lungs as he hit the earth, he heard a scream – his scream – as his leg twisted beneath his mount. Yet, somehow, the steed missed the rest of him. He was alive.

Alive, and once more surrounded by silence. The sun shone from an azure sky. The air was breathless as a corpse. And the birds and beasts silent as a forgotten tune.

The Earl of Doom Brae looked down at his stricken son, then up towards the heavens. "Ye Gods," the Earl whispered. "A witch she surely must be."

The transformation was immediate. The elder man stood in the field, stunned and transfixed. Only the moans of his son brought him back to the present. "Get up, son. We need to find the wench before someone else does."

"I can't. I can't move."

"Yes you can, you lily-livered oaf. Come."

The Earl of Doom Brae reached down for his son, took him by the arm. He was about to haul him to his feet when he noticed the blood on Felix's lower leg. Blood surrounding a rip in the Viscount's stockings. Through which a shard of white bone poked. The tibia was broken. A Greenstick fracture.

Mortimer's horse had bolted in the storm. Felix's mount lay stricken alongside its rider, fetlock at the same cruel angle as the Viscount's. The Earl looked around for help. Saw the building attached to the stables, with its heavy wooden door pulled shut.

"Trotter! Trotter!! Get yourself out here. I need help."

The smithy door opened with the reluctance of a lamb led to slaughter. Piggy Trotter emerged and ambled towards the Earl and his son. "Get a move on, Trotter. Live up to your name."

Piggy sauntered on, hands dug deep in the pocket of his apron. "Leg's broken," he said with obvious understatement.

"I can see that with my own eyes, you clodpole."

Trotter knelt beside the horse, gently stoking its mane, cooing softly. He looked around. "Your boy's legs gone, too."

"It's my boy I'm talking about, fool. Here; help me move him to the stable."

"It be painful as the devil's scrape for him."

"Just take his arm, damnit."

Piggy shrugged but did as instructed. Felix screamed all the way to the stable block as the men half-carried, half-dragged him across field and cobbles.

Piggy let go the moment they entered the building. "I be excusing myself now, my lord. I got a horse to attend to." He left without waiting for approval. Felix was in no state to disagree and his father was too engrossed with his son to notice.

"Where did you leave Goodchild? I'll fetch the rum wanton myself."

Felix face contorted in pain. Through a grimace, he managed to say, "East side. Second to last enclosure." He hesitated. "Father. Be warned. The sight will be gruesome. Please remember I was protecting the honour of our family. I did what I had to do."

Felix closed his eyes and rested his head on a hale bay while Mortimer furrowed his owl-like eyebrows. His son's warning worried him. He knew he'd incapacitated the girl, but how far had he taken it?

Mortimer shrugged. It was too late now. The deed was done. He inhaled, drew in the stench of horse dung and sodden straw, and tried to reassure the Viscount.

"I'll go seek her. Worry not: I'll see she's moved far from this place. She'll be sent to a work house up London way. She won't last more than a month before she's pox-ridden. It'll be as good as putting her to the test, and much less public."

The Earl sloped off to find the girl. "Wait here," he said over his shoulder.

Felix would have laughed at the irony were he not in such pain.

CHAPTER EIGHT

He sat with arms folded high against his chest. A scowl darkened his face as he glowered down at a tiny pewter plate littered with gingerbread crumbs. Alongside it, a coffee cup lay curdling, an oily film across the surface.

"Oh, for goodness sake. Cheer up, Hank. You said you liked authentic and it don't come more authentic than this."

"But I want a chilli dog."

From the tone in the voice, Mae expected it to be accompanied by a stamp of feet and juvenile bawl. "Honey, I don't think chilli dogs are popular amongst Brits even in this day and age, let alone nearly three hundred years ago."

"And the coffee's undrinkable. Tastes like swamp water."

Mae rolled her eyes at the couple sharing their table. She forced the last of her game pie into her mouth and made a tumbleweed motion with her hand to indicate she'd speak once her mouth was empty.

"Should have gone for the pie. It's awesome." She dabbed flakes of pastry from the corner of her mouth with her little finger. "And it says here on the menu the coffee's from what is now Yemen. It's where the family imported it from in them there days."

"Well, it still tastes like mud."

"It's probably ground," the man opposite Hank offered, earning a sneer in return.

Hank's stomach let out the rumble of a flatulent hippopotamus. He snatched the menu from Mae, signalled to a waitress and ordered a slice of apple pie, "And a Pepsi."

The maid pushed back her frilled linen bonnet. "Sorry, sir. We have fruit juice, freshly pressed lemonade, or water. Unless you'd care to partake in a flagon of ale. Or perhaps a gin, or mead?"

"So, you got no Pepsi. What sort of place is this? Water. Just water."

He shooed away a pair of sparrows who pecked at a few discarded crumbs at his feet while the maid offered a slight curtsy which didn't extend to a smile.

While he waited at the courtyard table, Hank studied the splendour of the manor house, and the thought he'd soon be striding the ancient corridors lightened his mood.

By the time the maid returned with his sweet dish, Hank was deep in conversation with his table companions. "Say, waddya make of it so far?"

The man, Clint Reubens, shielded his eyes from the sun as he replied, "Cool. I expected a boring mausoleum, but the trip's been more than that. I love the fact we experience what the Pendlebury's did back in the day. Not just get talked at, know what I mean?"

Hank nodded. "I sure do. Never come across anything like this place before. Kinda like a theme park but the way it's all set up is real neat. And we haven't even started inside the ol' place yet."

The man's wife, Althea, a tiny mouse-like woman with staring eyes, snickered. "I hope it's better than the witch in the woods. I thought it was a cheap effect. It let the place down, I reckon."

Hank gave her a stern look. "Hey, I thought it was awesome. Felt I could almost touch her."

The woman shrugged and slid her eyes to her husband. "Each to his own, I guess."

But Hank didn't hear her. The sparrows at his feet fluttered away as a shadow darkened the table. A huge magpie landed with the beat of heavy wings. Its splendid black and white plumage and oil-blue wing feathers belied its scavenging habits which earned it the title the Thief of Birds.

Mae recoiled from it, but Hank watched, enraptured. He felt compelled to meet its cold stare, even while he sensed its coal-black eyes search for something deep within him.

In the unfathomable depths of the bird's gaze, Hank saw a faint colour rise in its eyes, no more than a pin-prick of light; a luminous green light. And a voice chilled him to the bone. A voice he felt, rather than heard, whisper, "I shall steal your soul."

An intense surge, as if he were inside a car which crested a rise too fast, dragged his stomach downwards. Only it didn't stop. It kept going, hauling him further and further with it.

His field of vision swam. Images on the periphery swirled and drew inwards like water down a plughole until only the magpie remained visible. Whilst everything else moved downwards, it spread its wings and rose like a phoenix but, to Hank, it seemed to have merged with him; become part of him.

He closed his eyelids until everything around him disappeared into a black hole of emptiness.

When he opened them, he was alone at the table. The others had left him. Something else was different, too. Maids in bonnets and puffed-out skirts still fussed around the courtyard but there were no other customers. There wasn't, he realised, any other tables.

Hank had been sat opposite the aviary, the orchard behind it. Now, he realised, he was looking over open fields. No birdcages, no fruit trees. Just rugged fallow land on which cattle grazed; land interspersed with hawthorn bushes and a few feeble saplings.

A chubby woman with rosy red cheeks broke off her business and offered him a benevolent smile. The woman bustled over to him and, to Hank's open-mouthed astonishment, ruffled his hair.

He heard the woman speak. "Are you alright, H…"

"…ank? Hank? Are you still with us?"

Hank blinked several times at the sound of Mae's voice.

"Huuh?"

Mae's tone was etched with concern. "You sure you're ok, honey? I mean, really sure?"

Hank tutted. "Yeah. Course I am. What makes you think otherwise?"

Mae exchanged glances with her table companions. It was the mousey woman who spoke. She gave Hank a curious look. "You drifted off from us there."

"And you weren't too good out in the fields earlier," Clint added.

Hank wanted to ask how they hadn't seen the illusion, too, but decided against it given the tone of the conversation. Instead, he gave a dismissive wave. "I'm good. Just pondering how these guys do the FX, that's all. Some technology they must have."

"I'm pretty sure they'll never tell us," Clint said. "Now, you sure you're ok?"

"Sure, I'm sure." He wrinkled his nose. "Hey, what's that goddamn awful smell?"

The others sniffed the air. "Nope. Can't catch it," the man said.

"You're kidding me, right? It's rank."

Althea gave a Mona Lisa-like smile, but the conversation was interrupted by the waitress taking their plates, asking if everything had been to their satisfaction.

Mae kicked Hank under the table to elicit a "Yeah, all good, thanks."

The waitress-cum-maid reached across Hank for Mae's plate. As she raised it, Hank caught the acrid scent again.

"There - that's it. It's coming from your plate. What've you had again?"

"Game pie. But there's none left. I ate it all so it can't be that. Just left a sprinkling of the garnish. Some greens, a little tomato and some mushroom."

Hank clicked his fingers. "That's it. The smell. It's those damn stinkhorn from the wood. You trying to poison your customers?", he accused the waitress.

She frowned and smiled at the same time. "I assure you, sir, you are mistaken. We only use the finest field mushrooms. All freshly picked and perfectly edible."

Mae kicked Hank again. "It's totally fine. THEY were totally fine. Hank, you gone crazy today, boy."

The maid curtsied one last time before leaving Hank and Mae to their disagreement; a disagreement cut short by the arrival of the Wilberforce Long character and his harlequin-coloured garb.

"My Lords and Ladies", he bowed and scraped. "I trust you enjoyed our delicacies. You shall now be escorted into the house where, amongst many things, you shall witness how and where our meals are prepared."

After a beat, he continued. "It will, of course, have the Doom Brae twist. All may not be as it seems. Why, you may ask? Then I shall tell you. The kitchen is where the Doom Brae Witch worked."

Hank's face brightened at the news. As Wilberforce used a brass-headed cane to direct various groups to their respective guides, Hank and Mae stood to leave. Hank extended his hand across the table. "Been good talkin' to you guys. Hey, you never said where you folk from."

It was Althea who answered. "We're from Danvers, Massachusetts."

"All-righty. Can't say I know it."

"You will, but probably by its former name."

"Which is?"

"Salem Village"

CHAPTER NINE

Mortimer slipped around the hairpin bend of the stable and entered the eastern leg.

The Earl hesitated. He sensed it immediately. The air held a heaviness he'd never experienced. It remained acrid, still reeked of horse urine and more - yet, it was different; altered in some way.

He inspected the dung clinging to his riding boots, raised each foot in turn and scraped them against the wall while he gathered his thoughts. The noise echoed to eternity. It did so because everything else was mummified by absolute silence. No noise entered from outside, the horses remained hushed, even Felix's whimpering couldn't penetrate the invisible barrier.

Nevertheless, Mortimer knew what he must do. He strode over the cobbled slime until he reached the pen Felix said held the girl. Again, he listened. Again, he heard nothing.

He leant against the swing door, pushed it open, and entered the paddock.

Inside, the enclosure was immaculate; the air fragrant with the scent of a dozen posies. The contrast with the pungent ammonia aroma elsewhere caused the Earl's eyes to tear up.

Through a watery film, he observed a fresh bale of straw suspended from the rafters, untouched. Clean water filled a polished trough to overflowing. And the cobbled floor stood swilled, brushed and unsullied.

What grabbed the Earl of Doom Brae more than anything was the fact Louisa Goodchild was not there and, he was sure, never had been.

Mortimer hurried back to his son, checking each pen as he went. Confusion and panic rose in the Earl with each empty paddock he encountered. All were bereft of livestock, let alone Louisa Goodchild.

By the time he returned to Felix, he was breathless and splattered by midden. "She's not there. You left the girl elsewhere. Think, man. Think. Where did you leave her?"

Felix didn't reply. He was febrile and semi-conscious. Mortimer Pendlebury slapped his son's face. Pinched the flesh of his arm. Reached for a pail of foul-smelling water and tipped it over Felix's head.

The Viscount woke with a splutter. A waterboatman scuttled down his cheek. Spiders clung to his hair. "You found her?" he slurred.

"No, I didn't 'find' her. The girl wasn't there. You were mistaken."

Felix shifted position. Filth pooled around him. "I am not mistaken."

"You told me you encountered her in Bluebell Wood."

"I did."

"Then, why move her to the stables?"

Felix mopped sweat and stagnant water from his forehead. "My head was as a pan of broth, my thoughts muddled. I knew not what I was doing."

The Earl rested alongside his son. Thought for a moment. "It was the hex. She wanted protection. She needed to be discovered. The witch made you move her so she'd be found; so she could bring disrepute to Doom Brae. In truth, she wishes to ensnare us all."

"Father. You know I told a falsehood. The Goodchild girl is a kitchen maid, not a witch."

"I thought so, too, Felix. I truly believed you made up a faradiddles story to cover your actions. But the wench has disappeared into thin air. She brought on the storm. She had your steed throw you to the ground."

"My lord, 'tis not so."

Mortimer glowered at his son. "It is, Felix. It is true. We must both believe it and we must make others believe it, too."

Felix didn't hear him. He had slipped back to a state of delirium, all colour drained from his face, his skin slick with sweat.

Mortimer stood. Wiped his hands on his breeches and spoke to himself. "And I tell you, son, if the wanton can't be found to send to exile, then it must be Edwin I send away. He cannot know of this. None of it."

The Earl struggled to load the unconscious Viscount onto a hay wain, took a circuitous route to the rear of Doom Brae manor, and handsomely tipped a trusted footman to see Felix settled into his chamber where he was to remain undisturbed at all costs.

Mortimer, changed out of his riding gear, sat in the drawing room, unable to relax. A fire roared in the grate, and within its sparks and flames, the Earl saw the rumination of a plan take shape, blossom, and bloom like a red rose.

He'd resolved the first of his dilemmas. The Earl reached for the bell-pull by his chair and heaved on the knotted rope.

Minutes later, the Earl of Doom Brae ran a finger beneath his nose and pushed the snuff box across the table to his youngest son. Edwin nodded his gratitude. He took a pinch of the shredded leaves between his fingers and inhaled lightly. His nose twitched left and right as the tobacco hit.

The men were dressed informally, Lord Edwin in a frilled-collar blouse worn beneath a fan-tailed coat of rich blue; the Earl a buttoned, short black waistcoat and a white shirt tied at the neck by black silk cravat. Both wore natural hair.

"Tell me about your day," the elder man asked.

"I took a walk in the woods this morning." It wasn't a lie. His father needn't know he'd been outfoxed by a kitchen maid.

"Ah," Mortimer nodded sagely. "Splendid day for it. Did you encounter anything of interest?"

Edwin hesitated. Did his father know? Surely Louisa hadn't besmirched her reputation by revealing their friendship. Yet, why else had she avoided him the entire day? He settled for a simple, "No. sir."

The Earl steepled his fingers. Rested his chin on their tips. "And this afternoon?"

"I took tea in the library and read." It was a lie, of course. He'd spent it on a fruitless search of the manor, unable to ask servant or maid if they'd seen Miss Goodchild.

"Good book, was it?"

"Swift's 'A Modest Proposal'. Quite preposterous theme. As if a family would sell their children for food, indeed."

Mortimer's Adam's apple dipped and rose as he swallowed. The gesture went unnoticed.

"So, father," Edwin continued. "I'm sure you didn't call me here to discuss literature."

Mortimer cleared his throat. The gilded tapestries on the wall muffled the sound.

"Indeed not. Edwin, your days must be long. Felix carries out his duties as Viscount. He will inherit the manor from me. But you, you spend your day at leisure. I think you should see more of our great land, learn about its heritage. Wisdom will make a man of you."

Edwin pursed his lips. The offer would give him time to clear his thoughts. Determine his real feelings for Louisa. But, was now the right time; when she had left him in the lurch for reasons he couldn't fathom?

"Do you have Westmorland in mind, sir? Yorkshire, perhaps?"

His father stood. Looked out through leaded windows towards the fringes of Bluebell Wood. "No. I was thinking of somewhere more distant."

"Such as?"

Mortimer reached for a decanter. Poured two generous brandies. "I met with Sir Humphrey Butters last week."

Edwin took a sip from his glass. "And?"

"He was telling me the Duke of All Anglia is in poor health. Consumption, Sir Humphrey believes. He has a houseful of women, and no men. He needs assistance to run his dukedom."

"No, father. He wouldn't ask for my help. I know this isn't true."

Mortimer fingered the heavy curtains. "You're a quick-wit, Edwin. I'm proud of you. You are right. He didn't ask. But I offered." He hadn't, but by the time Edwin arrived in Anglia, the Earl knew he'd have it arranged.

"But, sir. That must be a week's ride away."

The Earl waved a hand; a dismissive gesture. "Five days, at most."

Edwin set down his glass. Looked at his father. "You know, don't you?"

"About your dalliance with the fair wench from the kitchen? Yes, I know."

Edwin stood. "Then you'll know I can never leave here. Not now."

The Earl rammed his staff on the floor. "You can. And you will. I need an heir to continue the line beyond Felix. And the parents must be of good stock. A kitchen maid would never, ever do. Think of the shame. Where would that leave the Doom Brae estate?"

Edwin opened his mouth to protest but the Earl silenced him.

"Now," he continued, "The Duke of All Anglia has two daughters. One, the Marchioness Rosemary, is of your age and as fragrant as her name suggests, according to Sir Humphrey. Not only would she be perfect bride material, she will be excellent breeding stock. It would lead to the Pendlebury's holding both Doom Brae manor and the Duke's Broad Mill Estate. We'd create a dynasty, you, Felix and I."

Edwin spat out a laugh. "Then, it's clear as the nose on my face that I am not the only one with secrets."

"Explain yourself, boy."

"I shall. You see, you are wrong about two things. Firstly, I shan't go. I refuse. And, of greater significance, Felix has already assured you of succession. He has an heir. And you did not know. What says that about you?"

Edwin smiled. He could see he had struck a mortal blow to the Earl's argument. "Josias is his name. The boy must be near four or more by now. Born of a disease-ridden harlot from the village tavern. Yes, my lord: 'Good stock', indeed."

The Earl's face reddened. He could barely speak, such was his rage. "Get out," he stormed. "How dare you belittle your elder brother with your filibuster. I shall see you to the Duke myself if I have to."

"You forget, father. Not only do I have Louisa to remain here for, I now also have Felix. I have him by his nutmegs." He formed his hand into a claw as if to emphasise his point.

The Earl of Doom Brae sucked air through his teeth. Laughed with the malevolence of the devil. "My dear son, you don't have Louisa. I have her. And, if you don't leave for Anglia this very night, this very moment; you know I shan't hesitate…"

He let his voice trail off. He could tell by Edwin's eyes he believed the lie.

Lord Edwin Pendlebury left the room, and Doom Brae, a beaten man.

CHAPTER TEN

The woman with white hair so big it swirled above her head like a tub of frozen yogurt introduced the party of twelve guests to an elegant man dressed in a green waistcoat and cherry-coloured breeches. Despite his attire, his face shouted 21st Century. Probably because it was.

The man doffed his hat. "Thank you, Miss Batkins. Before I return you to Mary," he gave Miss Batkins an imperceptible bow, "It is my duty to give you some information about the majestic building before us." He offered the manor a flamboyant hand gesture.

The party before him shuffled their feet, keen to continue the tour.

"Doom Brae Manor was one of the first buildings to be constructed in the Palladian style. Note east and west wing are exact replicas of one another; a perfect mirror image."

The tourists raised their eyes over the man's head and nodded their understanding. Hank stifled a yawn.

"Also, we have Greek and Roman influences," he signalled to the marble statues either side of the entrance door, "as well as the typically artistic stonemasonry of our age." Another effete gesture towards the portico awning, edged as it was with ornate swirls and waves of white plaster so thick it resembled icing on a wedding cake.

"Do you notice anything else unusual about the manor? Something that hints at its age and the period of its construction?"

The man in the waistcoat filled the silence himself. "Look at the windows. Note how those of the ground floor are small, the first floor larger and those of the uppermost floor larger still. This is to bear the weight of the building. Windows are the weakest point of a building's shell, so there are fewer where most weight sits."

He paused long enough to draw his audience's attention back to him. "This feature was to play a significant part in the history of the manor, and one which makes its story such a momentous one."

Hank's attention wandered. His gaze flitted between the horse-and-carriage convoy, up the hill towards Bluebell Wood, and to the Greco-Roman statues. A puzzled frown crossed his features. He couldn't quell the feeling that something wasn't right; something had changed. He shook his head to clear his mind and refocused on the prepared speech.

"Finally, before you continue the tour of the manor with Miss Batkins, there are two more features I must point out." His voice adopted a serious timbre. "Features which make Doom Brae THE most appropriate of name for our manor."

The tourists hushed. They sensed the boring part had come to an end.

"If you look towards the roof of the manor, you will see it's lined with crenulations."

"Excuse me, sir. What are 'crenulations'?"

"My apologies. I should use the word 'battlement'. Notice how the roof wall is interspersed with gaps through which an archer releases his volley of arrows before taking shelter behind the raised elements. It is a mediaeval feature; a period in history which fascinated the third Earl of Doom Brae, and one which required Royal Assent during peace time."

The group looked at the feature anew. Tried to imagine it lined with bowmen.

"Legend has it, when the sky is clear and the moon is full, an apparition visits the manor gable and can be seen peering from between the crenulation."

Twelve pairs of eyes instantly homed in on the rooftop.

"It is said to be the ghost of Lord Edwin Pendlebury, youngest son of the third Earl of Doom Brae, returning to search Bluebell Wood for a sight of his long-lost love. A lover believed by some to be the Doom Brae witch."

A noise drew the group's attention and they saw the outline of a crouched figure dash across their line of vision. Hank drew his camera but was too late. The fake Lord Pendlebury was already descending the fire escape at the back of the manor. Hank tutted his disappointment and lowered his lens.

The guide addressed Hank. "Fear not, sir. You and your companions may yet get the shot you desire, for I said there were two features of the manor I wished to speak of. Please, if you look at the centre of the portico, just above the feature which resembles a semi-quaver."

Fingers pointed and cameras rose to the place the guide had indicated.

"You will see a statuette. This is a gargoyle; the only one you will see on the entire Manor."

Hank sensed something was about to happen. He trained his lens on the feature.

"It is in the form of a gryphon; a mythical beast, half-lion, half-eagle, which represents the guardian of the divine. Please, feel free to take photographs."

Hank readied his camera as he leaned into Mae. "Dollar to a dime that old bird is going to move," he whispered.

Sure enough, no sooner had he spoken than the head of the gryphon rotated from westward-facing to look directly at the group. Cameras clicked, phones captured the movement on video.

A puff of smoke masked the gryphon for an instant, accompanied by the sound of nails drawing down a blackboard. Or of a stone slab, like the cover of Dracula's tomb, dragging aside.

When the smoke cleared, the gryphon stood with eyes wide and wings spread. To a chorus of 'No way' 'Will you look at that' and a few 'Jeezus', the gryphon launched itself from the portico and circled the group several times, the animatronic mouth opening as its tongue lapped at air like a lizard.

Birds nesting in the manor's eaves fled for their lives while cameras attempted to track the animatronic beast's movement against the backdrop of stonework and sky as it soared and dipped above the crowds.

"JK Rowling, eat your heart out", Hank yelled as he set his camera on Continuous Shoot mode.

After four circuits, the gryphon settled on the Olympian figurine and posed for photographs before it returned to its rightful place above the portico. Another puff of smoke and, when it cleared, the gryphon was once more motionless as death.

Green-and-cherry-red man basked in the applause of the group while Mary Batkins and her ice-cream hair moved into place to lead them into the manor.

Hank saw an opportunity to review his footage while the handover took place. He flicked through the images, nudging Mae whenever he came to a particularly aesthetic shot.

Mary Batkins finished her introduction and ushered the party forward. They headed towards the manor entrance where the refrains of Bach-composed organ music greeted them.

Once again, Hank was left in their wake. He was staring at the image review screen of his camera. Amidst the series of shots of the gryphon in flight, towards the end, there was a series of blank images. Hank estimated there to be around sixteen frames of nothingness before the images reappeared.

He did a double-take between statue and screen.

He couldn't comprehend how he had a photograph depicting a gryphon perched on a discus held in the right hand of a statue.

Hank checked again. A shiver convulsed him.

The sculpture was shorn of right arm and hand. There was no discus on which a gryphon could alight.

CHAPTER ELEVEN

The shadow of flames licked the walls of the darkened room like serpent's tongues. Grotesque misshapen figures filled his field of vision; their silhouettes so large they towered from ground to ceiling. He heard voices speak in tongues, words he didn't comprehend.

His body felt oily-slick. He hadn't the strength to wipe rivers of sweat from his brow or raise his head. He was certain of only one thing.

He was in hell.

Felix Pendlebury returned to the land of Morpheus just as the door inched open. His father closed it behind him with silent precision and walked to the two men hunched over something on a table.

"How is he?" Mortimer asked.

The men removed their tall hats. "His condition is grave, my lord," the elder of the two men replied.

"How grave, Sir Hugo?"

Sir Hugo Parsons tweaked the end of his waxed moustache as he considered his reply. "The leg is cruelly infected. We have tried our utmost, but the infection remains."

"Let me see."

The younger of the visitors spoke. "Sir, I would not encourage it. It's best left to men of our profession."

"Nonsense, Pitt. This is my son we speak of."

The men with the hats looked at one another. Sir Hugo used his position of seniority to make the decision. "Very well."

Sir Hugo and the Earl moved to the bed. Sir Hugo spread elegant fingers and gently pulled back the bedsheets.

The stench hit the Earl first. The smell of rotting flesh. He pulled his head away as his son's limb became exposed.

Felix's lower leg was black as night, the skin suppurated and gangrenous. Leeches, gorged to bursting-point, clung to the open wound while the flesh beneath pulsed with maggot activity.

Mortimer Pendlebury reeled back. "Ye Gods. A foul sight."

Sir Hugo Parsons covered the leg immediately. "Indeed, sir. Now you understand the gravity of the situation."

Parsons rejoined Adam Pitt at the table lit by the feeble flame of two candles. Sir Hugo closed a book he and Pitt had pored over as the Earl joined them.

They stood in a silence punctuated only by groans and murmurs from the bed. "What do you suggest?"

Again, the medics hesitated. Without a word, Sir Hugo rotated the manuscript until its cover faced Mortimer.

'The Treatise of the Operations of Surgery'
By Joseph de la Charriere'.

The Earl furrowed his thick eyebrows, darkened irises beneath. "What is this?"

Sir Hugo licked an index finger and leafed through the book. It settled open at a page.

Mortimer stared at the sheet before him, head bowed. He leant against the table.

"There must be something else."

"Sir, it is with regret I say not."

The Earl directed the same question to Pitt.

"I agree with Sir Hugo."

The flame from the candle flickered and shone in Pendlebury's eyes. Sir Hugo Parsons and Pitt saw the page of a book reflected in them. It read:

'Chapter XXXVII
Of Amputations.'

The Earl let out a sigh of despair. "What about Fordyce? Is he of the same mind?"

"He is."

"Then where in God's name is he? I'm paying him good money to heal my son."

"My lord, I fear John has other important matters to attend to."

The Earl found a release for his anger. "Other matters? What 'other matters' are more important than this? I'll see he pays for his absence. Go find him. Bring him to me. Now."

A voice spoke from the doorway. "Is it me you seek, sir?"

"Fordyce, you blackguard. How dare you leave my son whilst taking my shilling? I swear, I'll…"

Fordyce struggled to raise a bag stuffed with contents into the Earl's line of sight. "Time is of the essence, sir. I took the liberty of seeking out what we need in anticipation of your consent."

In the dim of the chamber, the Earl missed the look Parsons, Pitt and Fordyce exchanged.

Mortimer's face softened. "Then, if all three of you eminent gentlemen agree, so be it. If I must exchange his leg for his life, then I shall. But I warn you – if I lose both, I promise I shall amputate you of something more valuable than your leg."

The three medical men offered words of caution, expressed warnings about the dangers of surgery, but reiterated it was the only option. They asked his permission to proceed.

"What, now? Here? In this room?"

Adam Pitt chose to speak. "Sir, that's precisely what we suggest. The time of year is right for surgery. The body is relaxed after a long summer and, as we approach autumn, the blood is calm and retains sufficient vivacity to reanimate the body."

Sir Hugo nodded his pleasure at his prodigy's depth of knowledge. "So, my lord. May we proceed?"

The Earl looked at his son on the bed. A man lost to delirium and fever. He saw a boy close to death.

"Do what you must."

The Earl helped the medics carry the semi-conscious Felix from his bed and lay him on the table. Fordyce began unpacking the contents of his bag. Alcohol, powder, needles, reels of thread, swathes of padding, and a block of wood. Only when a six-inch long blade and a curved and serrated knife emerge did Mortimer realise the enormity of what was about to occur.

Sir Hugo noticed the Earl cower. "You may wish to leave the room, sir. We shall do what we can to limit the pain, but it will not be easy. The Viscount may, with luck, slip unconscious but, if not…" He left the sentence unfinished.

Through gritted teeth, Mortimer replied, "I shall not leave my son." His Adam's apple bobbed thrice. "I will remain with him."

"Very well. Mr Fordyce, please administer our patient with gin."

Fordyce pinched Felix's nose, forcing the mouth to open. He poured the alcohol into the Viscount's mouth, much of it spilling to the floor as the patient gagged and spluttered.

While they waited for the alcohol to hit, Pitt wrapped a block of wood in linen, Fordyce began tethering the patient to the table, while Sir Hugo lined up an array of evil-looking equipment on a sideboard.

"I need to know…" Mortimer's words came out as a croak. He cleared his throat and tried again. "I want you to explain what you will do to my boy."

Sir Hugo nudged the handle of a knife a fraction of an inch so it aligned itself perfectly with the tool alongside it.

"We shall put a wad of padding beneath your son's knee to relieve the pressure of the cut. The wood shall be placed in his mouth so his teeth bite down on it, not his tongue."

Even in the quarter light of the chamber, Sir Hugo saw Mortimer pale. "Go on," the Earl insisted in a whisper.

"We shall begin by incising the upper layer of dermis with the sharpest of knives. The acuity of the implement and the effects of the gin mean this is the least painful part of the procedure."

Fordyce finished tying the last of the straps around Felix's midriff, ensuring the Viscount's arms were constrained inside the tether. Pitt leafed through the manual as Sir Hugo continued his mantra.

"Once I feel tendon and sinew or, more likely, bone, I shall switch knives." Sir Hugo raised a second knife, the curved one, while Pitt picked up the first and held it in the flame of a candle.

"At this juncture, Pitt will apply a ligature to the leg to prevent blood loss. We may need your assistance to pull tight on the ligature, sir, while my men prepare other material. When the blood has ceased letting, I shall cut quick with the crooked blade."

"To what end?" Felix queried.

"To ensure the stump is rounded, my lord. If it remains sharp, it is more difficult to bind, has a greater risk of infection, and shall cause discomfort when the Viscount's pantaloons and, in time, the false limb rub against the stump."

Mortimer screwed his eyes tight to prevent tears from falling. "And does that conclude the procedure?"

"Alas, by no means. I shall stitch the arteries to prevent further blood loss. Once I finish my work, Mr Fordyce will apply a pad of flour and alcohol to the stump to reduce infection. The alcohol causes great pain but, after the trauma of the amputation, with God's grace the Viscount won't notice it."

Sir Hugo checked over the equipment once more as he continued his explanation. "I shall use the sharpest of knives to skin a layer of flesh from above the knee, fold it over the remaining stump, and stitch in place."

"And then?"

"Then, my lord, we wait. And we pray."

Sir Hugo looked at Pitt and Fordyce. They nodded. Pitt moved to one end of the table and laid his hands on the shoulders of Felix. Fordyce placed his on the patient's upper thigh.

"Gentlemen, we shall begin."

Sir Hugo rested the sharp knife below the knee, inhaled deeply, and cut.

Felix's eyes shot open, wide and staring into hell. Teeth splintered as he clamped down on the wood, and his muffled scream echoed around the Earl's head.

"I swear I'll find the witch who did this to you, my boy. On my life, I shall find her."

CHAPTER TWELVE

Hank ran to join Mae and the rest of the party just as they exited the Grand Hall.

His camera swung from his shoulder like a wrecking ball, narrowly missing a priceless blue and gold vase. His footsteps reverberated in the opulent surroundings - until Batkins half-turned and offered him a glare.

He slowed his gait to a feverish walk, finally close enough to grab Mae by the elbow as the group entered the smoking room, first stop on the interior tour.

"What are you doing?" Mae's words came out hushed but there was no denying the frustration in her voice.

"You gotta see this. There's something going on here and I can't work it out, for the life of me."

"What do you mean?"

"Here, look at this." He twisted his shoulder-strap and held the camera, awkwardly, while Mae squinted at the screen.

"Is that it? You hold me back to look at a photograph? We can look at them back in the hotel, or on the coach." She glanced over her shoulder at the muffled voices behind the smoking-room doors. "We're missing the tour. Come on; let's go."

Hank held her still. "Tell me what you see."

"The front door, the Greek statue, the gargoyle-thing. What exactly am I looking for, Hank?"

"The gryphon. Where is it?"

"Like I said: it's on the statue. On the stump where its arm was. Now, can we go before I miss any more of this?"

She pushed open the door, drawing glances from the tourists, and joined them while Hank studied the image.

The gryphon was indeed nestled on what had once been the elbow of the ancient sculpture. Nestled on the stump, not the discus. Because there was no discus; nor any arm.

"Double-you-tee-eff?"

The next half-hour bypassed Hank. While the others gawped at the lavish royal suite, the spacious chambers and dressing rooms of the Pendlebury family, and the decorous corridors linking them, Hank tried to come to terms with his state of mind.

They toured the staff quarters, comparing and contrasting the dark, squalid rooms, rock-hard beds and bare furnishings, all while Hank's brain did its best to process the earlier events.

Batkins pointed paintings by Hogarth, put names to the faces of the Pendlebury's captured in oil, and explained how the Earl removed all images of Lady Elizabeth as they bore no resemblance to her appearance after her features were ravaged by smallpox.

While she did this, Hank settled on the only explanation possible: the electro-magnetism involved in the special effects somehow, and in some way, had interfered with his digital photographic equipment.

The more he thought about it, the more convinced he became. It was the one thing that made any sense. By the time they reached the library, Hank was once more at Mae's side, taking in Miss Batkin's litany with relish.

The company sat on rows of hardwood chez-longes, cushioned by plump fabric and gaudy upholstery. Like church pews front onto an altar, each bench faced the vast bookcase stacked with an array of hard-bound books, gold lettering on the spines. The collection adorned the entirety of the southern wall, from floor to ceiling.

At its centre, above the lectern where Miss Batkins had taken up position, Hank noticed a large sign advising pregnant women, those prone to seizures or anyone with a heart complaint or pacemaker, to make themselves known to a member of staff. 'NOW'. A woman did so and was led through a side-door.

From behind the bookcase, a series of dull thuds, muted laughter, and muffled shrieks emerged. Hank nudged Mae. "There's more fun in the next room, just you watch."

Miss Batkins gave an exaggerated cough in order to capture attention. When that failed, she clapped her hands in the brusque manner befitting her Head of Household status.

"Lords, ladies and gentlemen, I crave your attention. We are about to visit the hub of this wondrous estate. It is, of course, the kitchen. Before we enter, I must forewarn you that this is no ordinary kitchen, nor you ordinary visitors. You shall be privileged to witness scenes denied even the Earl of Doom Brae himself and, I assure you, your senses shall reel from what you will experience."

The audience gazed around the library as she spoke. They marvelled at the ornate ceiling, the lavish candelabra suspended from it, and the battery of torches pinned to the wall by solid gold fixings.

Miss Batkins addressed the tourists again. "Pray tell me, what sights do you expect to behold within? What delicacies will our staff be preparing for the Earl and his guests this evening?"

"Pheasant? Partridge? Grouse?" proposed one.

"Venison," said another.

A third, "How about pastries and fruit pies?"

"Lots of vegetables, I would imagine."

Miss Batkins nodded at each offering. "And what scents and aromas will greet you?"

A hand shot up. "The scent of warm, baking bread," a heavy-set woman offered.

Batkins' big hair wobbled like gelatine as she nodded her agreement. "Yes, you could expect to notice such an aroma. Anything else?"

"Steaks searing, or hogs being roasted over a fire," the man from the café, Clint Reubens, suggested.

"The smell of pan-fried dumplings," another observed.

Mae threw up her hand. "Spices."

"Ah yes. All sensible suggestions. But, alas, not."

She produced a handkerchief from the hidden depths of her skirts, depressed a bulbous swelling attached to a small bottle, and sprayed liquid onto her kerchief.

"Our age is very different to yours. Ingredients differ. Cooking methods do not resemble yours." She cast her eyes downwards. "And, I regret to say, hygiene is an issue for our ladies. We do not engage in the filthy habit of bathing and, with the heat, well…I'm sure you can imagine."

The party laughed as she dabbed her nose with the perfumed handkerchief. Miss Batkins glanced around like a spy in Red Square. She beckoned the audience to her. Her voice dropped to a stage whisper.

Colin Youngman

"You may have heard of a creature known as The Doom Brae Witch. Be forewarned. She has employ within our kitchen. You may observe some signs of her presence. Look for them. If you spot them, it may, just may, mean she's at work somewhere within."

She raised her voice once more. "Do not be afraid." The audience jumped at the resonance, then giggled at their reaction. "Our best alchemists have been hard at work. Attached to the rear of the seats before you, you shall find the results of their labours. They will offer you protection from her spells and curses. "

Hank stretched out a hand. Withdrew an object from a pocket. A pair of spectacles. "It's like Disney's Muppet 3-D, Mae."

He slipped them on as the bookcase slid open and the floor, complete with rows of chez-longes and anticipatory tourists, glided forward.

The bookcase closed behind them. They were in the kitchen.

And Batkins hadn't been wrong.

A device buried in the arms and supports of their seats assailed the party with a volley of stenches. Hank, Mae and their group gagged as the sour smell of sweat, spoiled and rotting vegetables, and mutton fat rained down on them like the blows of a heavyweight boxer.

A mix of live actors, holograms and animatronic cooks and maids crowded into the kitchen space. Above the heat and squalor, the scents gradually changed.

From the weighty reek of foul breath and fetid cheese, more pleasant smells emerged. Rich gravies, sweetmeats and the fresh citrus smell from platters overflowing with fresh fruit lightened the air and cleared the senses sufficient for the party to appreciate their surroundings.

In a corner, a dark object with luminous eyes seemed to survey the events. It lowered its head and lapped at a bowl at its feet. "A black cat," Hank observed. "I betcha the witch is gonna make a showing. That'll be her familiar."

His eyes scanned the actors, slid across to the work surfaces, over to the giant range on which a selection of meats turned on a spit, and upwards. Strung from the wall above the range, fowl and game hung awaiting maturity.

Alongside them, Hank spotted a leathery-creature, a lizard-like object and long-tailed vermin. He nudged Mae and pointed them out. "What did I tell you? 'Wing of bat, eye of newt, tail of rat'; all that nonsense. She's here."

He made the wooo-woo noise of a child imitating a ghost. Mae shrugged him off.

On stage, actors whizzed back and forth. Some carried plates laden with food, an elderly animatronic man in tailed coat leaned over a hologram of a rotund woman, in ubiquitous linen bonnet and apron, as she carved a joint.

Hank found it almost impossible to determine real from imagined. Towards the centre rear, another woman – hologram, actress or mannequin - stirred a steaming pan of broth with a huge ladle.

Then the lights failed.

Women jumped as the auditorium was plunged into darkness. Mae let out a nervous cry.

"Relax, honey. All part of the show."

A mighty crack, like a thunderclap, rent the air. The tour party jumped again. An electronic sizzle followed and the audience, man and woman, screamed as a burst of static lifted them from their seats. Nervous laughter ensued.

Slowly, a faint glow appeared. It grew in brightness, projecting a greenish light downwards from the ceiling until the pan of broth glowed under a phosphorous cone.

Except it wasn't a pan of broth any longer. It was a cauldron. An ugly, scarred crone sat alongside it. She stirred the bubbling, steaming contents as she turned her head towards the audience and extended a bony finger towards them.

The hologram was much more realistic than the one they'd seen in the woods, and they stiffened with fright as the crone rose from the kitchen floor and moved out and over until it levitated above them.

The tour party turned their heads and twisted their necks to watch as, in a burst of fireworks, the hologram fragmented into crystals and appeared to shower down upon them.

They flinched away from the 3-D effects before bursting into laughter and applause.

All except Hank. He hadn't seen any of it. His eyes were fixed on stage where three characters remained side-by-side.

A chubby rosey-cheeked woman, who seemed vaguely familiar, laid a protective hand on the shoulder of a young boy. On his other side stood a beautiful blue-eyed, flaxen-haired girl.

Hank knew instantly who she was. She tossed her head, hair cascading down her back like a shower of gold, and crooked a finger towards Hank, inviting him forward.

Hank rested his hands on his seat, pushed himself upwards, and glanced towards Mae.

By the time he looked back, the stage was bare.

CHAPTER THIRTEEN

The narrow staircase at the rear of the manor wound like the tight coils of a cobra.

Louisa Goodchild's bare feet caressed the cold stone with the tenderness of a lover's touch as she inched her way down from the servant's quarters. It was pitch black, yet she needed no light to see. She had taken this route many times over the last five weeks and knew it better than her own face.

Kitty Cook's chamber was cramped enough with just one occupant. With two, it was unbearably claustrophobic. So, by day, Louisa slept while Miss Cook worked, safe in the knowledge her presence would go undetected. No household member would lower themselves to enter a maid's room. Only Kitty's second cousin knew of her presence, and she had every reason to be grateful to him. He had saved her life.

As Louisa's recuperation garnered strength, she followed the man's advice. "The blood needs an opportunity to flow," he had told her. "It will provide the body with both vigour and vim and speed you to good health." So, by night, Louisa exercised.

She prowled the empty corridors and halls of Doom Brae Manor much as a spirit haunts the confines of its last abode. Now, at the foot of the staircase, she hesitated behind a heavy wooden door and pressed her ear against it.

She heard nothing.

Louisa depressed the latch. The door creaked as it inched open. She cringed and shrank into the shadows of the stairwell.

A lighter shade of darkness framed the doorway, but only silence entered. Louisa let out the breath she'd been holding and eased the door open some more. She peered through the crack and saw nothing ahead or to the left.

To see to the right, her one-sided blindness required her to open the door sufficiently for her to expose her head. She pulled back the hood of her robe and took another deep breath.

She twisted her neck and shot her head through the gap, retracting it like a strutting pigeon.

All clear.

Louisa laid her back against the door, closed her eye, and took in a lungful of air. She'd done this every night, yet she sensed tonight was somehow different. Tonight was the night she'd seek Edwin. She dreaded his reaction to her scars and sightlessness, but she needed him to know: know the truth about his brother, and the truth about her.

To do so meant entering the family's quarters on the first floor; quarters accessible only via by the gilded staircase at the far end of the manor, through the open expanse of the Great Hall, up to quarters where footmen and butlers were likely still on duty.

Louisa took her first pace into the hall. The dim embers of extinguished fires crackled in shallow alcoves, just enough light to illuminate macabre carvings. Louisa tip-toed across a black and silver marble floor, her robe and underskirts rustling softly in the stillness.

She waited at the foot of the staircase, grasping the domed topper of the handrail. She'd only ventured to the Pendlebury family's personal floor twice in three years. Never uninvited, and never at night. Time to make it a third.

Louisa moved so silently she appeared to float up the stairs. At its head, the corridor unfolded into the distance like a menacing tunnel. Decorative torches lined the wall at infrequent intervals, held in place by bronze sconces. None were lit.

A large candle, almost three feet tall and as wide in circumference, signified the Earl's chamber and provided the only source of light. Meagre though it was, it was enough to reveal the passage was empty.

Louisa's heart thumped like a drum in her chest as she began her slow walk. Conscious of the swishing of her robe, she raised it a few inches from the floor and lost herself in the silence.

Louisa's feet warmed to the thickness of the carpet, but all she sensed was the tickle of pile like a thousand insects beneath her feet.

She hesitated. A noise. She glanced left and right. No place to hide. There it was again. She retreated into shadow and crouched low.

A figure emerged from a side corridor. Tall. Dark clothing. Outdoor clothing. Not a member of household.

In the gloom, Louisa saw the shape pass Edwin, Lord Pendlebury's bedchamber. Onwards it went, beyond Edwin's dressing room, and into the candlelight outside the Earl of Doom Brae's chamber.

Louisa stood, revealing herself to the man's gaze. The man nodded in acknowledgement. He held a finger to his lips. Louisa smiled.

John Fordyce, Kitty Cook's second cousin, heaved his heavy case of elixirs into the next chamber, the room of Felix Pendlebury, and closed the door behind him.

The golden-haired girl hurried forth, safe in the knowledge there was no danger passing the Viscount's chamber, not with John Fordyce looking out for her. Yet, she couldn't afford to disturb the Earl. She paused outside Mortimer's room, and relaxed when she heard the heavy snores of a sleeping man.

Assured of more time, she half-turned so she could see the full length of the corridor with her good eye.

No-one followed. She threw the hood of her plum-coloured robe over her head and entered the darkness of Edwin's chamber.

She didn't need light to know he wasn't there. She knew his scent well enough. And the only odour here was that of a cold, empty, dusty, room. He hadn't slept here for some time, of that she was certain.

Nonetheless, something drove her towards his bed. She reached out. Touched the feather-filled pillows, the rich plumpness of the mattress, and dreamt she was under the covers with Edwin alongside her.

Louisa lost track of time. She could have been there seconds or minutes, but a noise outside the room brought her back. She ducked behind the drapes at the same moment the door opened.

She heard it close. Louisa waited several moments in suffocating silence. She tried to sense a presence. She heard no sound; no breathing, no movement; yet, when she sniffed the air, it bore the vague muskiness of a male.

Was he still in the room? At length, she peeked out.

The room was empty.

Louisa snuck into the corridor. The candle still flickered, and the sound of a somnolent Earl drifted to her ears. Relieved, Louisa scurried to the staircase and down its wide, carpeted steps.

She perched on a stool at its foot while she gathered her thoughts. High above her head, the feeble light of a gibbous moon filtered through a stained-glass window, providing relief to the gloom around her and the darkness in her heart.

She rested her head in her hands, her long hair flowing from the confines of her hood. Louisa knuckled her eye dry of tears at the same time as she heard the clash of doors on the floor above, and the sound of animated voices.

The voices came nearer, urgency in their tone. She heard her name. Somehow, they'd discovered her.

The woods. She'd be safe there. She raced toward the main entrance. The door opened before she reached it. Two footmen filled the frame.

She turned on her heels and headed back through the Great Hall. She twisted around so she could see over her shoulder. Louisa caught a glimpse of five men pouring down the staircase whilst another hurdled it. The two footmen joined the chase.

The Earl of Doom Brae strode nonchalantly behind them, Lupo, the crossbred hound, tethered to his wrist by a heavy chain.

Louisa careered down the corridor towards her only means of escape: the spiral stairway to the servant's quarters. She knocked over pedestals, the busts of Pendlebury family ancestors rolling into the path of her pursuers.

One of the Earl's men stumbled over them. The others sidestepped the obstacles with ease.

Louisa flew through the hall, past the sconces. The chasing pack gained on her. One of the footmen snatched a torch. Others followed suit. Set them ablaze.

The sudden flare disoriented Louisa for a moment. Her feet caught in her robe. She stumbled. Hit the wall with her shoulder. It sent her spinning across the corridor. She glanced back. Saw men charging towards her, faces contorted with rage, arms stretching out for her.

Louisa turned back and ran. Straight into the door leading to the stone staircase, and her one possible chance of escape.

She reached for the latch. Depressed it. Pushed against the door.

It didn't budge.

She put her shoulder against it.

Nothing.

It was bolted. From the inside.

She turned to face the men. Their appearance, distorted by the flickering torches, took on greater malevolence. To Louisa, there seemed many more men now, their numbers multiplied by the reflections in the mirror above their heads.

The Earl pushed his men aside. Lupo reared up on hind legs before Mortimer wrapped the dog's chain around his wrist to restrain it.

Mortimer stood in front of Louisa, his thick eyebrows furrowed, long nose casting dark shadow across his face. "Miss Goodchild. How are you, this eve?"

No response.

"Cat got your tongue, has it? A black cat, one presumes." He chuckled. The Great Dane Wolfhound emitted a long, low growl.

Louisa tried to remain calm whilst her mind worked overtime. Who had betrayed her? She knew for sure it wouldn't be Kitty. Fordyce? He had his opportunity upstairs. If he, why wait? If not them, then who?

"How did you find me?" Her voice came out flat, yet confident.

The Earl chuckled again, so quietly it screamed. "Who would have thought a man who has worked with fire all his life could be so afraid of his own forge?"

"Piggy Trotter! What have you done with him?"

"Fear not. The rapscallion is safe. Or, should I say, safer than you."

Louisa shuddered.

"There is someone here with me who would very much like to meet you," the Earl continued.

She glared at him with her one eye as the men parted like the Red Sea. Felix Pendlebury hopped forward, his weight born by a wooden crutch.

Louisa almost smiled. "An eye for a leg. Fair exchange, I'd say."

"Seize her!"

The men stepped forward. Took hold of her gown. Before Mortimer could instruct them to lead her to the dungeon, the door behind Louisa creaked open.

The staircase swarmed with people like bees round their queen. In the shadows, she made out her friends from the kitchen. Sadie Bishop was there. Emily Jones, too. She noticed Alfred Pooley towards the rear, and Kitty Cook in front of him; all drawn from their quarters above by the commotion.

Mortimer and Felix looked at each other open-mouthed, their plan thwarted. They had no plausible reason to haul Louisa away.

Louisa saw their dilemma. She became imbued with fresh confidence. She grinned at them, deliberately exposed the hideously-scarred side of her face to the men and spoke directly to Mortimer and Felix.

"A plague on both your houses," she quoted.

She saw the Earl's countenance change. Renewed hope showed in his eyes. He tried to disguise a smile. 'What have I said?' Louisa wondered.

"Hear her!" the Earl proclaimed, extending a trembling finger in her direction. "From her own mouth come the words and hexes of a witch!"

Panic showed in Louisa's eye. The company on the stairs gasped. Kitty mouthed 'No', but she could see doubt show on the faces of some of her friends.

The Earl addressed his men. "What is to be done with her?"

"Let the waters decide. Test her!" shouted one.

"Too good for her. Burn her, I say!" insisted another, raising his torch aloft.

As he did so, the shaft barely touched the mirror above him, insufficient for anyone to notice but enough to send the heavy frame crashing to the floor.

Glass shattered in an explosion. Uproar followed. Voices all shouting at once. The Great Dane howling. Bedlam on the staircase, panic amongst the company of the Earl's men.

The party fell silent. Louisa wondered why.

She looked at Mortimer, his face impassive.

Felix, too, remained unmoved. Until he slid slowly down the wall, a slug-trail of blood left behind, and an eight-inch shard of glass protruding from his stump of a leg.

Louisa looked at the sea of faces, and realised she'd sealed her own fate. Now, all bar Kitty Cook believed Louisa Goodchild was a sorceress.

The Doom Brae Witch was born.

CHAPTER FOURTEEN

The party remained abuzz with the drama and sensory-overload of the kitchen escapade.

Mary Batkins had handed the baton back to Wilberforce Long as the tour built towards its climax. He still looked as though he'd been colour-coordinated by a blind man.

Long ramped up the tension with stories of mysterious goings-on through the ages, interwoven with snippets of historical detail. Wilberforce Long led the group to the rear of the servants' quarters and stood outside a low, windowless access door while the group gathered around him.

"We stand outside the only access and egress point our house staff are permitted to use. Not for them the grandeur of the main staircase, the magnificence of the entrance hall, or the Palladian splendour of Doom Brae Manor's exterior. No, our servants, maids and kitchen staff all use what I believe you good folk would name 'the tradesmen's entrance.'"

He tapped his staff against the door. "Behind this door, you will find a stairwell. It leads us to the lower reaches of the manor, to the eastern corridor. At its foot, directly across the corridor, another door awaits us."

Wilberforce held a silence. He straightened his wig. Pulled at an earlobe. Pretended to wonder whether to say more. "The door of which I speak leads downwards. Some say it leads to hell. In a trice, you shall discover the truth."

A blast of icy air expelled itself over Hank and his group. They all shivered, most laughed.

"One-by-one, you are about to learn how difficult even the simplest of tasks is for our hardworking people. Their rations are meagre. The Earl gives prominence to his personal staff." He sniffed haughtily. "I am fortunate to count myself amongst the lucky souls."

An image projected itself above Long's head. He feigned shock before reading out the words projected against the wall. It warned those with mobility problems, fear of confined spaces or poor eyesight to excuse themselves from the attraction.

"It is most important you do as the magical words forewarn. I wish you to experience what the people of our house go through each and every night. Contrary to what you may imagine, candles are not freely available in the quarters. Cost is one reason, the risk of fire another. One candle per week is as all we are granted. And its flame is soon extinguished. So, ladies and gentlemen, imagine it is night. You have been summoned from your quarters by one of their lordships. You must attend to their needs."

He indicated the door. "One-by-one, please step into the dark, forbidding world of Doom Brae Manor."

Wilberforce Long disappeared into a service lift disguised behind a colourful three-tiered dressing screen. A mysterious voice issued the guests with instructions from a speaker in the ceiling. 'Take great care,' 'Enter one-by-one,' 'Do not enter until called', and 'Follow the light'.

The door creaked open unaided and the first tourist stepped into the darkness, giggling nervously as she did so.

Hank passed the wait exchanging small talk with folk nearby. Baroque music filtered around, the strident organ and harpsichord tones periodically interrupted by an electronic voice declaring 'Will the next guest please enter the unknown.'

After Mae disappeared through the door, Hank quickly flicked through some of the pictures on his camera until the door opened. He knew the drill. He stepped inside even as the voice invited him through.

Inside, it was darker than anything he'd ever experienced. Hank reached out until he felt rough stone beneath his fingertips. He extended his other arm. His hand rasped against the wall even before he needed to flex his elbow.

Hank waited for the light. None came. He felt for the edge of the step with his foot. Gingerly, he stepped down. Once one foot was planted, the other followed.

Still no light.

He clung to the handrail. Took another step. Then another. The silence clawed at him. Hank whistled a tune. It echoed around the well-like staircase as if a runaway train approached.

He stopped whistling. Waited for the light.

Still nothing.

He began to sweat. Felt his pulse rate increase. Not knowing who or what may wait on the next step disoriented him. The walls closed in. He spread his arms. No, they were the same distance away.

Hank took another step. Increased his pace. Began taking two at a time. He stumbled. Grabbed at the handrail. Was the rail closer to him? Was he about to be squashed between stone?

Blood pounded his temples. He sat on the cold, bare stair. Held his head. Flicked sweat away. How much further? And, where was the damn light?

Hank stood once more. His head swam. He steadied himself, took another step and, around the next turn, saw the light. A faint green glow, little more than a pin-prick, but something to focus on.

He made his way toward the light, almost running now, his footsteps echoing so it sounded like half a dozen men raced downward.

Without warning, he rushed headlong into a door. Relief flooded through him. He reached for the handle. Opened the door.

Only to find yet more blackness beyond.

Hank almost cried, then he remembered Wilberforce Long's instructions. Another door lay opposite. He reached out. Touched it. And heard the comforting sound of voices beyond.

He heard something else, too; an indistinct tapping from somewhere nearby. He listened. Yes, someone was drumming on a window. Yet, how could they? It was daytime. If there was a window, there'd be light.

Then, what was it?

His hands touched the wall. He ran his fingers up it until they rested on something solid. The rapping came more insistent, and closer by. He folded his fingers around the object. It felt familiar. He touched something else. Glass. Glass within a frame. Yet, not a window.

With creeping certainty, Hank realised someone was knocking not on a window, but on a mirror.

Worse, they were knocking from INSIDE the mirror!

The door behind him flung open. Light bathed the corridor. Hank turned, wide-eyed.

"That was boring, wasn't it?" the last of the tourists said as he emerged.

CHAPTER FIFTEEN

A horse drawn carriage trundled a pathway beneath the protective shield of an archway of trees. Alongside the coach, sodden flora bowed their heads like hooded dowagers in the face of nature's deluge.

Kitty Cook, face set, stared straight ahead. Little Henry huddled into her as she stretched an arm around his shoulder. He hadn't listened to Kitty's words of discouragement. Despite her pleas, Henry had clung to her like ivy to bark. Nothing would stop him being with her today.

She kissed the top of the boy's head. For the first time, Henry didn't need words to make himself understood. His doleful eyes said it all.

He shifted on the uncomfortable bench seat and watched the muddy track wander onwards. "Mu-hug," he grunted.

Kitty ruffled his hair. "Couldn't have put it better myself," she said as the coach slowed to a halt amidst a gathering horde of peasant folk.

The village of Elderkirk, in the parish of Doom Brae, was little more than a scuff on the map; a stain best avoided even by highwaymen. Yet, today, its narrow, filthy streets buzzed with the excitement of villagers, young and old.

The throng of humanity lay before the coach like a giant cow-pat. Through the carriage windows there drifted a stench of greasy, unwashed clothes, foul breath and flatulence. Kitty flung open the carriage door, grabbed Henry by the hand, and clambered out.

They made their way towards the riverbank, ignoring the shouts, curses and raucous laughter of the villagers. "This be the day of all days," a black-toothed hag shouted at no-one in particular.

"Come to educate your boy, have you?" another said to Kitty as they jostled and squeezed their way through the crowd.

"The village never seen nowt like it; not in my lifetime nor my father's or my father's father," hailed a manure-splattered farmhand. "Who'd have thought it? A witch trial in Elderkirk."

The words hit Kitty in the stomach. This was real. This was happening. And nothing was going to stop it.

Above the crowd, a thick haze of smoke rose to meet the leaden skies in a grim embrace. Grey clouds puffed from the unsteady chimneys of abandoned homesteads and, beyond the last of the houses, villagers lit bonfires by the riverbank to relieve their bones of the morning chill while others ignited pyres to ward off spirits.

Kitty and Henry hurried as best they could past the last row of cottages and left behind the sweet, pungent aroma of emptied chamber pots. The waif ran into the back of Kitty. She'd stopped dead.

Across the river, a rickety platform had been erected. Alongside it, by the river itself, stood a strange, wooden device. A roughly-hewn frame, a long plank at a 90-degree angle with a cross bench tethered to it. Ropes and pullies at either end.

Kitty had never seen such a thing, but she knew what it was.

A ducking stool.

Henry made a noise beside her. He grasped Kitty's hand even tighter as he shielded his eyes with the other.

"We don't have to stay, Henry. We can leave this place."

Henry shook his head. "Mah."

She looked up to the slate grey heavens. "Then, offer a prayer, dear child."

A great roar rose from the masses. Gentlemen raised their hats high, women waved their handkerchiefs. Urchins climbed onto their father's shoulders for a clearer view.

Kitty Cook swayed back and forth to catch a glimpse through the forest of people. The Earl of Doom Brae and three manservants stood atop the platform. Another man, short and stout, clambered up to join him. He exchanged words with the Earl's men, who hoisted Viscount Felix Pendlebury onto the platform.

The crowd gasped at the sight of the infirm Viscount, wooden prop tethered to his ragged stump by broad leather straps. A woman, her face powdered chalk-white to disguise pock marks and lesions, pushed her way to the front of the mob. She dragged a child of about four to her side. She bent to whisper something to the boy, pointing out the one-legged man.

The street urchin looked at Viscount Felix anew. This was no longer just another cripple: the boy was seeing his father for the first time.

The stout man stepped forward, a footman holding an umbrella over him to protect his finery from the downpour.

Murmurs rose from the audience. "He shields beneath an umbrella," "What man hides under such a thing?" and, to chortles, "I wager he's loose in the haft."

The man raised his arms, exposing even more extravagant cuff beneath his coat-sleeves. The crowd fell silent.

"Good folk of Elderkirk, welcome. Greetings, too, to those who have travelled far to witness this historic occasion." He bowed towards better-dressed gentry gathered together on the fringe of the crowd. "My name is Silas Grindrod, magistrate and high sheriff of this shire."

The muttering began once more. While Grindrod regained control of the audience, Kitty Cook shepherded Henry away from the river bank, towards the elite. "'Tis safer this way. We're likely to land a facer should the mob turn a mill" Kitty explained.

Silas Grindrod resumed his address. "I thought I had seen the last of these days, but ne'er. The laws of the land remain and, though seldom invoked, they remain for good reason. The devil can still do his work, and we must remain vigilant to his shamming."

The villagers rose in agreement. Pitchforks pointed skywards, handkerchiefs fluttered, and Kitty Cook feared the worst.

"Which brings us to today. It is alleged there is a witch among us. This is no dung-speak; the allegation comes from none other than Mortimer Pendlebury, our much-loved Earl of Doom Brae."

More cheers. Grindrod silenced them with the wave of his cane.

"Bring forth the accused."

Kitty and Henry clambered up a bank turned to muddy slime by the feet of many dozen villagers. They stopped, balanced precariously, on hearing Grindrod's words.

Men hauled a figure onto the platform. The accused wore a flowing, plum-coloured robe. She was bare-foot, hands bound behind her back. A rough hood of sackcloth had been pulled over her face and knotted at collar-bone level.

"Oh, my poor, poor innocent," Kitty gasped, hand to mouth. Henry offered a pained grunt, but their voices were drowned out by the buzz of excitement, anticipation and fear which ran through the crowd.

"The wench beneath the hood is Louisa Goodchild. She must remain covered in case she chooses to bewitch you."

A lady in voluminous whale-bone skirt shouted, "What tomfoolery. Witchcraft is no more. Set her free."

Kitty Cook and Henry weren't alone. She was buoyed by the knowledge others fought on Louisa's behalf, too. Buoyed, that is, until the majority of the crowd drowned out the lady's protests.

"Silence!" the magistrate commanded. The noise continued. Grindrod rapped his cane on the platform six times before order was restored. He read out the charges.

'Hexed Viscount Felix Pendlebury into carnal relations.'

'Conferred with beasts to bring about heinous injuries to the Viscount.'

'Placed a curse upon the Pendlebury family before many a witness.'

'Brought life to inanimate objects causing pain and suffering to Viscount Pendlebury.'

With each charge, the mob became more enraged. Kitty feared they were about to storm the platform and take justice in their own hands. Henry became agitated by her side, croaking and grunting. She squeezed his hand, more for her comfort than the child's.

"…and, finally, the wit…" Grindrod corrected himself in time, "The accused caused Lord Edwin Pendlebury to vanish into thin air."

"Nooo!" The crowd started at the muffled wail from beneath the hood; the first time Louisa had spoken.

Kitty set her mouth grim. If she'd ever had any doubts about Louisa, the final charge brought absolute clarity. "He talks nonsense. Lies, all of it. The Earl would rather cut a wheedle than slice bread," she muttered.

"I agree." The lady in the whale-bone skirt was next to Kitty. "But he has standing in the village. I fear the end will be no good." The lady glanced at Henry. "Your son?"

"Yes. Yes, he is. He's my boy," Kitty answered without thinking.

Despite the circumstances, Henry beamed and hugged Kitty tighter than ever before.

"Gentlefolk," Grindrod commanded from the platform, rain falling so heavily it rebounded up to his knees. "It does not befall me alone to decide the fate of Miss Goodchild. You all know we need a jury for this trial."

Hands shot up. Willing volunteers. All with crazed, gleeful looks on their faces.

A man doffed his three-cornered hat towards Kitty "They're desperate to see a spectacle; that's all they want. They have no interest in justice". Kitty Cook took solace from another supporter.

From the platform, Grindrod continued his address. "Please, please. No more raised hands. Hear me out." The crowd settled. "As we know, the Earl is a good man. He wishes justice to be served, and for it to be served well."

Whispers of agreement came from the throng on the riverbank.

"For that reason, the Earl, as is his right, chooses not to place the burden on twelve men alone. He wishes you all to decide."

A roar like thunder rolled through the crowd. Hats were flung high in the air. Staff and canes held aloft, children shouted from where they perched on their fathers.

Kitty, Henry and their companions exchanged puzzled glances as Grindrod hushed the crowd.

"The Earl is truly magnanimous, is he not?" Silas Grindrod asked of the masses.

Cries of "Hear him," "Hip Hip," and a muted chorus of "For he's a jolly good fellow" all drifted from the masses.

"What in God's name is the man up to?" the man in the three-cornered hat said.

Kitty didn't look at him. "He's turning them up sweet, that's what he's doing," she answered.

"Good lord; of course. He's a devious one, is the Earl." The man's voice contained a trace of admiration despite his distaste.

Grindrod spoke with gravitas. "Folk of the jury. Now is the time for you to decide. Do we free Louisa Goodchild, the kitchen maid; or put Louisa Goodchild, the Doom Brae witch, to the test of a greater power?"

CHAPTER SIXTEEN

Across the corridor from the darkened staircase, the tour party sat cross-legged in front of Wilberforce Long; schoolkids at story time.

They were in a bare chamber scarcely large enough to contain them. To their left, the door through which they'd entered. To the right, a set of ancient stone steps led down into blackness.

Long stood in a spot where a single beam of light shone upwards, directed at his chin so his face showed as a patchwork of light and shade. Water from a concealed tap slicked the rough pebbled wall behind him. Hidden from view, engineers twiddled consuls which steered radio-controlled rats around the party.

Wilberforce recounted the legend of the Doom Brae witch trial in his quaint Georgian cant. His version wasn't historically accurate, but it still engaged and enthralled his audience.

Applause reverberated around the chamber as Long took his bow. When the echoes faded away, he announced a change in the schedule.

"Good folk, at this point, I am expected to escort you, at your own peril, down to the Doom Brae Manor dungeon. The dark exhibits it contains betray our Earl's love for malevolent days of yore."

Wilberforce noticed some of the tourists face drop. "Fear not, for see them you shall. However, before you do, we have some special visitors amongst us today. I have recounted the tale of the Doom Brae witch. Now, I have the pleasure to introduce you to Mrs Althea Reubens."

"Hey, that's our friend," Hank whispered to Mae.

"Mrs Rubens lives in a village known to us all, and she has kindly agreed to share the story of her home with us. Ladies and gentlemen, please welcome Mrs Reubens."

Wilberforce led the applause as Althea rose nervously. Long manoeuvred her into position above the light. Althea cleared her throat and slid her eyes downwards.

"Thank you, Mr Long. I know you're all eager to move on, and so am I. But our host thought you'd be interested in what I have to say. Why? Because I come from Salem Village, that's why."

Ears pricked up and backs straightened at the mention of the name.

Althea Reubens snickered. "Thought that would grab your attention. It was interesting to learn the background to Miss Goodchild's trial, because there are many parallels with events in Salem. Back in the late seventeenth century, Salem was, shall we say, a difficult place to live."

She looked at her husband. "Clint would say it still it has its problems. Nowadays, it's black against white, rich versus poor."

Sage nods of empathy greeted her words.

She continued. "Back then in Massachusetts, neighbour battled neighbour over real estate, family set itself against family over petty jealousies and rivalries, much like the Pendlebury family Mr Long has just told us about. And it was family strife, in a home as far removed from Doom Brae Manor as you can imagine, which precipitated events in Salem."

Althea's voice grew stronger as she gained in confidence. She even raised her eyes to meet her audience.

"A young girl, Betty Parris, was accused by her older cousin, Abigail Williams, of having 'powers beyond nature'. Betty, so it is said, bore marks on her body of 'unnatural origin'. What is more, her cousin accused her of 'moving objects without physical force'.

Wilberforce Long interrupted. "Indeed, dear lady. Just as the Doom Brae witch forced the mirror from the wall."

"Yes; except in Salem, things didn't stop there. Others claimed they'd witnessed similar events elsewhere, in both young and old, male as well as female. Rumour and mistrust spread like wildfire. Folk saw an opportunity to incriminate their neighbour. By the end of May 1692, no fewer than sixty-two people were under arrest."

Heads shook within the group, low whistles coming from some. Hank spoke up. "You know us Yanks; always bigger and better." The group laughed.

"Are there any other similarities between Doom Brae and Salem?" Long asked, keen to move things along.

Althea flushed. "Yes, there is. While Louisa Goodchild had her dalliance with Lord Edwin, and the Viscount is said to have used the girl to his advantage, many of the Salem accused were brought to account for a lack of Puritanical values. Girls and women were accused of attracting men by Malleus Maleficaram."

"Kindly explain, dear lady."

"Of course. My apologies all. Malleus Maleficaram is an ancient log which documents tales and legends of men having…," she hesitated, " 'Encounters' of the flesh with demons. it details incidents of men having their minds swayed, and of the prophecy of evil events. In short, Mr Long, of behaving exactly as Miss Goodchild was accused."

A member of the group raised her hand. "Sorry to interrupt, but you did say sixty-two were arrested, didn't you? I did hear you correctly?"

Althea nodded.

"And were all found guilty?"

"Actually, no. Twenty were executed. Fewer than most imagine but, of course, far too many."

The temperature in the chamber had plummeted. Breath came in clouds from those who spoke. Shivers convulsed the few who still wore their summer garb.

Even Wilberforce Long, in his heavy apparel and triangular wig, looked pasty. He folded his arms and rubbed the palms of his hands against them. "Tell us, Mrs Reubens, why were the unfortunate score found guilty whilst others walked free?"

"Much of the testimony was verbal from those who claimed to witness the events. Of course, many of these weren't neutral or unbiased accounts. In fact, they rarely were. So, in the majority of cases, the magistrate demanded corroborating evidence."

"Such as?"

"They were asked to recite the Lord's Prayer in the belief that those who did the devil's work were unable to speak the Lord's words."

Most the group stood, now; stamping their feet for warmth.

Hank buried his hands deep in his pockets. His nose shone red against pale, cold flesh. "Surely they all passed this test, though. What made the twenty stand out from the others?" he asked.

"Simple. When entering a pact with the Devil, it's claimed he uses a claw or a branding iron to mark the witch as his own. Quite simply, all sixty-two were checked for such marks."

Frost clung to the chamber's walls. Water no longer trickled down them. Instead, it froze in a glassy pool.

"And, the twenty all bore ugly moles, skin blemishes, fleshy folds, or vivid scars." Althea's words to the group were solemn.

"In short, they bore Satan's mark."

CHAPTER SEVENTEEN

Silas Grindrod strode over the platform like a player across his stage, the baying mob his audience.

"Think well before you cast your verdict," Grindrod said. "The Earl and Viscount wish you to consider the evidence in full course. Above all, they wish justice to be served."

Mortimer and Felix looked at one another. The elder man swallowed. This was the moment where his plan stood or fell. Either the crowd were with him, and the family shame died with the Goodchild girl, or his dynasty faced ruination.

The magistrate moved alongside Louisa. In solemn tones, he addressed the crowd. "People, it is time to decide."

He grasped the sack over her head and whipped it off, displaying her face for the first time.

Gasps rent the air. People shouted all at once.

Grindrod rammed his cane. Waited for the noise to subside. He pointed his staff towards his right; where Kitty, Henry and the others stood.

"Let you have say," the magistrate commanded.

The majority, wooed by Louisa's beautiful looks, golden hair, and serene appearance yelled "Free her," "She is surely innocent," "Let the girl go."

A considerable number dissented, persuaded by Grindrod's rhetoric, but most voted in her favour. Kitty's heart skipped a beat. Henry jumped twice, a laugh gurgling from him.

Grindrod addressed the mass to the left. "What say you?"

They had no doubts.

"She bears the mark of the devil." "Satan has claimed her." "She has forsaken the lord and let the brand of the beast sit upon her."

"The test. The test – she must face the test!"

The heart which had skipped a beat only moments earlier now resided in Kitty's stomach. The mob had been exposed to Louisa's ruined aspect; her appearance the deciding factor.

Kitty now understood the Pendlebury's tactics. Tears filled her eyes. Louisa's destiny lay in the hands of a hundred or so folk in the centre of the crowd; folk who didn't know her kind heart, easy ways, or loving nature.

Folk who knew only what the Earl, through Grindrod, had told them.

At the rear of the platform, Mortimer Pendlebury screwed his eyes tight until only ragged folds showed. Felix held his breath and wobbled precariously as he struggled to maintain balance on the slick platform. Neither could bear the tension.

Centre stage, Silas Grindrod stepped from beneath the shelter of his umbrella. With a dramatic flourish, he pointed to the remainder of the crowd.

Rain pounding the river, hammering against trees and foliage, and the steady drip-drip of drops upon waterlogged turf, was the only sound.

Kitty prayed. Henry prayed.

Finally, a single voice emerged above the silence.

"She has two faces."

Another voice: "The devil creeps over her, inch by inch."

And another, louder. "A sure sign. The wench be a witch."

Cries of assent grew. "Let the water decide." "Test her."

Bedlam followed.

Guards grabbed Louisa. Dragged her to the stool. The crowd jostled for the best vantage point. Scuffles broke out. Men wrestled with each other. A couple tumbled into the river and were washed away, still fighting.

Kitty Cook sat in the mud and the filth and cried. Henry sat beside her, making what he intended to be noises of comfort amid his own tears. The other couple walked away, arm-in-arm, no desire to see more.

In the distance, Kitty saw men fasten Louisa to the stool. Four others clung to the rope as if their lives depended on it. Above the frenzy, she heard Grindrod's voice. "Wench, what say you?"

Louisa spoke to the crowd, head aloft. "I am not afraid of death, as you are the truth. Every night, the spider eats its own web and spins anew the following day. That is all death is to me. I devour my old life and prepare to build a stronger, better one next time."

She turned to face the Pendlebury's. "But those who know not the ways shall forever be ensnared in their own web."

At that, Grindrod gave a signal. "Release the ropes."

Kitty Cook, ashen-faced, hauled Henry away, back towards their waiting carriage, as Louisa entered the water.

By the riverbank, the Earl and Viscount watched the distorted outline of Louisa struggle beneath the waters. She tossed back and forth in her tethers. Her hair fanned outwards, golden reeds afloat in the river's ebb. After a few moments, Louisa's struggles ceased. The raging waters flowed by, undisturbed by air bubbles.

Grindrod looked at the Earl. He shook his head and displayed the palm of his hand. "A few moments more," he said through clenched lips. "To provide surety."

The crowd stilled. Wondered how long before the Earl released her. Just as they became uncomfortable, he nodded.

"Bring her up," Grindrod ordered. Four men hauled on the rope. The stool broke the surface, Louisa still shackled to it.

The girl emerged, her pallor more greyish blue than deathly white. Louisa's head hung forward onto her chest. River water streamed from her hair and clothing. A patch of green moss clung to her forehead.

Unease settled over the crowd. A witch should survive the test. Water would renounce her in the way she'd renounce Holy Water. Had they killed an innocent? Women sniffled into handkerchiefs, their menfolk hid their guilt.

The Pendlebury's exchanged smiles. It was over. They'd preserved their dynasty, gained retribution, and silenced Goodchild forever.

They offered their hands to Silas Grindrod, who gave a reverential bow in return. The crowd began to disperse. One of the Earl's men stepped forward. He cut the first of Louisa's bonds.

And screamed like a stuck hog.

Her one eye had shot open, blood red, madness within.

The crowd swivelled at the commotion. They turned in time to see the dead girl toss back her head. Water streamed from her hair, the droplets freeze-framed in a strobe-light flash of lightning.

Her blood-curdling shriek filled the air. "May the devil have his day. Let him touch them from afar. Take them all, and ne'er cease 'til the Pendlebury line be no more. So it be!"

The crowd rushed in all directions, some in panic, others to better see what had happened, still more to escape the witchery.

Shouts echoed around the village. A powdered-faced woman broke away from the stranger she'd accosted, just in time to see a surge of villagers force her four-year old son towards a smouldering pyre.

Someone made a grab for him. The hands pushed him away. The boy slithered on waterlogged mud, did the splits. The child struggled to his feet. Slipped once more and, with arms windmilling, tumbled from the riverbank into the raging foment.

The woman prepared to scream, but only swallowed dirt as she was pushed to the ground and trampled in the stampede.

Not five minutes after the Doom Brae Witch had spoken, the river's currents sucked Josias Pendlebury-Shanks from view.

Mortimer cowered at the rear of the platform. A tremulous wave of fear shook his voice. "She IS a witch. It is proven. Dunk her again. Commit her to the water. Now!"

Many of his men had fled but the strongest remained. He levered the stool, and the words of the Lord's Prayer caught in Louisa's throat as she entered the foaming river waters.

"Leave her overnight. Guard her. Do not raise her from the river 'til morning. Then, burn the witch," Felix bellowed.

Beneath the ferment, Louisa Goodchild remained still. After she'd unleashed her curse upon the Pendlebury family, all of nature had whispered its secrets to her. She wasn't afraid. Today was her beginning, not her end.

Those who remained by the bank witnessed a ghostly green glow, the shade of the Aurora Borealis, glimmer in the river's depths.

The phenomena rose to the surface, broke through, and hovered above. It pulsed to a heartbeat's rhythm then sunk back to the water, gradually fading to oblivion.

The river flowed dark and turbulent once more.

CHAPTER EIGHTEEN

A disembodied voice crackled in the ear of the man charged with playing the Wilberforce Long character. Long pressed a finger against the hidden earpiece and gave a thumbs-up to the CCTV camera disguised within a bowl of fruit.

"Ladies and Gentlemen: may I have your attention for a moment? At this stage of your tour, we would normally take you straight through to the dungeons before concluding your visit with a carriage tour of the grounds. If I could pray your forbearance, we have a change to our schedule."

The group shuffled their feet to keep warm in the frigid air.

"We owe thanks to our friend for her interesting tales from Salem. They were, I'm sure you'll agree, well-worth hearing. However, as a result, we have caused quite a tailback behind us. We will, therefore, come back to the horrors of the Doom Brae dungeon in a short while and take our trip round the grounds first. Our carriages await, so I shall escort you to your coachmen and, when you return, we shall conclude your visit with the nightmarish cellar dungeons. Should your nerves permit, that is."

The dungeon was always the highlight of the tour and Wilberforce feared the announcement wouldn't go down well. On this occasion, he needn't worry. The party were more than happy to escape into the warmth of late afternoon.

Hands shot to foreheads to shield their eyes as they stepped into brightness after hours inside the manor. A line of coachmen in brown breeches and long brown frieze coats trimmed with extravagant gold brocade, aided passengers into their carriage and quickly set off in convoy.

By chance, Hank and Mae found themselves sharing a coach with the Reubens. Hank sat back and watched livestock graze in the fields whilst Mae engaged in chat-chit with the couple.

Hank learned the Reubens had family in New Port Ritchie, Florida. Clint's brother worked for the Port Charlotte Fire and Rescue Service, where Mae's cousin Alwyn spent some time.

Hank stifled a yawn. In the warmth of the sun, and with the gentle rocking motion of the carriage, he felt his eyelids droop.

His eyes opened as the carriage lurched and jolted. He looked around while he regained his senses, before smiling at Althea who sat opposite. She fixed him with her beady eyes and smirked back.

They were alone.

"Where are the others?" Hank asked.

"They wanted a look around the stables. Our driver will pick them up on our way back."

"When was this?"

"Five minutes ago, I guess."

Hank furrowed his brow. "Gee. Thought I'd just rested my eyes."

Althea laughed, a curious high-pitched sound. "You've been out almost quarter of an hour now. Been a long day, has it?"

"It sure has. Enjoyed it, though."

He tried to get his bearings. The fields to the left were overgrown, no sign of cattle. A copse of saplings lay to his right; ahead, a brooding mass of woodland. "Where are we?"

"Doom Brae."

"I know that." He felt guilty for snapping at Althea. "I thought your stories of Salem were darn interesting, Althea," he offered by way of apology.

Althea sat with hands folded in her lap while she continued to fix him with her stare. "Thank you. But they weren't stories. It's fact."

Hank nodded. "I guess."

"No guessing about it." The coach lurched left and right as it left the track and crossed open grassland, but her head barely rocked. "It's all fact."

"Real sad. Twenty innocent people executed over a load of bull. Can't imagine it, can you?"

"I certainly can. But it wasn't a load of bull, Hank. Sure, some were innocent. But, not all."

Hank poo-pooed. "What? You trying to tell me they were witches? You need get a job here, Althea, if you think that."

"I didn't say they were all witches." Althea didn't blink; just penetrated Hank with her stare. "Only some of them were."

"You serious?" Hank's voice wavered. He put it down to the coach's motion but wasn't entirely sure. "You don't believe all that old smoky, do you?"

Althea's voice remained calm, quiet, and emotionless. "As a matter of fact, I do."

Hank spat out a laugh. "Witches and wizards? Gryffindor and Slytherin? Why would you think any of that was real?"

"Because I'm one of them."

Hank waited for the punchline. She remained silent. He waited for her odd high-pitched laugh. None came.

"Come on, lady. You're trying to tell me you're a witch? Get real, man."

Althea shrugged. "Whatever."

"I bet you a hundred bucks. Make it a thousand bucks. Put a spell on me."

Althea's laugh came this time. "Then, you'd better show me the colour of your money. I already have."

"What?"

"Cast a spell. Why do you think you fell asleep? Why do you think Clint and Mae explored the stables? Because I made 'em."

Hank shook his head. "Lady, I thought you were a bit strange, but never imagined you were this deluded. Why would you want to do that?"

Althea just smiled and stared right through him. "Driver. Stop the coach, please."

The coachman pulled back the reins. The horse gave a whinny and tossed his mane.

"Wait. What are you doing?"

"Get out the coach, Hank. We're going for a little stroll."

He didn't know why, but he clambered out. Althea followed. They stood at the fringe of Bluebell Wood.

Hank fidgeted with his hands. "Are we supposed to be here without a guide? I mean, isn't this the part where the T-Rex bursts outta the trees?"

"No need to worry, Hank. I don't communicate with the beasts. Not often, anyway. I can't move inanimate objects. And, I'm a bit old in the tooth for the seduction spell, don't you think?

"Then, you're not a witch. Come on, let's get back for Clint and Mae."

Althea was already inside the wood. Against his better judgement, he followed. He found her in a clearing beside an ancient, fallen tree. He watched Althea, her hands still clasped together, eyes closed.

Her nostrils flared as she breathed through her nose. She snapped her eyes open and spoke.

"You sense her too, don't you, Hank? That's why I brought you here. You can sense the Doom Brae witch."

He laughed, but it was a nervous one. "Yeah, I sure do. Gandalf's here, too. And look, there's Tinkerbell hiding in the tree."

"I know you feel her presence. You saw her here, in the woods. And in the courtyard café. The manor, too. You've sensed her in so many places." She fixed him with her icy stare. "Don't deny it, Hank. I know you have."

He hesitated. Shrugged. "Maybe. Say, does that make me Professor Dumbledore?"

Althea stood in the shadows, almost invisible. When she spoke, it was as if her voice came from a wizened oak. "Don't jest, Hank. I may not do all those things Wilberforce Long said of the Doom Brae witch, but 'witch' is a very broad term. Some of us are Sayers who foretell the future. Others are Seers. They see things from the past. Things they can't possibly know."

She fixed Hank with her cold eyes. "You're neither of those. So, what are you? A transmigrant?"

"Whoa. I'll have you know I'm a happily married man and…"

"A transmigrant is a soul shifter. He, or she, moves from host-to-host. Half-believers explain it away as reincarnation."

Hank shivered. Violently. He felt neither cold nor warm; just unnerved. He knew the woman from Salem was talking nonsense, yet she scared the hell out of him.

"Well, Althea. It's been real interesting talking to you, but can we go back to our carriage now? I'd like to finish this tour before the manor closes."

The mouse-like woman gave a half-smile and led him by the hand to the coach. As they clambered in, she spoke.

"You can deny it all you like. But, same as you, I feel things. Sense them. What I can't figure is why you can sense her. You haven't got other powers. You intrigue me, Hank; you really do. I've never come across a non-believer with a gift."

He opened his mouth to speak but, instead of words, all that came out was a yawn.

His eyelids fluttered. Mae sat alongside him, Clint and Althea opposite. All three were engaged in a discussion about the impact of cutbacks on Port Charlotte fire and rescue emergency services.

Try as he might, Hank couldn't harvest the vague recollections of a hazy dream.

CHAPTER NINETEEN

Hellfire reflected in the curved surface of the glass. As it gently rotated, a grotesque distortion of Mortimer Pendlebury's face appeared to float within the flames.

"Good health." The Earl raised the glass and sipped a generous measure of brandy. "Quite a day, my boy."

Felix remained silent as they chinked glasses.

Father and son sat in the drawing room of the manor's west wing. A roaring fire blazed in defiance of the wind and rain's fury outside. Lupo lay spread-eagled in front of the grate, a giant paw holding down the remnants of a gnawed bone. His tail thwacked in rhythm with the mantel clock's pendulum.

The men remained still as statues. At length, Mortimer stood and walked to the window. Rain smeared the leaded glass like Angel's tears. In the darkness, he watched the vague outline of trees bow and scrape in deference to the elements.

"Quite a day, indeed," he repeated. "But it is over. The fuss will soon depart. All that shall remain is the memory of how the Pendlebury family preserved the village from evil wickedness. Our family reputation is enriched, not besmirched."

The Earl looked at his silent son. "You remain troubled. Speak of it."

Felix swallowed the remains of his brandy and reached for the decanter. "What of Edwin? He must be told."

"Why?"

"You must ask 'why'? He will raise merry hell, that is why. Edwin won't be taken in by tales of witchery."

Mortimer snorted. "You still call them tales after what we beheld today? Nay, lad. They aren't tales. Besides, we have the good folk of Elderkirk to bear witness. Let him hear from them, not us."

Silence enveloped them once more save for the howl of the wind and the insistent rap of rain. Lightning's distant flare illuminated the room. Thunder followed, barely audible above the gale.

Lupo sat up, alert; bone ignored. He sniffed the air, circled, let out a brief, menacing growl, and settled again.

Mortimer retook his seat. "'Tis the heavens rejecting the sorceress, it is plain."

"Sir, we must get news to Edwin. He is not fly to the time of day. If he hears news from others, he will suspect deceit. We must keep him sweet. Doom Brae needs an heir beyond my inheritance The Earldom needs a line of succession." Felix rubbed at his stump of a leg. "And no-one shall wish to pair with a cripple like me."

One corner of the Earl's mouth curled upwards. "Felix, pray tell: do you think I am 'fly to the time of day', as you call it?"

"No, father."

"I see." Mortimer held the silence. "Then, you must know I am already aware you have an heir. Josias is his name, I believe."

The Viscount flushed. Cast his eyes downwards. "You know."

"Yes, I know."

"Edwin?"

"Who else?"

"The child doesn't know me. He is not worthy of the Pendlebury name. He can't be allowed to inherit the manor, which is why we need Edwin to spread seed and to remain part of our line."

Lupo pricked his ears again. They stood pointed and erect. A bass rumble emerged from the depths of his throat. The Earl admonished him, but the growl continued.

"You should have told me, Felix. I could have arranged for the boy to be..." he hesitated, "...removed."

Felix continued to inspect the rug at his feet. "I did remove the next one."

"The next one?" Mortimer roared. "How many side-slips of yours are out there, by heaven?"

"No more, sir. I swear there's only Josias. The other is not yet born. But you shall not hear of him, or her. A few florins and a word in Captain Woodcott's ear saw the wench sail far from these shores as soon as I discovered she was with child."

"Ye Gods, man. I'm beginning to think I exiled the wrong son."

Outside, the wind howled like a dervish. A freak gust drove down the chimney, carrying spirals of smoke into the room. Lupo leapt up, tail trembling between his hind legs. The hound yelped pitifully and bolted towards the closed door. It cowered there, whimpering to be let out.

The smoke cloud drifted towards the window where it hovered in the shadows, an amorphous olive-green mass, before its poisons snuffed out the candle's flame. The Earl of Pendlebury tisked as he walked to the window to reignite the tallow.

A blaze of incandescent lightning, so bright it blinded the Earl, projected his silhouette across the canvasses of family ancestors. Thunder roared like a voracious predator.

More lightning. Simultaneous thunder. Again, and again.

Felix shivered. "Father, I need my bed. My limb pains me and the day has been long."

"Nonsense, Felix. You need more brandy to warm your bones. I'll summon my man."

The Earl reached for the bell-pull as the manor creaked and groaned around them like an arthritic man rising to his feet. His fingers touched the velvet rope.

And the building lurched as if caught in an earthquake, throwing the Earl of Doom Brae to the floor. Mortimer found himself face down in Lupo's drool.

He brushed himself down, embarrassed at his fall. "What in God's name was that? No-one will sleep with this storm raging," the Earl said as he clambered to his feet. "A nightcap. Just one. Then we shall retire. Drink with me, Felix. Let us move on from today."

The door flew open. A footman entered as Lupo dashed out, sending the interloper head-over-heels. The man dragged himself to his feet, and then doubled-up, gasping for breath, hands on knees.

"What the Devil, Moncur? I shall have you flogged. Knock first, man."

Moncur looked up, his face florid, chest heaving. The bows of his wig lay unfastened around his shoulders. His shirt-tails hung over his breeches like a nightgown. He opened his mouth to speak but hadn't the strength. Waved his hand instead.

Mortimer and Felix exchanged perplexed glances. The sound of thunder rumbled in the distance. The sound came closer. Advanced towards them.

Not thunder.

Finally, Moncur found his words. "Sires, you must leave. At once. Lightning has struck. It has penetrated the eaves of the West Wing. The timber is alight. Sir, the manor – it's ablaze."

Mortimer set towards the door. Realised his infirm son wouldn't make it. He turned back to help him.

The roar intensified, and the ball of flame which had rumbled along the corridor like a snowball downhill came to a dead halt in the doorway.

Intense heat filled the drawing room. Fingers of flame probed the walls and furnishings, reaching out for the Earl and Viscount.

The sound of breaking glass, the screams of servants, the roar of fire, the vitriol of the storm - all combined to baffle the senses and served to cause panic.

Mortimer spun round, trapped, frantically searching for an exit. The smell of thick, acrid smoke choked the Earl. Wood splintered in the distance, walls crumbled and tumbled, came crashing down at the far end of the corridor.

Priceless oil paintings singed in the heat. Tapestries curled in on themselves, soon spitting flames onto rug and carpet which flared in sympathy.

"Felix. Take my hand. Come."

Felix hobbled towards his father. He reached out, their fingers almost touching, before the ceiling split asunder. A blazing roof beam hung between them. Flames licked upwards; up towards the inferno bearing down from the floor above.

A curtain of fire lay between father and son.

"Felix. I shall return. I shan't desert you."

The younger man stood, paralysed by fear, wide-eyed and helpless. Mortimer shared a long gaze with him before the sound of breaking glass spurred the Earl onwards.

The ground floor window had shattered, showering the table with glass. Oxygen fed the flames, the fireball hungrily licking its way towards the source. It was now or never, Mortimer knew.

He dashed across the room. Vaulted atop the table. He ripped off his wig as he smelt it burn. Heat singed his eyebrows. He levered himself into the frame. Glass shredded his fingers, arms and stomach as he struggled to squeeze through the narrow exit.

Felix barely heard the words, "I will be back, I promise. Trust me, son" before he found himself alone in hell.

Outside the window, Mortimer rolled himself in mud. His clothing cooled so it no longer scalded the flesh beneath. For a moment, he luxuriated in the sweetness of driving rain before he dashed off into a wind that bit and snapped at him like a rabid dog.

Inside what was left of the drawing room, Felix prayed. He recited every prayer he'd ever heard and made a few of his own. He thought of his father, of Edwin, of Josias and the boy's harlot of a mother. Last of all, he thought of Louisa Goodchild.

He looked down to pray again. And froze at what he saw. Now, his thoughts weren't of Louisa. They were of the Doom Brae witch.

The Earl of Doom Brae emerged from the outbuilding and stood stock-still. He faced the manor. Its stonework glowed red with the heat of the firestorm within. Part of the West Wing was little more than rubble, a mix of black char and glowing redness; lava from a volcano.

He thought of the priceless antiquities within, the loss of his legacy, and the ruination of his reputation. Most of all, he thought of Felix, imprisoned within what was left of its walls.

Members of the household stood at a safe distance, staring at the remnants of the manor as the Earl slithered and slipped his way across a field of mud, a thick rope trailing behind him like a serpent.

He stood beneath the same window he'd squeezed through. It was too high. He couldn't reach it. He looked at it in desperation.

Part of the frame remained. The Earl fashioned a noose and tossed it at the frame. Three times he tried, three times he fell short.

"I'm back," he screamed towards the wall. "I said I wouldn't leave you. Have patience."

At the fourth attempt, the rope snagged. Mortimer scrambled up. The top of his head appeared in view. Swiftly, he unknotted the rope with his teeth and one hand as he clung to the frame with the other.

"Felix – I have a rope. I shall throw it to you." He ducked as a chunk of masonry plummeted downwards. "Hold fast and I shall haul you out."

He grasped the frame so he could heave himself up. His skin blistered with the intense heat of the stone. Gritting his teeth, he hauled himself into the frame. It was a ground floor window; a tight, narrow space. Could he manoeuvre himself sufficiently to cast the rope?

"Here I am," he shouted triumphantly, barely concealing a laugh. "I am back for you, son."

Mortimer looked through the window for the first time. Despite the raging heat, he was chilled to the bone.

The walls were blackened. Thick smoke filled the air, but crimson flames provided sufficient light for Mortimer to see.

Viscount Felix Pendlebury lay on his back surrounded by the fallen portraits of his ancestors, his eyes wild. But their gaze wasn't on his father. They were fixated on his peg leg.

The peg-leg which burned brightly. Flames consumed it, ravenously making their inexorable way towards the rest of his body.

Mortimer watched, aghast. He couldn't bear to look, yet he couldn't turn away.

A growl filled his ears. Not thunder. Not fire. He knew what it was.

He looked upwards. Saw the crack appear in the wall. Watched it widen as if fingers prized it apart. Stone crumbled, small and pebble-like at first, before larger chunks rained down.

Finally, in an explosion audible in Elderkirk, the entire wall of the West Wing collapsed upon him.

All that remained of the Earl were his legs, protruding from the rubble of Doom Brae Manor.

CHAPTER TWENTY

The slow, doom-laden beat of timpani heralded the convoy's return to the manor.

Bass rhythms grew louder while the company clambered from their carriages, until the battery became painful. They felt the beat throb and pulse within them as the volume increased even more.

Suddenly, they were plunged into silence.

Hank's ears sang as if he'd left a rock concert. He rubbed them until they reddened. Some of his fellow-tourists plugged fingers in their own. Others shook their heads to exorcise the ghostly echoes.

So pre-possessed were they that they failed to notice their three principal guides, Wilberforce Long, Erasmus Fairbody and Mary Batkins, emerge from the manor.

Long stepped forward. Hank saw Wilberforce's lips move but it was a while before his words seeped through the residual buzz in his ears.

"… conclude your visit," were the first words to register. "The dungeons await you. So, too, does none other than the Earl of Doom Brae himself, Mortimer Pendlebury. Ladies and gentlemen, I beseech you to show his lordship respect. The Earl does not suffer fools gladly. You will be wise not to incur his wrath."

Mary Batkins and the gamekeeper, Fairbody, moved to join Wilberforce Long.

The man in the stuffed crust pizza wig concluded his speech. "Ladies and Gentlemen, it has been our pleasure to escort you around our wondrous home. But now, we must leave you. The dungeon is not a place to trifle with. We dare not enter. Good luck, dear friends. I fear you shall need it."

The party filed past the three guides, the late-afternoon sun casting their long-legged spidery shadows over the Roman and Grecian guardians and across the manor walls.

Some of the trippers thrust coins and notes into the hands of the Georgian characters as they snaked past. Mae fumbled in her purse and handed the proceeds to Hank to pass on.

He shook Long by the hand. "Hope I didn't embarrass you earlier. About the wig, I mean."

Long smiled. "No sir. I've heard a lot worse dressed like this, I assure you."

Mary curtsied in appreciation as Hank handed over a few dollars.

"I'm pleased you managed to see all the tour," the Erasmus character said. "You had me worried at one point."

Hank laughed. "Gee, seems a long time ago now. Thanks for your concern. Honestly, I feel right at home here. This is my kinda' place," he said, taking a good look round. "And I'm swell. Real fine."

He watched the backs of Clint and Mae disappear down a flight of steps. Althea walked a few paces behind.

"At least, I think I am," Hank concluded.

He caught up with them outside a heavy wooden door adorned by rusted metal fittings. A tall haughty-looking man stood in front of the party. Two muscular men holding axes guarded the entrance.

None spoke.

When the last of the stragglers joined them at the foot of the stairs, the gentleman pushed at the door. It swung open with an exaggerated groan. The party of twelve stepped inside, into cold and darkness.

They jumped when the door clanged shut behind them, the noise deliberately amplified to provoke a startled action.

The drum beat began again, much softer and all the more menacing because of it. A single torch flared. The group blinked at the sudden light.

They were in a large cellar, dank and musty. Stone columns held up the ceiling. In contrast to the manor's opulence, there was nothing ornate about the pillars. No carvings, decorations. Just plain, bare stone.

The guards led them forward, into the middle of the chamber. More torches flared, flooding the space with light and shade.

A platform sat against one wall. Above it, three oil-paintings; the Earl of Doom Brae, Viscount Felix Pendlebury, and his younger brother, Lord Edwin. Left and right of the platform stood two suits of armour; a nod to the Earl's fascination with all things mediaeval.

A tall, high-backed chair, an ermine throw tossed over it, sat centre-stage. A smaller chair, less-intricately carved, remained empty next to it.

The party whispered to one another as they studied the artefacts. A burst of trumpets made them jump. A door opened. Two bewigged gentlemen emerged. One walked regally to the centre chair. The other hobbled behind, supported by crutches.

The men mounted the platform. Hank's eyes slid between the portraits on the wall and the seated men. The Earl and Viscount.

The Earl had a long, hawkish nose and looked like he sported eyebrow wigs. Hank nodded. The actor bore a passing resemblance to the gent depicted in the portrait. The man portraying the Viscount was less of a lookalike.

A huge dog, a Great Dane, perhaps, lumbered on stage and plonked itself at the Earl's feet with a groan.

Mae nudged Hank. "I feel I'm on a Game of Thrones set," she whispered.

Hank looked at the armour, the portraits and the hound. "I was thinking more Scooby-Doo."

"Silence!" the Earl of Doom Brae roared. "I shall not have peasants speak in my presence. My name is Mortimer Pendlebury. I am the third Earl of Doom Brae. This is my son and heir, Viscount Felix. My other son, Lord Edwin," he smirked, "Is indisposed."

Each member of the party sensed he was talking directly to them. "I gather you folk have born witness to my estate. What say you?"

Caught in the moment, lost in the virtual world of the setting, no-one spoke.

The Earl smiled. "Good. You remain silent. You learn your lessons well." The man stood. "My informants tell me you know of this place. So, it will come as no surprise to you to discover that I call this my playroom." He rubbed his hands together and laughed like a pantomime Abanazer.

"Come. Follow me. I wish to show you a few of my toys."

A trapdoor opened beneath the Earl and he slid from view in a puff of dry ice. The guards solemnly ushered the tour party down a short flight of steps until they stood at the lowest point of the manor.

Mortimer Pendlebury emerged in front of a floor-to-ceiling red velvet curtain. "I take pleasure in the history of our land. But my pleasure comes not from our conquests, our heraldry, or our status in the world. It comes from our inventions and our ingenuity. It comes, my citizens, from things like this."

The velvet curtain swished aside. The audience drew breath. They now stood in an even larger antechamber. It held an array of equipment the like of which they'd never before seen.

Clint sidled up to Hank. "No wonder they don't let kids see this place. It gives me the creeps."

Hank was about to speak when he observed the Earl's eyes upon him. He contented himself with a nod.

Mortimer Pendlebury walked the length of the dungeon. In a far corner, a see-saw like object towered above them all. A mannequin, trussed like a chicken, sat upside down on a wooden chair.

The actor playing the role of Pendlebury tenderly ran a finger over a wooden support. "This is my favourite toy. Pray, do your eyes recognise it?"

No-one spoke.

"You have permission. You may speak when I address you."

Althea Reubens broke the silence. "It's a ducking stool."

The Earl applauded; a slow clap which echoed in the stone cellar. "Very well done, my friend. You observe well. Tell me, dear, what be it used for?"

"The test. It's used to determine the guilt or innocence of a witch." Althea fixed the Earl with her bird-like stare. "Of course, it doesn't work."

Clint groaned. He knew this was a charade, yet the act was so mesmeric he felt sure Althea had sealed her fate.

"Oh, but it does work, my dear. I assure you."

"Not every time."

Despite everything, Clint grabbed Althea by the arm. Dragged him to her.

"Your man is most wise, madam. He knows when you should hush. You are fortunate the stool is already occupied, or I would have you sit upon it. But, as you see, occupied it is. This is the very stool", the word 'REPLICA' flashed onto the wall, prompting laughter, "On which the guilt of the Doom Brae Witch herself was proven. And here she is – Miss Louisa Goodchild."

The stool lowered into a well built into the floor. An effect threw up a swell of water as the Louisa mannequin disappeared from view.

The Earl took a dozen paces to his left. The guards ensured the party followed his every move. A table with attachments and bindings, pulleys and rollers, lay in front of Mortimer. In the cool of the chamber, an audience member at the front of the group shivered. He yawned involuntary as his body craved extra oxygen to warm him.

The gesture didn't go unnoticed by the Earl. He walked up close to the man, so close their noses touched. "Do I bore you?"

The man shook his head and shivered once more.

"You deny it. I see. Then, I must know the truth. Guards, take him."

Hank spoke through gritted teeth. "This guy plays a real good part, Mae."

His wife nodded. She, too, wasn't prepared to be caught speaking out of turn.

The guards feigned brutality as they led the man to the table and laid him upon it. When the tethers were fastened, they stepped aside for Mortimer Pendlebury.

"This, of course, is not a British invention. It was first used by Emperor Nero. But we became masters in its use. This, my friends, is the infamous rack."

The Earl moved to one end of the bench and grasped a handle. He wrenched it towards him. The machinery creaked and groaned. A recorded scream shrieked from beneath the table.

The audience laughed, but the sniggers stopped. Abruptly. The man really was being stretched. His fingers inched towards the edge of the table. The screams grew louder.

Hank watched, open-mouthed. He snapped his fingers. "I got it, Mae. I know how it works. He's not being stretched. The table's being made shorter. How cool does it look, though?"

Mortimer Pendlebury left the rack, tutting as he did so. He confronted Hank. "Well, well, well. I can't decide if you are six-bottled or a nincompoop. Either way, you shall pay for your insolence." The Earl stage-whispered to the tourists. "Methinks I have just found my next exhibit."

Hank's face creased in smiles. "Yes! Hey, Mae, hold this for me, will you?" He passed her the camera. "Make sure you get some good shots, yeah? Now, where do you want me, guys?"

The guards stepped forward. Took an arm each and frog-marched Hank to a Russian Doll-like creation. Mae fiddled with the camera and hoped she was getting the shots Hank wanted.

The guards opened the door. The inner door was lined with sharpened nails, knifes and blades. They pointed in every direction.

The Earl of Doom Brae addressed the audience in sinister tones. "The time is late. My table shall soon be set, and I need garner an appetite for it. This, my good friends, is the last of my playthings. I grant you leave to speak of it without impunity."

A young woman in skinny jeans and cropped T-shirt raised a hand. "Speak, girl."

She didn't. Instead, she stood in front of the Earl and tugged at her T-shirt. The Earl laughed. The girl turned to face the audience.

The T-shirt bore the name of a rock group.

Iron Maiden.

The tour party grinned at the girl's motion, then they nodded. All were familiar with the infamous device.

"It is," Mortimer Pendlebury concurred. "And we have an occupant. Our friend – our RUDE friend – is about to experience it. Note there can be no escape for the blackguard. The blades point every which way. Once the door closes, his end is assured."

Hank couldn't wait to step into the sarcophagus, but he hesitated. "Hey, wait. Can I have a photograph? Mae, come here. Clint," he signalled the man forward. "C'mon Althea." He looked around. "Where's Althea?" He thought he saw her leave the cellar. "Oh, never mind. Let's get the show on the road. Smile, peeps."

The character playing the Earl stepped in, aware the coaches waited outside, engines running. "We shall have no such wizardry here. Guards? The maiden awaits."

Hank felt the Earl's men push him inside. One leant close to him. "Don't worry, sir. Look." The actor pressed the palm of his hand against a patch of nails. They immediately retracted into the shell of the maiden. He moved his hand higher. Did the same thing. "And again, see?"

Hank winked at him. "Thanks, but I already guessed the trick."

The guards stepped aside. The Earl walked to the casket. Laid a hand against it. "Goodbye, my friend," he smiled.

He gave the door a shove. It swung shut, slowly. Mae clicked away, capturing Hank's smiling face.

The device clicked shut with a satisfying thunk. There were no phony screams, no amplified music, nothing. Nothing except a pool of blood flowing from the base of the casket.

The lights came on. The party applauded and bent to gather their belongings, ready to leave.

They saw the Earl and his men exchange glances. One of the guards ran a finger through the fake blood. Held it to his lips. Only when he staggered back, and the other actors dashed towards the cabinet did they begin to suspect something was wrong.

Mae missed the signs. She was engrossed in getting the best shots for Hank. She hoped he'd be proud. She was still snapping away when the sarcophagus door swung open.

Mae stopped clicking.

Hank was impaled to the inner door, run through by dozens of sharpened spikes.

The onlookers screamed, wept, cried out.

Hank hadn't cried out. He couldn't.

The first spike penetrated his throat and rendered him silent.

CHAPTER TWENTY-ONE

A shroud of silence blanketed the darkened room. Tawdry gifts and tat hid in alcoves, their crassness discretely veiled from view.

Near the gift shop exit door, four chairs, arranged in a semi-circle, sat beneath a single dimmed uplighter. Two were occupied: one by a uniformed policewoman, the other by Hank's wife.

Hank's widow.

A handkerchief lay crumpled in Mae's lap. The WPC held the distraught woman's hand while a medic in green coveralls crouched in front of Mae. She handed her a flimsy plastic cup and a handful of sedatives. Once she was sure Mae had swallowed them, the medic moved to one side.

A door creaked open in the distance. A blast of sound entered the room, alien and discordant. DI Cotton closed the door behind him and silence returned, save for Mae's snuffles and the squeak of Cotton's shoes.

He took a seat alongside Mae. "How are we now?" He cringed at his words. He hated this part of the job. Wasn't comfortable with the grieving relative thing. Although he directed his words at Mae, he looked at the WPC.

Sandra Senior patted the woman's hand and rolled her eyes. Cotton shrugged his shoulders; a 'what am I supposed to say' gesture.

"I'm… I don't know what I am." Mae raised the handkerchief and blew her nose.

Cotton left his seat and squatted in front of her, knees cracking like popping candy. He raised the woman's chin with the tips of his fingers and looked into bleary eyes. "I'm truly sorry for your loss."

He tilted his head, a signal for Senior to follow him to the far side of the room. As she did so, the medic slipped into the vacated seat.

The detective and Sandra walked through the gift-shop, his shoes squeaking like a church mouse, where they waited outside the door which signified the dungeon's exit.

"We're just about done here," DI Cotton said to her. "Witness statements taken. All give a consistent story. Forensics checked the equipment in there. It's all working as it should."

"So, we're no further forward? There's no gadgetry involved? No-one meant to trigger something but didn't, either deliberately or by accident?"

Cotton gave Sandra a look. "Senior, I do believe you're questioning my competence."

"No, sir. Sorry, sir…"

"Relax, Sandra. I'm not being serious. No, the spikes are inlaid on a series of panels. They're designed to automatically retract under pressure. They've always done it before – thankfully – and they're doing it again now. Every time. They just didn't work when it mattered."

They heard laughter from inside the dungeon. Cotton stuck his head around the door. "Shut up, you lot. We've got a widow in here. I don't think she'll find much to laugh at, do you?"

Cotton and Senior looked towards Mae. She hadn't heard anything. She was lost in her own world.

"And before you ask," he continued to Senior, "Harris has run checks on all staff working here. Nothing on any of them. No links to the victim. Mo Khalif's done the belt-and-braces check on the tour party. He's drawn a blank, too."

Sandra sighed. "Where do we go from here, sir?"

"We go home, that's where. There's no crime here. It was an accident, that's all. A mysterious one, but an accident all-the-same. It's for the Health and Safety Executive to solve the mystery. I'll wait for the Family Liaison crew to arrive but you're free to go, Sandra."

The door behind Mae and the medic opened. The cool of night entered alongside a woman wearing a leather jacket, silk-scarf and mid-length skirt. The woman shook Mae's hand, held it for a few moments, and took a seat next to her.

"Speak of the devil," the DI said. "I need a word with the wife before the FLO takes over. You get yourself home. It's late. I'll be right after you."

Cotton took a deep breath and headed for Mae and the FLO. He shared a grim smile with the Liaison Officer. He knew her. She'd make sure the widow got whatever help she needed. Still, he knew he was compelled to offer more condolences.

Cotton knelt again, not too close, not too far, from the tearful Mae.

"I have to go now. This has been a terrible day for you. It'll be no consolation for you, but I'm satisfied this has been a dreadful accident. There's no more for me to do here. I'll leave you with Teresa. She'll support you in any way she can, right up until the time you're ready to fly home."

Mae nodded. "Thank you, officer. You've been very kind."

Cotton felt a knot tighten in his throat. He coughed before continuing.

"Now, I know you've only just met Teresa so, before I go, are you sure there's no-one I can get to help you; anyone back home you want me to inform?"

The woman released a fresh flood of tears. Cotton rubbed the stubble on his chin. He wished he'd never spoken.

Mae shook her head. "No. There's no-one. Absolutely no-one. We're both only children of only children, Hank and me. Our parents are long gone. No brothers. Sisters. Aunts or Uncles, nieces or nephews."

She sat silent for a moment as the realisation struck her. "It's the end of a generation."

Cotton stood. Shook Mae by the hand. He felt more doleful than usual. Her words – the end of a generation – hit him hard.

The DI realised he'd witnessed not only the end of a life, but the end of a family line.

Cotton stepped outside into darkness, case file tucked under his arm. The cover contained only the most basic information; date and location.

And the name of the victim.

Hank Pendlebury.

**

DI Cotton removed the file from beneath his arm. He stood in night air that was warm, silent and peaceful. The rhythmic pulse of blue light from the vehicles guarding Doom Brae Manor's drive cast a sub-aquatic glow across the estate.

Cotton sauntered across to the patrolmen. After a quick exchange, the lights were extinguished. One car crunched away from the manor towards the highway. The other pulled in front of the house, waiting for Mae Pendlebury.

A single coach stood in the moonlight. Cotton made his way to it, clambered up the steps, and spoke to its occupants.

"I've spoken to most of you already, but for those I haven't met personally I am DI Cotton of Southern Borders police. I'd like to thank you for your co-operation today. I appreciate it's been a long and difficult day for you. I've no wish to delay you any longer than necessary, so I'm pleased to say you're free to go now. Thanks again, folks. Driver, it's all yours."

Cotton stepped from the coach. It spluttered to life, sides shuddering like the awakening of a beast. From outside, Cotton heard the driver speak into the microphone, his tone subdued.

"Because there's no public transport out here this late, I've agreed to drop off some of the manor staff in town. I'm sure you'll appreciate they've had a rough day, too, and they also had to stay behind to talk to the police. I promise I'll get you back to your hotel as soon as I can."

The driver took silence as approval. He released the handbrake and pulled away into the night.

The interior of the coach remained ghostly quiet. No-one spoke. Some of the occupants looked down at the floor. A couple sent text messages to worried relatives. Many more looked out the window, seeing only their haggard reflections gaze back at them in the nocturnal black mirror of night.

A woman dressed in maid's costume yawned. Alongside her, a man dressed as a farm hand wondered how long it would be before the manor opened for business again.

Clint and Althea Reubens had taken it worse than most. Clint sat upright, pale, drawn and red-eyed. Althea sat still as stone, hands clasped in her lap, trying to remain stoic.

The coach came to a halt at the junction with the highway. The click-click of its indicators sounded like a mantel clock counting out time. Subconsciously, a woman checked her watch.

Ten minutes to midnight.

Wilberforce Long glanced out the window. He allowed himself a melancholic smile at what he saw. For the first time, he could see what the man meant. Hank had been right. His wig did look like a stuffed crust pizza slice. Long removed it and bounced it on his lap.

Behind him, an elderly traveller rummaged in his pocket for a mint. He watched the reflection of his friend sat next to him as he donned a pair of glasses and opened the glossy Doom Brae Manor brochure.

Further back, the final Georgian couple sat in silence, hand-in-hand. The woman looked towards the man for support and comfort. He tried to reassure her with his eyes.

The girl turned towards the window. Her reflection showed a serene smile below ice-blue eyes and long, flaxen hair. At least, that's what it would have displayed. But the window revealed no reflection.

There wasn't one.

Louisa Goodchild laid her head on Edwin's shoulder and fell into a peaceful slumber.

**

Early morning, and the kitchen sprang to life like the breaking of dawn. Pots and pans boiled, eggs sizzled, and milkmaids delivered urns of fresh milk.

Kitty Cook stood aside from the chaos and observed the maelstrom around her. "Looks like she's out gallivanting with His Lordship again," she mumbled to herself. "Oh well, I'll have to cover for her once more. There'll be no rest for the wicked again today."

Kitty turned on her heel, tripped over something hidden beneath her eye-line, and landed face down onto the grease-stained floor.

Her eyes rose before the rest of her. They came to rest on a pair of scruffy cloth shoes.

Skinny legs, engrained in grime, protruded from the shoes. Beaten leather trousers, three-quarter length, held in place by a frayed rope lay beneath a ripped and rancid brown blouse-shirt.

Kitty Cook struggled to her feet and wiped her grazed hands on her pinafore.

"Shoo, shoo. Be on your way, young fellow me lad, whoever you are. We can't be having you getting in the way."

The boy didn't move.

"Now, I don't know how you got in here, but I knows the way out." She held out a hand. "Come on. There's work to be done in here. Quick, quick – out we go."

The boy held out a hand, but not to grasp Kitty's. Instead, he offered over a stained and crumpled sheet of paper. Spidery scrawls ran across it.

"What's this? Speak, boy. Cat got your tongue?"

The boy clasped his hands together, a begging motion. He offered a smile so sad it hurt. He pointed to a scar near his voice box.

"A fine pair we are," Kitty continued. "I can't read, and you can't talk."

The boy laughed a silent laugh and thrust the paper into Kitty's hand.

"You're asking the wrong one here, lad. I can barely spell my own name. I'll see if I can find Mr Pooley, shall I? Old Alfred's sure to help."

The urchin shook his head. Besides, Alfred Pooley was nowhere to be seen. Reluctantly, Kitty Cook unfolded the note and began to read aloud, the best she could.

"*Help me.*" So far so good, she thought, though she feared what trouble the boy was in. "*I am lost. I have*, oh dear: whatever is that word? *to stay.*"

Kitty hesitated while she tried to fill in the blanks. "Nowhere, is that what it says? You have nowhere to stay?"

The boy nodded, his face wreathed in a smile which wormed its way into Kitty's heart. Despite herself, she knew she couldn't offer him shelter.

"*I come from…* No, don't know what that one says, neither *…and need a place to sleep. I* something *won't stay long.*"

Kitty looked around. Could the boy hide here, after all?? He's a tiny thing and the house very large.

"*I* something *to be quiet. I promise*, that's it, promise, *I won't say a word.*"

The rascal made his soundless laugh again. Kitty laughed out loud with him.

"*Please. I'm a good boy. I don't steal. I don't lie. I don't…*" Kitty passed on the last word. "I'm sure you are, and I'm sure you don't, whatever it is."

She ruffled the boy's hair. His hand went to it, as if it reminded him of something. He looked puzzled.

Kitty had all but made up her mind. "You're a sweetie, do you know that? How can I resist? But you promise you'll stay down here. Mustn't let the masters see you. The Earl will throw you to the dragons if he so much as sets eyes on you." She winked at the boy. He winked back. She returned to the note.

"*My name is.*" Kitty struggled to read. "Henry? Is that what it says? Your name is Henry? Well, Henry, you come with me and keep your head as hidden as a fly on a cow's…" she stopped herself in time. "Don't let anyone see you. You're my secret."

The boy's face beamed. He took Kitty's hand. As she led him past the range, she screwed up the note and dropped it on the flames.

The paper charred, took alight at the edges, and slowly flipped itself over as the heat consumed it until only the final line remained visible.

Flames licked the lingering fragment of paper and the last few words were lost forever. Words that read:

"*My name is Hank.*"

****

****

****

BOOK TWO

The Second Telling of the Doom Brae Witch.

*The historical thread of The Doom Brae Witch extracted to present a stand-alone tale of wicked despots, family jealousies and vengeance.
18th Century Britain; a time when witches and heretics were not quite gone, yet alone forgotten.*

The dawn sun cast gilded shadows over a patchwork quilt of golden corn and lush fallow land. Swallow and swift darted overhead, horses whinnied in a stable bank, and dormice clung to ears of corn like sailors in the rigging.

Louisa Goodchild remained oblivious to the idyll around her. She sprinted over the fields, at once breathless and adrenalin-fuelled. She hopped twice on one foot while she removed a shoe, then pulled off the other. Louisa hoisted her skirts and set off once more, glancing behind at her pursuer.

Lord Edwin Pendlebury, youngest son of the Earl of Doom Brae, ran after her. He, too, gasped for breath in the thin air. Neither his tight leather boots nor his long-tailed jacket helped his cause but, ever-so-slowly, he closed the distance between them. He stumbled as he ran, clawed ape-like at the ground as he continued uphill, before he regained his footing.

Louisa glanced back once more, golden hair streaming behind her like maypole ribbons. Far below, Doom Brae manor was little more than an ornate doll's house amidst neglected gardens as she increased her stride and veered right towards Bluebell Wood.

Before she knew it, Edwin had reached her. His hand touched her back, enough to send her tumbling, and she felt his weight upon her.

Louisa's breath came in sharp bursts. Her bosom heaved and quivered above her corset. But she found the energy to giggle. Lord Pendlebury laughed, too. They lay next to each other, panting in unison, unable to speak from the exertion.

Gradually, their breathing subsided. Louisa's hair fanned over the grass like a cluster of buttercups. Eyes the colour of sky searched Edwin Pendlebury's face as it hovered inches above hers. She felt his breath, warm and welcoming as a summer breeze, as he lowered his face to hers.

Lord Pendlebury rolled onto his back. Gazed up at cotton-bud clouds. He released a sigh. "Does he need to know? Is it of such importance?"

She pushed herself onto her elbows. "Of course, it is."

"Why? If it's what we desire…"

"Because he's your father. He's the Earl. You have so much to lose."

Edwin closed his eyes. "I have nothing to lose but you. All this," he made a circular motion with his hand, "All this shall belong to Felix when father passes. He is father's heir, not I."

"Then, we should tell him."

"I wish it could be so."

A heavy silence hung over the couple. Louisa spoke first. "Tell him, Edwin."

He shook his head. "You don't know father as I do. You see him as the Laird of Doom Brae, he sees you as a maid. And I see him for what he is."

"You talk in riddles, Edwin."

"It's better that way, believe me."

"So, what now?"

His eyes sparkled. "Now, I kiss you."

"My good Sir, you wouldn't be taking advantage of a kitchen-maid, would you?" she teased.

Lord Pendlebury laughed. The sound reminded Louisa of warm treacle. "I am the master of the house, Miss Goodchild, and a huntsman by nature. You must do as I ask."

She recognised the jest in his voice. "Then, pray, allow this maiden time to compose herself. And you to enjoy the chase of the hunt." She glanced towards the woods, not thirty yards away. "Allow your quarry to secrete itself in a hiding place. Your pleasure will be all the greater for it, I assure you."

Edwin felt himself stir. "Then a hunt it shall be. You have until I count to one hundred. Now, go. Before I change my mind."

She feathered her lips against his cheek. "A mere taste of things to come," she breathed, before dashing off towards the shade of trees.

Once inside the wood, she turned sharply left, followed the line of trees, before she took a right turn and hopped over a brook.

"…seventy-three, seventy-two, seventy-one."

It was dark inside the wood; darker than she'd expected. Louisa ducked under a bramble bush, stepped over a fallen tree.

The earth felt moist where the sun had yet to penetrate, the ground slick beneath her stockinged feet. Wet leaves licked her arm like serpent's tongues, knotted bark formed dozens of eyes watching her progress, and wispy fingers of mist sought out her ankles as the forest floor warmed. The dankness absorbed most sound. She barely heard Edwin count down.

"Forty-six, forty-five, forty-four…"

A squirrel startled her as it bolted up a tree-trunk. She headed deeper into the woodland. Another fallen tree, larger heavier and thicker than the one before, barred her path. She circumnavigated it, hunkered down behind it amidst a mushroom patch, and waited.

"…three, two, one. Ready or not, here I come."

Louisa couldn't hear him from her hiding place. She was deep in the woods. She wondered if she was too deep, if he'd ever find her.

Her lips curled and her nostrils flared at a carrion smell behind her. She looked at the fungi sprouting from the floor of Bluebell Wood. For a moment, her memories took her back to her childhood; to a time when her mother would send her into the woods to gather material for her effacations. Louisa knew what these were.

Stinkhorn.

Phallus Impudicus.

She sniggered and hoped Edwin would find her.

Time passed slowly. Louisa's ears strained for any sign of Edwin, but she heard nothing. Flies buzzed around the stinkhorn. She flapped them away, wishing she had a tail with which to perform the task. Irritated, she chose to move location.

Perhaps Edwin would hear her, even if she couldn't hear him. She opted to move towards the fringes of Bluebell Wood; to a place where she'd be found more easily. She smoothed her skirts, looked around - and realised she didn't know which-way-was-which.

She was lost.

Louisa gazed upwards, tried to gauge the position of the sun in relation to her own. She thought about crying out but resisted. He'd think her foolish, helpless and child-like. That's what she was, but she couldn't show it. Why would he want her, a mere kitchen-maid, if he knew the truth?

She heard a rustle in the trees ahead of her. Twigs snapped. Branches moved. And a full-grown doe and her fawn emerged feet from her. Girl and beast stared into each other's eyes, a magical moment, and then the deer turned and bolted back from where they had appeared.

With an enlightened heart, Louisa spun around as a figure stepped from the trees. "Edwin, at last. You'll never believe…"

She cut the sentence short.

It wasn't Edwin.

The man's riding crop flayed the side of her face twice. Her vision blurred, everything within it turned red and, mercifully, she was only vaguely aware of what happened next.

**

By the manor's entrance, a liveryman tended to a handsome horse and the black carriage to which it was attached. The horse pawed the ground, breath snorting from nostrils like steam from a dragon.

A dark-haired man in frilled collar strode by, taking the stone steps two at a time. A footman gave the well-heeled gent a deferential bow as he pulled open the manor doors and allowed the man to march into the hall.

The gent's clogs echoed around the stone hall. He ignored the tapestries on the walls, the stag's head set above the ornate fireplace, and the portraits lining the high-ceilinged corridor as he hurried to his destination.

He paused outside a solid oak door and waited for the flush to subside from his cheeks. He regulated his breathing and brushed loose grass from his leggings before inhaling deeply.

A footman stood further along the corridor. He gesticulated towards the dark-haired man. Viscount Felix Pendlebury gave him a disdainful look, ignored him, and rapped on the drawing room door. Without waiting for a response, he heaved it open.

Inside, a huge dog, Great Dane with a hint of Wolfhound, lay in front of a marble fireplace. Lupo raised his head, looked the intruder over, and plopped it back on his paws.

Behind the hound, two men sat at an oblong table, facing each other. One, a round-faced, chinless man with snub nose and powdered wig, used a compass pointer to indicate features on a technical drawing spread across the desk. The other, Mortimer Pendlebury, the third Earl of Doom Brae, was a hawk-faced man with bushy eyebrows which expressed annoyance at the interruption.

"My lord," Felix Pendlebury bowed, "May I speak with you?"

The man glared at him from beneath his bushy eyebrows. "I expressly declared I was not to be interrupted. I shall have words with Maltby. He should not have let you enter."

"Sir, it is important. I would not have interrupted were it not."

The man sighed. "Mr Brown," the Earl said to his seated guest, "This is my eldest son, the Viscount Pendlebury. He takes after his mother. He has no manners."

The other man laughed. "I have no wish to come between a man and his son. I shall leave you with my drawings. My carriage and driver have waited long enough. May I suggest we reconvene next month and agree on my fee? I assure you, I am more than capable of delivering you the finest Pleasure Gardens in the county, your grace."

"That suggests your services shall not come cheap. We shall discuss it next month." The men stood and shook hands. "Thank you for your time, Mr Brown. It's been most rewarding."

The chinless man nodded, straightened his coat tails and swept out of the room, giving Viscount Pendlebury a faint nod as he swept past.

"Felix, my boy. Your timing is impeccable. That Lancelot Brown is a truly insufferable gabster." Mortimer laughed. "Please, take a seat."

Felix Pendlebury fanned his jacket tails behind him as he lowered himself onto the high-backed chair. He gripped the heads of the gargoyles carved on the arms with such force his knuckles turned white.

The mannerism didn't escape the Earl's attention. "Felix, my boy. What have those poor griffins done to deserve such harsh handling? Come, relax. Let's share a brandy."

"Father, I have grave news."

The older man regarded his son, chin resting on steepled fingers. "Spit it out, man."

"I'm afraid I must tell you there is a witch abroad. Here, in this very house."

Mortimer Pendlebury spat out a laugh. "Nonsense, my boy. There hasn't been a witch in these parts for nigh on two-score years. The year 1720, I believe. Your tale is too smoky by half."

"If I hadn't witnessed it myself, I would ne'er believe it, too. But I'm afraid I did more than witness it. I, myself, have fallen foul of her spells and witchcraft."

A beam of sunlight from a high window fell across the younger man's eyes, rendering them unreadable. The rest of his face lay in shadow.

The Earl of Doom Brae studied his son for a long time from beneath his furrowed eyebrows. "Pray tell."

Felix lowered his head. "I dare not, father, for it brings great shame upon me and this household."

"You came here for a reason so spit it out, man."

Felix swallowed. "Sir, I was walking in the woods when I came across her. She had bewitched a doe and foal from the estate. They stood at her side, as if in communication. I disturbed her before she could cast her malevolence on them but, alas, in her spite she turned herself on me."

"Really? You expect me to believe this bag of moonshine? Tell me, what evil did she cast upon you?"

Felix looked around the room, at its high ceilings and the portraits lining the wall. The eyes of his forefathers appeared to train themselves on him. He cast his eyes downwards. "I failed to see her runes or hear her words, but I lost track of time and space. When I awoke, she lay beneath me."

He paused. Ensured his words registered. "Of course, I tried to fight her off once I came to. I raised my horsewhip to her. I fought a brave battle and eventually I beat her off. But I fear it was too late. She had taken my honour."

Mortimer Pendlebury remained silent, his mouth a thin line. "And the creature was of this household, you say?"

"Yes, sir. I'm afraid she is. She works in the very kitchens where our food is prepared. I believe the name she goes by is Louisa Goodchild."

"Goodchild? Is that the tempting armful who dallies with Edwin?"

Felix met his father's gaze, struggled to suppress a smile. "Yes, sir. It is she."

"Then the succubus must pay. Come, we must find her at once. Put her to the test."

The Earl stood. Felix followed suit, head bowed not in deference but to disguise the smirk on his face.

"One thing, Felix."

"Yes, sire?"

"Next time you wish to have your way with one of the household, don't come to me with your damned hum and poppycock. Keep your member in your breeches, where it belongs."

**

The air in the kitchen was thick with the stench of boiling vegetables. Steam belched from monstrous pots and pans. Maids stirred the contents with heavy metal spoons. Others turned a hog roasting above the range whilst still more polished silverware or inspected delicate china for chips and flaws.

The appropriately-named Kitty Cook stood aside from the chaos, mopped her brow with a cloth pulled from her waistband, and puffed out her rose-red cheeks. She raised her head towards the window high above her but could see nothing through the misted-over glass. It was like looking through cataracts.

Kitty felt a tug at her skirts. She smiled benevolently. "Not now, Henry. I'm full of busy." She ruffled the eight-year old urchin's hair.

Henry didn't have a surname. He didn't have a mother or a father, either. Henry was an eight-year old orphan taken in by the kitchen staff. Henry was also persistent.

He pulled at Kitty's skirts again, this time with the urgency of a dog dragging a branch. The mute child made a guttural sound, his eyes wide and pleading.

"Whatever's the matter with you, child?"

Henry made the noise again in response. He raised an arm and seemed to point at the wall. Kitty followed the line of his outstretched arm towards a rack of saucepans.

"You want to help, is that it? The kitchen's no place for you." Kitty made as if to touch a hot pan, let out an 'ouch' sound, and shook her hand. "Hot. Too dangerous for one as small as you."

The boy shook his head. Exasperation showed in his face. He repeated the stabbing motion towards the wall. Pulled on Kitty's apron once more. Made the sound for a third time.

Kitty tried to understand. She stood, arms akimbo, and watched the urchin tilt his head to one side and rest it against clasped hands.

"Sleep? Is that what you want? Are you knocked-up tired?"

The boy shook his head. Then, he made a slashing motion and held a finger against his cheek.

The cook's brow furrowed in bewilderment. "I don't know what you want."

The boy heaved at her with even greater urgency. Mind made up, Kitty glanced around to ensure no-one watched, wiped her hands on her apron, and took the boy's hand. "Show me."

He dragged her out the kitchen into the cool of a stone corridor, pushed her out a side door, and led her up towards Bluebell Wood.

Kitty doubled over, breathless from the uphill scurry. "Henry. Slow down. I'm fagged to death. Let's wait a while." The boy refused to wait. Beckoned her to follow. With a look of resignation, the cook did so. She wheezed and coughed but trudged after the boy until she saw him clamber over a dry-stone wall.

"Wait. I can't climb like you young whipper-snapper. I go by the gate." Henry took no heed. He was already inside the stable block.

Five minutes later, Kitty Cook entered the stables. When her rasping breath eased, she was struck by the silence. The horses were eerily quiet. Some would be out working the fields, others tethered to carriages, a few perhaps mounted for the hunt. But there should be horses here. Indeed, she knew there were; she'd seen their heads as she entered, and she could smell them. Yet, there was scarcely a sound.

"Henry? Henry? Where are you, boy?" She knew he wouldn't answer – couldn't answer – but Kitty needed to fill the silent void.

Mottled sunlight filtered through glassless windows, golden fingers scrabbling at the cobbled floor. The rest of the interior was dark and forbidding.

"Henry?" Kitty's voice was hushed now, caution in her tones. She looked into one pen. It was empty. She moved to the next. Empty, too, save for a mass of soiled straw, and brasses and harnesses hanging from the wall.

Kitty moved on. A grey mare met her gaze. The old horse didn't whinny or flick her tail. She just stood, fixing Kitty with her big brown eyes.

She moved to the next, and the next; one empty, one with another occupant, silent and still as the mare.

"What's happened here?" she asked it. "I wish you could tell me."

Kitty reached the end of the row of pens. She did a hairpin turn and began searching the eastern side of the stables. She found nothing but vacant paddocks or stock-still, silent horses.

Until she reached the penultimate stable.

Louisa Goodchild lay bent and broken, her head lolled to one side. Her bodice was ripped, skirts filthy and unkempt. Henry sat by her, Louisa's hand in his, while a young foal tenderly nuzzled her.

Kitty hand shot to her mouth. "Oh, my poor child."

At the sound of Kitty's voice, the foal moved in front of the stricken girl as if to protect her. It snorted and pawed the stable floor, eyes flared, the whites exposed, as Kitty stepped towards Louisa.

Kitty backed off. Henry left Louisa's side. He brushed the foal's mane and made his guttural croak. The foal immediately backed away, allowing Kitty space to enter.

The cook looked between boy, horse, and Louisa. Not for long, but long enough for something to register. She offered a faint smile and nod of deference to the foal and rushed to Louisa's side.

She ripped off a piece of her apron, doused it in a trough of pea-green water, and held it to Louisa's brow. She brushed a wisp of the girl's hair aside. "My dear, dear child. What have you done to yourself? Let's get you back to the house."

Kitty heard a terrified Henry make a noise. She glanced towards him. He shook his head so fast she thought it would spin off his shoulders.

"Henry, we must help her." She bent to hoist the girl to her feet. Louisa's head rolled aside, exposing a cruel, deep wound across the right-hand side of her face.

And an eye resting on her cheek beneath an empty socket.

Kitty Cook stumbled backwards into a pile of steaming dung, gagged by bile in her throat. Before she passed out, she heard Henry make his unearthly cough again, a double-barrelled explosion of air.

She could have sworn it sounded like "Viscount."

**

Outside a stone annex to the stable block, a man watched two horses and their riders approach over the brow of the hill. The man wore a course brown shirt which struggled to contain his stomach. A tan leather apron reached down to his knees, covering battered and worn breeches.

The man was bare headed and, though most of his face was hidden behind a mask of white whiskers, the flesh that showed through revealed a brandy-faced complexion born from years in front of the forge and nights nursing flagons of ale.

George 'Piggy' Trotter studied the horses as they beat their way towards the stables. Fine, strong beasts; beasts he'd shod only that morning. The riders handled their mounts with aplomb. There again, Piggy thought, they'd had plenty of practice. They had precious little else to do.

As he watched, one of the horses pulled-up abruptly. Felix Pendlebury, astride the stallion, dug his heels into the horse's flanks. The spurs made no impact. The horse didn't budge.

Felix snapped his crop against its shoulders, and again higher-up, against its withers. His mount stayed still, no movement other than the steam of its breath.

The other rider circled his horse and pulled-up alongside the first. "Felix, you'd think you were atop a queer prancer not the finest steed," the Earl laughed. "Come on man, get your beast moving. Dig your heels in; get those bleeders working on him."

"Father, I swear this pile of backward-breeze is good for nothing but glue."

The elder man chortled again. He dismounted his horse and landed in the turf with a thud and a tinkle of spurs. He took his son's mount by the bridle. Patted the white blaze on its nose. The beast watched him suspiciously, eyes flared.

"Get a haste on. We need to find this Goodchild girl, this 'witch' as you call her, afore anyone else finds her in a mood for a-hexing."

Felix stopped beating his horse. He sat still. "Listen. Do you hear it?"

The Earl strained to hear. "You imagine it. I hear nothing."

"Precisely, my Lord. Nothing. No birdsong. No insects. No farmhands or stable-lads toiling in the field. There's nothing."

Mortimer cocked his head as he listened again, waiting for something, anything. And then he heard it. Little more than a breeze, it whispered across open fields.

Ears of corn rubbed together, the sound of a pensive man scratching his beard, before the wind reached the trees. It strengthened within the forest. Conifers swayed to Mother Nature's overture and pine needles seemed to sing a sweet melody.

Piggy Trotter heard it, too. He gave a knowing smile, pushed himself off the smithy wall, and stepped inside; making sure the door was closed behind him.

Out of nowhere, the skies darkened, purple and indigo clouds blanketed the sun like a bruise spread over flesh. The wind whipped to a frenzy. Branches, ripped from trees, flung themselves at the gentry and their steeds.

Crows, dozens of them, rose from where they nested in Bluebell Wood until the flock formed a shield which blocked out all remaining light. Their cacophony of caws drowned out even the howl of the wind.

The men's horses broke from their trance. Stripes of chalky white sweat flecked their flanks, their lips curled back, froth foamed their gums. They pawed at the earth, ears flat, eyes wide.

The Earl sensed it first. "Felix. Dismount. You won't hold him." He shouted to make himself heard above the gale. He made a frantic grab for his hat as the wind tore it from him and tossed it to the field's border.

"No. You doubted my horsemanship. I'll show you my worth."

The steed tossed its head. Cantered backwards. Then, as a crack of thunder filled the air like musket-fire, it reared up on itself, fetlocks clawing at the sky.

"Get down, Felix. Now!" the Earl urged.

Too late. The stallion had passed the point of no return. Its balance had shifted. It reared beyond the vertical plane and whinnied as it tipped over backwards with Viscount Felix Pendlebury still in the saddle.

Felix felt it happen. Knew he had nowhere to go. He launched himself free at the last moment, but his left ankle caught in a stirrup. He dangled from it, head downwards, as the weight of the horse bore down upon his neck. Felix closed his eyes, waited for the impact, hoped it would be quick.

As if in slow motion, Felix felt the air expel from his lungs as he hit the earth, he heard a scream – his scream – as his leg twisted beneath his mount. Yet, somehow, the steed missed the rest of him. He was alive.

Alive, and once more surrounded by silence. The sun shone from an azure sky. The air was breathless as a corpse. And the birds and beasts silent as a forgotten tune.

The Earl of Doom Brae looked down at his stricken son, then up towards the heavens. "Ye Gods," the Earl whispered. "A witch she surely must be."

The transformation was immediate. The elder man stood in the field, stunned and transfixed. Only the moans of his son brought him back to the present. "Get up, son. We need to find the wench before someone else does."

"I can't. I can't move."

"Yes you can, you lily-livered oaf. Come."

The Earl of Doom Brae reached down for his son, took him by the arm. He was about to haul him to his feet when he noticed the blood on Felix's lower leg. Blood surrounding a rip in the Viscount's stockings. Through which a shard of white bone poked. The tibia was broken. A Greenstick fracture.

Mortimer's horse had bolted in the storm. Felix's mount lay stricken alongside its rider, fetlock at the same cruel angle as the Viscount's. The Earl looked around for help. Saw the building attached to the stables, with its heavy wooden door pulled shut.

"Trotter! Trotter!! Get yourself out here. I need help."

The smithy door opened with the reluctance of a lamb led to slaughter. Piggy Trotter emerged and ambled towards the Earl and his son. "Get a move on, Trotter. Live up to your name."

Piggy sauntered on, hands dug deep in the pocket of his apron. "Leg's broken," he said with obvious understatement.

"I can see that with my own eyes, you clodpole."

Trotter knelt beside the horse, gently stoking its mane, cooing softly. He looked around. "Your boy's legs gone, too."

"It's my boy I'm talking about, fool. Here; help me move him to the stable."

"It be painful as the devil's scrape for him."

"Just take his arm, damnit."

Piggy shrugged but did as instructed. Felix screamed all the way to the stable block as the men half-carried, half-dragged him across field and cobbles.

Piggy let go the moment they entered the building. "I be excusing myself now, my lord. I got a horse to attend to." He left without waiting for approval. Felix was in no state to disagree and his father was too engrossed with his son to notice.

"Where did you leave Goodchild? I'll fetch the rum wanton myself."

Felix face contorted in pain. Through a grimace, he managed to say, "East side. Second to last enclosure." He hesitated. "Father. Be warned. The sight will be gruesome. Please remember I was protecting the honour of our family. I did what I had to do."

Felix closed his eyes and rested his head on a hale bay while Mortimer furrowed his owl-like eyebrows. His son's warning worried him. He knew he'd incapacitated the girl, but how far had he taken it?

Mortimer shrugged. It was too late now. The deed was done. He inhaled, drew in the stench of horse dung and sodden straw, and tried to reassure the Viscount.

"I'll go seek her. Worry not: I'll see she's moved far from this place. She'll be sent to a work house up London way. She won't last more than a month before she's pox-ridden. It'll be as good as putting her to the test, and much less public."

The Earl sloped off to find the girl. "Wait here," he said over his shoulder.

Felix would have laughed at the irony were he not in such pain.

**

Mortimer slipped around the hairpin bend of the stable and entered the eastern leg.

The Earl hesitated. He sensed it immediately. The air held a heaviness he'd never experienced. It remained acrid, still reeked of horse urine and more - yet, it was different; altered in some way.

He inspected the dung clinging to his riding boots, raised each foot in turn and scraped them against the wall while he gathered his thoughts. The noise echoed to eternity. It did so because everything else was mummified by absolute silence. No noise entered from outside, the horses remained hushed, even Felix's whimpering couldn't penetrate the invisible barrier.

Nevertheless, Mortimer knew what he must do. He strode over the cobbled slime until he reached the pen Felix said held the girl. Again, he listened. Again, he heard nothing.

He leant against the swing door, pushed it open, and entered the paddock.

Inside, the enclosure was immaculate; the air fragrant with the scent of a dozen posies. The contrast with the pungent ammonia aroma elsewhere caused the Earl's eyes to tear up.

Through a watery film, he observed a fresh bale of straw suspended from the rafters, untouched. Clean water filled a polished trough to overflowing. And the cobbled floor stood swilled, brushed and unsullied.

What grabbed the Earl of Doom Brae more than anything was the fact Louisa Goodchild was not there and, he was sure, never had been.

Mortimer hurried back to his son, checking each pen as he went. Confusion and panic rose in the Earl with each empty paddock he encountered. All were bereft of livestock, let alone Louisa Goodchild.

By the time he returned to Felix, he was breathless and splattered by midden. "She's not there. You left the girl elsewhere. Think, man. Think. Where did you leave her?"

Felix didn't reply. He was febrile and semi-conscious. Mortimer Pendlebury slapped his son's face. Pinched the flesh of his arm. Reached for a pail of foul-smelling water and tipped it over Felix's head.

The Viscount woke with a splutter. A waterboatman scuttled down his cheek. Spiders clung to his hair. "You found her?" he slurred.

"No, I didn't 'find' her. The girl wasn't there. You were mistaken."

Felix shifted position. Filth pooled around him. "I am not mistaken."

"You told me you encountered her in Bluebell Wood."

"I did."

"Then, why move her to the stables?"

Felix mopped sweat and stagnant water from his forehead. "My head was as a pan of broth, my thoughts muddled. I knew not what I was doing."

The Earl rested alongside his son. Thought for a moment. "It was the hex. She wanted protection. She needed to be discovered. The witch made you move her so she'd be found; so she could bring disrepute to Doom Brae. In truth, she wishes to ensnare us all."

"Father. You know I told a falsehood. The Goodchild girl is a kitchen maid, not a witch."

"I thought so, too, Felix. I truly believed you made up a faradiddles story to cover your actions. But the wench has disappeared into thin air. She brought on the storm. She had your steed throw you to the ground."

"My lord, 'tis not so."

Mortimer glowered at his son. "It is, Felix. It is true. We must both believe it and we must make others believe it, too."

Felix didn't hear him. He had slipped back to a state of delirium, all colour drained from his face, his skin slick with sweat.

Mortimer stood. Wiped his hands on his breeches and spoke to himself. "And I tell you, son, if the wanton can't be found to send to exile, then it must be Edwin I send away. He cannot know of this. None of it."

The Earl struggled to load the unconscious Viscount onto a hay wain, took a circuitous route to the rear of Doom Brae manor, and handsomely tipped a trusted footman to see Felix settled into his chamber where he was to remain undisturbed at all costs.

Mortimer, changed out of his riding gear, sat in the drawing room, unable to relax. A fire roared in the grate, and within its sparks and flames, the Earl saw the rumination of a plan take shape, blossom, and bloom like a red rose.

He'd resolved the first of his dilemmas. The Earl reached for the bell-pull by his chair and heaved on the knotted rope.

Minutes later, the Earl of Doom Brae ran a finger beneath his nose and pushed the snuff box across the table to his youngest son. Edwin nodded his gratitude. He took a pinch of the shredded leaves between his fingers and inhaled lightly. His nose twitched left and right as the tobacco hit.

The men were dressed informally, Lord Edwin in a frilled-collar blouse worn beneath a fan-tailed coat of rich blue; the Earl a buttoned, short black waistcoat and a white shirt tied at the neck by black silk cravat. Both wore natural hair.

"Tell me about your day," the elder man asked.

"I took a walk in the woods this morning." It wasn't a lie. His father needn't know he'd been outfoxed by a kitchen maid.

"Ah," Mortimer nodded sagely. "Splendid day for it. Did you encounter anything of interest?"

Edwin hesitated. Did his father know? Surely Louisa hadn't besmirched her reputation by revealing their friendship. Yet, why else had she avoided him the entire day? He settled for a simple, "No. sir."

The Earl steepled his fingers. Rested his chin on their tips. "And this afternoon?"

"I took tea in the library and read." It was a lie, of course. He'd spent it on a fruitless search of the manor, unable to ask servant or maid if they'd seen Miss Goodchild.

"Good book, was it?"

"Swift's 'A Modest Proposal'. Quite preposterous theme. As if a family would sell their children for food, indeed."

Mortimer's Adam's apple dipped and rose as he swallowed. The gesture went unnoticed.

"So, father," Edwin continued. "I'm sure you didn't call me here to discuss literature."

Mortimer cleared his throat. The gilded tapestries on the wall muffled the sound.

"Indeed not. Edwin, your days must be long. Felix carries out his duties as Viscount. He will inherit the manor from me. But you, you spend your day at leisure. I think you should see more of our great land, learn about its heritage. Wisdom will make a man of you."

Edwin pursed his lips. The offer would give him time to clear his thoughts. Determine his real feelings for Louisa. But, was now the right time; when she had left him in the lurch for reasons he couldn't fathom?

"Do you have Westmorland in mind, sir? Yorkshire, perhaps?"

His father stood. Looked out through leaded windows towards the fringes of Bluebell Wood. "No. I was thinking of somewhere more distant."

"Such as?"

Mortimer reached for a decanter. Poured two generous brandies. "I met with Sir Humphrey Butters last week."

Edwin took a sip from his glass. "And?"

"He was telling me the Duke of All Anglia is in poor health. Consumption, Sir Humphrey believes. He has a houseful of women, and no men. He needs assistance to run his dukedom."

"No, father. He wouldn't ask for my help. I know this isn't true."

Mortimer fingered the heavy curtains. "You're a quick-wit, Edwin. I'm proud of you. You are right. He didn't ask. But I offered." He hadn't, but by the time Edwin arrived in Anglia, the Earl knew he'd have it arranged.

"But, sir. That must be a week's ride away."

The Earl waved a hand; a dismissive gesture. "Five days, at most." Edwin set down his glass. Looked at his father. "You know, don't you?"

"About your dalliance with the fair wench from the kitchen? Yes, I know."

Edwin stood. "Then you'll know I can never leave here. Not now."

The Earl rammed his staff on the floor. "You can. And you will. I need an heir to continue the line beyond Felix. And the parents must be of good stock. A kitchen maid would never, ever do. Think of the shame. Where would that leave the Doom Brae estate?"

Edwin opened his mouth to protest but the Earl silenced him.

"Now," he continued, "The Duke of All Anglia has two daughters. One, the Marchioness Rosemary, is of your age and as fragrant as her name suggests, according to Sir Humphrey. Not only would she be perfect bride material, she will be excellent breeding stock. It would lead to the Pendlebury's holding both Doom Brae manor and the Duke's Broad Mill Estate. We'd create a dynasty, you, Felix and I."

Edwin spat out a laugh. "Then, it's clear as the nose on my face that I am not the only one with secrets."

"Explain yourself, boy."

"I shall. You see, you are wrong about two things. Firstly, I shan't go. I refuse. And, of greater significance, Felix has already assured you of succession. He has an heir. And you did not know. What says that about you?"

Edwin smiled. He could see he had struck a mortal blow to the Earl's argument. "Josias is his name. The boy must be near four or more by now. Born of a disease-ridden harlot from the village tavern. Yes, my lord: 'Good stock', indeed."

The Earl's face reddened. He could barely speak, such was his rage. "Get out," he stormed. "How dare you belittle your elder brother with your filibuster. I shall see you to the Duke myself if I have to."

"You forget, father. Not only do I have Louisa to remain here for, I now also have Felix. I have him by his nutmegs." He formed his hand into a claw as if to emphasise his point.

The Earl of Doom Brae sucked air through his teeth. Laughed with the malevolence of the devil. "My dear son, you don't have Louisa. I have her. And, if you don't leave for Anglia this very night, this very moment; you know I shan't hesitate…"

He let his voice trail off. He could tell by Edwin's eyes he believed the lie.

Lord Edwin Pendlebury left the room, and Doom Brae, a beaten man.

**

The shadow of flames licked the walls of the darkened room like serpent's tongues. Grotesque misshapen figures filled his field of vision; their silhouettes so large they towered from ground to ceiling. He heard voices speak in tongues, words he didn't comprehend.

His body felt oily-slick. He hadn't the strength to wipe rivers of sweat from his brow or raise his head. He was certain of only one thing.

He was in hell.

Felix Pendlebury returned to the land of Morpheus just as the door inched open. His father closed it behind him with silent precision and walked to the two men hunched over something on a table.

"How is he?" Mortimer asked.

The men removed their tall hats. "His condition is grave, my lord," the elder of the two men replied.

"How grave, Sir Hugo?"

Sir Hugo Parsons tweaked the end of his waxed moustache as he considered his reply. "The leg is cruelly infected. We have tried our utmost, but the infection remains."

"Let me see."

The younger of the visitors spoke. "Sir, I would not encourage it. It's best left to men of our profession."

"Nonsense, Pitt. This is my son we speak of."

The men with the hats looked at one another. Sir Hugo used his position of seniority to make the decision. "Very well."

Sir Hugo and the Earl moved to the bed. Sir Hugo spread elegant fingers and gently pulled back the bedsheets.

The stench hit the Earl first. The smell of rotting flesh. He pulled his head away as his son's limb became exposed.

Felix's lower leg was black as night, the skin suppurated and gangrenous. Leeches, gorged to bursting-point, clung to the open wound while the flesh beneath pulsed with maggot activity.

Mortimer Pendlebury reeled back. "Ye Gods. A foul sight."

Sir Hugo Parsons covered the leg immediately. "Indeed, sir. Now you understand the gravity of the situation."

Parsons rejoined Adam Pitt at the table lit by the feeble flame of two candles. Sir Hugo closed a book he and Pitt had pored over as the Earl joined them.

They stood in a silence punctuated only by groans and murmurs from the bed. "What do you suggest?"

Again, the medics hesitated. Without a word, Sir Hugo rotated the manuscript until its cover faced Mortimer.

'The Treatise of the Operations of Surgery'
By Joseph de la Charriere'.

The Earl furrowed his thick eyebrows, darkened irises beneath. "What is this?"

Sir Hugo licked an index finger and leafed through the book. It settled open at a page.

Mortimer stared at the sheet before him, head bowed. He leant against the table.

"There must be something else."

"Sir, it is with regret I say not."

The Earl directed the same question to Pitt.

"I agree with Sir Hugo."

The flame from the candle flickered and shone in Pendlebury's eyes. Sir Hugo Parsons and Pitt saw the page of a book reflected in them. It read:

'Chapter XXXVII
Of Amputations.'

The Earl let out a sigh of despair. "What about Fordyce? Is he of the same mind?"

"He is."

"Then where in God's name is he? I'm paying him good money to heal my son."

"My lord, I fear John has other important matters to attend to."

The Earl found a release for his anger. "Other matters? What 'other matters' are more important than this? I'll see he pays for his absence. Go find him. Bring him to me. Now."

A voice spoke from the doorway. "Is it me you seek, sir?"

"Fordyce, you blackguard. How dare you leave my son whilst taking my shilling? I swear, I'll…"

Fordyce struggled to raise a bag stuffed with contents into the Earl's line of sight. "Time is of the essence, sir. I took the liberty of seeking out what we need in anticipation of your consent."

In the dim of the chamber, the Earl missed the look Parsons, Pitt and Fordyce exchanged.

Mortimer's face softened. "Then, if all three of you eminent gentlemen agree, so be it. If I must exchange his leg for his life, then I shall. But I warn you – if I lose both, I promise I shall amputate you of something more valuable than your leg."

The three medical men offered words of caution, expressed warnings about the dangers of surgery, but reiterated it was the only option. They asked his permission to proceed.

"What, now? Here? In this room?"

Adam Pitt chose to speak. "Sir, that's precisely what we suggest. The time of year is right for surgery. The body is relaxed after a long summer and, as we approach autumn, the blood is calm and retains sufficient vivacity to reanimate the body."

Sir Hugo nodded his pleasure at his prodigy's depth of knowledge. "So, my lord. May we proceed?"

The Earl looked at his son on the bed. A man lost to delirium and fever. He saw a boy close to death.

"Do what you must."

The Earl helped the medics carry the semi-conscious Felix from his bed and lay him on the table. Fordyce began unpacking the contents of his bag. Alcohol, powder, needles, reels of thread, swathes of padding, and a block of wood. Only when a six-inch long blade and a curved and serrated knife emerge did Mortimer realise the enormity of what was about to occur.

Sir Hugo noticed the Earl cower. "You may wish to leave the room, sir. We shall do what we can to limit the pain, but it will not be easy. The Viscount may, with luck, slip unconscious but, if not…" He left the sentence unfinished.

Through gritted teeth, Mortimer replied, "I shall not leave my son." His Adam's apple bobbed thrice. "I will remain with him."

"Very well. Mr Fordyce, please administer our patient with gin."

Fordyce pinched Felix's nose, forcing the mouth to open. He poured the alcohol into the Viscount's mouth, much of it spilling to the floor as the patient gagged and spluttered.

While they waited for the alcohol to hit, Pitt wrapped a block of wood in linen, Fordyce began tethering the patient to the table, while Sir Hugo lined up an array of evil-looking equipment on a sideboard.

"I need to know…" Mortimer's words came out as a croak. He cleared his throat and tried again. "I want you to explain what you will do to my boy."

Sir Hugo nudged the handle of a knife a fraction of an inch so it aligned itself perfectly with the tool alongside it.

"We shall put a wad of padding beneath your son's knee to relieve the pressure of the cut. The wood shall be placed in his mouth so his teeth bite down on it, not his tongue."

Even in the quarter light of the chamber, Sir Hugo saw Mortimer pale. "Go on," the Earl insisted in a whisper.

"We shall begin by incising the upper layer of dermis with the sharpest of knives. The acuity of the implement and the effects of the gin mean this is the least painful part of the procedure."

Fordyce finished tying the last of the straps around Felix's midriff, ensuring the Viscount's arms were constrained inside the tether. Pitt leafed through the manual as Sir Hugo continued his mantra.

"Once I feel tendon and sinew or, more likely, bone, I shall switch knives." Sir Hugo raised a second knife, the curved one, while Pitt picked up the first and held it in the flame of a candle.

"At this juncture, Pitt will apply a ligature to the leg to prevent blood loss. We may need your assistance to pull tight on the ligature, sir, while my men prepare other material. When the blood has ceased letting, I shall cut quick with the crooked blade."

"To what end?" Felix queried.

"To ensure the stump is rounded, my lord. If it remains sharp, it is more difficult to bind, has a greater risk of infection, and shall cause discomfort when the Viscount's pantaloons and, in time, the false limb rub against the stump."

Mortimer screwed his eyes tight to prevent tears from falling. "And does that conclude the procedure?"

"Alas, by no means. I shall stitch the arteries to prevent further blood loss. Once I finish my work, Mr Fordyce will apply a pad of flour and alcohol to the stump to reduce infection. The alcohol causes great pain but, after the trauma of the amputation, with God's grace the Viscount won't notice it."

Sir Hugo checked over the equipment once more as he continued his explanation. "I shall use the sharpest of knives to skin a layer of flesh from above the knee, fold it over the remaining stump, and stitch in place."

"And then?"

"Then, my lord, we wait. And we pray."

Sir Hugo looked at Pitt and Fordyce. They nodded. Pitt moved to one end of the table and laid his hands on the shoulders of Felix. Fordyce placed his on the patient's upper thigh.

"Gentlemen, we shall begin."

Sir Hugo rested the sharp knife below the knee, inhaled deeply, and cut.

Felix's eyes shot open, wide and staring into hell. Teeth splintered as he clamped down on the wood, and his muffled scream echoed around the Earl's head.

"I swear I'll find the witch who did this to you, my boy. On my life, I shall find her."

**

The narrow staircase at the rear of the manor wound like the tight coils of a cobra.

Louisa Goodchild's bare feet caressed the cold stone with the tenderness of a lover's touch as she inched her way down from the servant's quarters. It was pitch black, yet she needed no light to see. She had taken this route many times over the last five weeks and knew it better than her own face.

Kitty Cook's chamber was cramped enough with just one occupant. With two, it was unbearably claustrophobic. So, by day, Louisa slept while Miss Cook worked, safe in the knowledge her presence would go undetected. No household member would lower themselves to enter a maid's room. Only Kitty's second cousin knew of her presence, and she had every reason to be grateful to him. He had saved her life.

As Louisa's recuperation garnered strength, she followed the man's advice. "The blood needs an opportunity to flow," he had told her. "It will provide the body with both vigour and vim and speed you to good health." So, by night, Louisa exercised.

She prowled the empty corridors and halls of Doom Brae Manor much as a spirit haunts the confines of its last abode. Now, at the foot of the staircase, she hesitated behind a heavy wooden door and pressed her ear against it.

She heard nothing.

She depressed the latch. The door creaked as it inched open. She cringed and shrank into the shadows of the stairwell.

A lighter shade of darkness framed the doorway, but only silence entered. Louisa let out the breath she'd been holding and eased the door open some more. She peered through the crack and saw nothing ahead or to the left.

To see to the right, her one-sided blindness meant she needed to open the door sufficiently for her to expose her head. She pulled back the hood of her robe and took another deep breath.

She twisted her neck and shot her head through the gap, retracting it like a strutting pigeon.

All clear.

Louisa laid her back against the door, closed her eye, and took in a lungful of air. She'd done this every night, yet she sensed tonight was somehow different. Tonight was the night she'd seek Edwin. She dreaded his reaction to her scars and sightlessness, but she needed him to know: know the truth about his brother, and the truth about her.

To do so meant entering the family's quarters on the first floor; quarters accessible only via by the gilded staircase at the far end of the manor, through the open expanse of the Great Hall, up to quarters where footmen and butlers were likely still on duty.

Louisa took her first pace into the hall. The dim embers of extinguished fires crackled in shallow alcoves, just enough light to illuminate macabre carvings. Louisa tip-toed across a black and silver marble floor, her robe and underskirts rustling softly in the stillness.

She waited at the foot of the staircase, grasping the domed topper of the handrail. She'd only ventured to the Pendlebury family's personal floor twice in three years. Never uninvited, and never at night. Time to make it a third.

Louisa moved so silently she appeared to float up the stairs. At its head, the corridor unfolded into the distance like a menacing tunnel. Decorative torches lined the wall at infrequent intervals, held in place by bronze sconces. None were lit.

A large candle, almost three feet tall and eighteen inches in circumference, signified the Earl's chamber and provided the only source of light. Meagre though it was, it was enough to reveal the passage was empty.

Louisa's heart thumped like a drum in her chest as she began her slow walk. Conscious of the swishing of her robe, she raised it a few inches from the floor and lost herself in the silence.

Louisa's feet warmed to the thickness of the carpet, but all she sensed was the tickle of pile like a thousand insects beneath her feet.

She hesitated. A noise. She glanced left and right. No place to hide. There it was again. She retreated into shadow and crouched low.

A figure emerged from a side corridor. Tall. Dark clothing. Outdoor clothing. Not a member of household.

In the gloom, Louisa saw the shape pass Edwin, Lord Pendlebury's bedchamber. Onwards it went, beyond Edwin's dressing room, and into the candlelight outside the Earl of Doom Brae's chamber.

Louisa stood, revealing herself to the man's gaze. The man nodded in acknowledgement. He held a finger to his lips. Louisa smiled.

John Fordyce, Kitty Cook's second cousin, heaved his heavy case of elixirs into the next chamber, the room of Felix Pendlebury, and closed the door behind him.

Louisa hurried forth. There was no danger passing the Viscount's chamber, not with John Fordyce looking out for her, but she couldn't afford to disturb the Earl. She paused outside Mortimer's room, and relaxed when she heard the heavy snores of a sleeping man.

Assured of more time, she half-turned so she could see the full length of the corridor with her good eye.

No-one followed. She threw the hood of her plum-coloured robe over her head and entered the darkness of Edwin's chamber.

She didn't need light to know he wasn't there. She knew his scent well enough. And the only odour here was that of a cold, empty, dusty, room. He hadn't slept here for some time, of that she was certain.

Nonetheless, something drove her towards his bed. She reached out. Touched the feather-filled pillows, the rich plumpness of the mattress, and dreamt she was under the covers with Edwin alongside her.

Louisa lost track of time. She could have been there seconds or minutes, but a noise outside the room brought her back. She ducked behind the drapes at the same moment the door opened.

She heard it close. Louisa waited several moments in suffocating silence. She tried to sense a presence. She heard no sound; no breathing, no movement; yet, when she sniffed the air, it bore the vague muskiness of a male.

Was he still in the room? At length, she peeked out.

The room was empty.

Louisa snuck into the corridor. The candle still flickered, and the sound of a somnolent Earl drifted to her ears. Relieved, Louisa scurried to the staircase and down its wide, carpeted steps.

She perched on a stool at its foot while she gathered her thoughts. High above her head, the feeble light of a gibbous moon filtered through a stained-glass window, providing relief to the gloom around her and the darkness in her heart.

She rested her head in her hands, her long hair flowing from the confines of her hood. Louisa knuckled her eye dry of tears at the same time as she heard the clash of doors on the floor above, and the sound of animated voices.

The voices came nearer, urgency in their tone. She heard her name. Somehow, they'd discovered her.

The woods. She'd be safe there. She raced toward the main entrance. The door opened before she reached it. Two footmen filled the frame.

She turned on her heels and headed back through the Great Hall. She twisted around so she could see over her shoulder. Louisa caught a glimpse of five men pouring down the staircase whilst another hurdled it. The two footmen joined the chase.

The Earl of Doom Brae strode nonchalantly behind them, Lupo, the crossbred hound, tethered to his wrist by a heavy chain.

Louisa careered down the corridor towards her only means of escape: the spiral stairway to the servant's quarters. She knocked over pedestals, the busts of Pendlebury family ancestors rolling into the path of her pursuers.

One stumbled over them. The others sidestepped the obstacles with ease.

Louisa flew through the hall, past the sconces. The Earl's men gained on her. Snatched the torches. Set them ablaze.

The sudden flare disoriented Louisa for a moment. Her feet caught in her robe. She stumbled. Hit the wall with her shoulder. It sent her spinning across the corridor. She glanced back. Saw men charging towards her, faces contorted with rage, arms stretching out for her.

Louisa turned back and ran. Straight into the door leading to the stone staircase, and her one possible chance of escape.

She reached for the latch. Depressed it. Pushed against the door. It didn't budge.

She put her shoulder against it.

Nothing.

It was bolted. From the inside.

She turned to face the men. Their appearance, distorted by the flickering torches, took on greater malevolence. To Louisa, there seemed many more men now, their numbers multiplied by the reflections in the mirror above their heads.

The Earl pushed his men aside. Lupo reared up on hind legs before Mortimer wrapped the dog's chain around his wrist to restrain it.

Mortimer stood in front of Louisa, his thick eyebrows furrowed, long nose casting dark shadow across his face. "Miss Goodchild. How are you, this eve?"

No response.

"Cat got your tongue, has it? A black cat, one presumes." He chuckled. The Great Dane Wolfhound emitted a long, low growl.

Louisa tried to remain calm whilst her mind worked overtime. Who had betrayed her? She knew for sure it wouldn't be Kitty. Fordyce? He had his opportunity upstairs. If he, why wait? If not them, then who?

"How did you find me?" Her voice came out flat, yet confident.

The Earl chuckled again, so quietly it screamed. "Who would have thought a man who has worked with fire all his life could be so afraid of his own forge?"

"Piggy Trotter! What have you done with him?"

"Fear not. The rapscallion is safe. Or, should I say, safer than you."

Louisa shuddered.

"There is someone here with me who would very much like to meet you," the Earl continued.

She glared at him with her one eye as the men parted like the Red Sea. Felix Pendlebury hopped forward, his weight born by a wooden crutch.

Louisa almost smiled. "An eye for a leg. Fair exchange, I'd say."

"Seize her!"

The men stepped forward. Took hold of her gown. Before Mortimer could instruct them to lead her to the dungeon, the door behind Louisa creaked open.

The staircase swarmed with people like bees round their queen. In the shadows, she made out her friends from the kitchen. Sadie Bishop was there. Emily Jones, too. She noticed Alfred Pooley towards the rear, and Kitty Cook in front of him; all drawn from their quarters above by the commotion.

Mortimer and Felix looked at each other open-mouthed, their plan thwarted. They had no plausible reason to haul Louisa away.

Louisa saw their dilemma. She became imbued with fresh confidence. She grinned at them, deliberately exposed the hideously-scarred side of her face to the men and spoke directly to Mortimer and Felix.

"A plague on both your houses," she quoted.

She saw the Earl's countenance change. Renewed hope showed in his eyes. He tried to disguise a smile. 'What have I said?' Louisa wondered.

"Hear her!" the Earl proclaimed, extending a trembling finger in her direction. "From her own mouth come the words and hexes of a witch!"

Panic showed in Louisa's eye. The company on the stairs gasped. Kitty mouthed 'No', but she could see doubt show on the faces of some of her friends.

The Earl addressed his men. "What is to be done with her?"

"The test! The test!" shouted one.

"Too good for her. Burn her, I say!" insisted another, raising his torch aloft.

As he did so, the shaft barely touched the mirror above him, insufficient for anyone to notice but enough to send the heavy frame crashing to the floor.

Glass shattered in an explosion. Uproar followed. Voices all shouting at once. The Great Dane howling. Bedlam on the staircase, panic amongst the company of the Earl's men.

Then, the party fell silent.

Louisa wondered why.

She looked at Mortimer, his face impassive.

Felix, too, remained unmoved. Until he slid slowly down the wall, a slug-trail of blood left behind, and an eight-inch shard of glass protruding from his stump of a leg.

Louisa looked at the sea of faces, and realised she'd sealed her own fate. Now, all bar Kitty Cook believed Louisa Goodchild was a sorceress.

The Doom Brae Witch was born.

**

A horse drawn carriage trundled a pathway beneath the protective shield of an archway of trees. Alongside the coach, sodden flora bowed their heads like hooded dowagers in the face of nature's deluge.

Kitty Cook, face set, stared straight ahead. Little Henry huddled into her as she stretched an arm around his shoulder. He hadn't listened to Kitty's words of discouragement. Despite her pleas, Henry had clung to her like ivy to bark. Nothing would stop him being with her today.

She kissed the top of the boy's head. For the first time, Henry didn't need words to make himself understood. His doleful eyes said it all.

He shifted on the uncomfortable bench seat and watched the muddy track wander onwards. "Mu-hug," he grunted.

Kitty ruffled his hair. "Couldn't have put it better myself," she said as the coach slowed to a halt amidst a gathering horde of peasant folk.

The village of Elderkirk, in the parish of Doom Brae, was little more than a scuff on the map; a stain best avoided even by highwaymen. Yet, today, its narrow, filthy streets buzzed with the excitement of villagers, young and old.

The throng of humanity lay before the coach like a giant cow-pat. Through the carriage windows there drifted a stench of greasy, unwashed clothes, foul breath and flatulence. Kitty flung open the carriage door, grabbed Henry by the hand, and clambered out.

They made their way towards the riverbank, ignoring the shouts, curses and raucous laughter of the villagers. "This be the day of all days," a black-toothed hag shouted at no-one in particular.

"Come to educate your boy, have you?" another said to Kitty as they jostled and squeezed their way through the crowd.

"The village never seen nowt like it; not in my lifetime nor my father's or my father's father," hailed a manure-splattered farmhand. "Who'd have thought it? A witch trial in Elderkirk."

The words hit Kitty in the stomach. This was real. This was happening. And nothing was going to stop it.

Above the crowd, a thick haze of smoke rose to meet the leaden skies in a grim embrace. Grey clouds puffed from the unsteady chimneys of abandoned homesteads and, beyond the last of the houses, villagers lit bonfires by the riverbank to relieve their bones of the morning chill while others ignited pyres to ward off spirits.

Kitty and Henry hurried as best they could past the last row of cottages and left behind the sweet, pungent aroma of emptied chamber pots. The waif ran into the back of Kitty. She'd stopped dead.

Across the river, a rickety platform had been erected. Alongside it, by the river itself, stood a strange, wooden device. A roughly-hewn frame, a long plank at a 90-degree angle with a cross bench tethered to it. Ropes and pullies at either end.

Kitty had never seen such a thing, but she knew what it was.

A ducking stool.

Henry made a noise beside her. He grasped Kitty's hand even tighter as he shielded his eyes with the other.

"We don't have to stay, Henry. We can leave this place."

Henry shook his head. "Mah."

She looked up to the slate grey heavens. "Then, offer a prayer, dear child."

A great roar rose from the masses. Gentlemen raised their hats high, women waved their handkerchiefs. Urchins climbed onto their father's shoulders for a clearer view.

Kitty Cook swayed back and forth to catch a glimpse through the forest of people. The Earl of Doom Brae and three manservants stood atop the platform. Another man, short and stout, clambered up to join him. He exchanged words with the Earl's men, who hoisted Viscount Felix Pendlebury onto the platform.

The crowd gasped at the sight of the infirm Viscount, wooden prop tethered to his ragged stump by broad leather straps. A woman, her face powdered chalk-white to disguise pock marks and lesions, pushed her way to the front of the mob. She dragged a child of about four to her side. She bent to whisper something to the boy, pointing out the one-legged man.

The street urchin looked at Viscount Felix anew. This was no longer just another cripple: the boy was seeing his father for the first time.

The stout man stepped forward, a footman holding an umbrella over him to protect his finery from the downpour.

Murmurs rose from the audience. "He shields beneath an umbrella," "What man hides under such a thing?" and, to chortles, "I wager he's loose in the haft."

The man raised his arms, exposing even more extravagant cuff beneath his coat-sleeves. The crowd fell silent.

"Good folk of Elderkirk, welcome. Greetings, too, to those who have travelled far to witness this historic occasion." He bowed towards better-dressed gentry gathered together on the fringe of the crowd. "My name is Silas Grindrod, magistrate and high sheriff of this shire."

The muttering began once more. While Grindrod regained control of the audience, Kitty Cook shepherded Henry away from the river bank, towards the elite. "'Tis safer this way. We're likely to land a facer should the mob turn a mill" Kitty explained.

Silas Grindrod resumed his address. "I thought I had seen the last of these days, but ne'er. The laws of the land remain and, though seldom invoked, they remain for good reason. The devil can still do his work, and we must remain vigilant to his shamming."

The villagers rose in agreement. Pitchforks pointed skywards, handkerchiefs fluttered, and Kitty Cook feared the worst.

"Which brings us to today. It is alleged there is a witch among us. This is no dung-speak; the allegation comes from none other than Mortimer Pendlebury, our much-loved Earl of Doom Brae."

More cheers. Grindrod silenced them with the wave of his cane.

"Bring forth the accused."

Kitty and Henry clambered up a bank turned to muddy slime by the feet of many dozen villagers. They stopped, balanced precariously, on hearing Grindrod's words.

Men hauled a figure onto the platform. The accused wore a flowing, plum-coloured robe. She was bare-foot, hands bound behind her back. A rough hood of sackcloth had been pulled over her face and knotted at collar-bone level.

"Oh, my poor, poor innocent," Kitty gasped, hand to mouth. Henry offered a pained grunt, but their voices were drowned out by the buzz of excitement, anticipation and fear which ran through the crowd.

"The wench beneath the hood is Louisa Goodchild. She must remain covered in case she chooses to bewitch you."

A lady in voluminous whale-bone skirt shouted, "What tomfoolery. Witchcraft is no more. Set her free."

Kitty Cook and Henry weren't alone. She was buoyed by the knowledge others fought on Louisa's behalf, too. Buoyed, that is, until the majority of the crowd drowned out the lady's protests.

"Silence!" the magistrate commanded. The noise continued. Grindrod rapped his cane on the platform six times before order was restored. He read out the charges.

'Hexed Viscount Felix Pendlebury into carnal relations.'

'Conferred with beasts to bring about heinous injuries to the Viscount.'

'Placed a curse upon the Pendlebury family before many a witness.'

'Brought life to inanimate objects causing pain and suffering to Viscount Pendlebury.'

With each charge, the mob became more enraged. Kitty feared they were about to storm the platform and take justice in their own hands. Henry became agitated by her side, croaking and grunting. She squeezed his hand, more for her comfort than the child's.

"…and, finally, the wit…" Grindrod corrected himself in time, "The accused caused Lord Edwin Pendlebury to vanish into thin air."

"Nooo!" The crowd started at the muffled wail from beneath the hood; the first time Louisa had spoken.

Kitty set her mouth grim. If she'd ever had any doubts about Louisa, the final charge brought absolute clarity. "He talks nonsense. Lies, all of it. The Earl would rather cut a wheedle than slice bread," she muttered.

"I agree." The lady in the whale-bone skirt was next to Kitty. "But he has standing in the village. I fear the end will be no good." The lady glanced at Henry. "Your son?"

"Yes. Yes, he is. He's my boy," Kitty answered without thinking.

Despite the circumstances, Henry beamed and hugged Kitty tighter than ever before.

"Gentlefolk," Grindrod commanded from the platform, rain falling so heavily it rebounded up to his knees. "It does not befall me alone to decide the fate of Miss Goodchild. You all know we need a jury for this trial."

Hands shot up. Willing volunteers. All with crazed, gleeful looks on their faces.

A man doffed his three-cornered hat towards Kitty "They're desperate to see a spectacle; that's all they want. They have no interest in justice". Kitty Cook took solace from another supporter.

From the platform, Grindrod continued his address. "Please, please. No more raised hands. Hear me out." The crowd settled. "As we know, the Earl is a good man. He wishes justice to be served, and for it to be served well."

Whispers of agreement came from the throng on the riverbank.

"For that reason, the Earl, as is his right, chooses not to place the burden on twelve men alone. He wishes you all to decide."

A roar like thunder rolled through the crowd. Hats were flung high in the air. Staff and canes held aloft, children shouted from where they perched on their fathers.

Kitty, Henry and their companions exchanged puzzled glances as Grindrod hushed the crowd.

"The Earl is truly magnanimous, is he not?" Silas Grindrod asked of the masses.

Cries of "Hear him," "Hip Hip," and a muted chorus of "For he's a jolly good fellow" all drifted from the masses.

"What in God's name is the man up to?" the man in the three-cornered hat said.

Kitty didn't look at him. "He's turning them up sweet, that's what he's doing," she answered.

"Good lord; of course. He's a devious one, is the Earl." The man's voice contained a trace of admiration despite his distaste.

Grindrod spoke with gravitas. "Folk of the jury. Now is the time for you to decide. Do we free Louisa Goodchild, the kitchen maid; or put Louisa Goodchild, the Doom Brae witch, to the test of a greater power?"

**

Silas Grindrod strode over the platform like a player across his stage, the baying mob his audience.

"Think well before you cast your verdict," Grindrod said. "The Earl and Viscount wish you to consider the evidence in full course. Above all, they wish justice to be served."

Mortimer and Felix looked at one another. The elder man swallowed. This was the moment where his plan stood or fell. Either the crowd were with him, and the family shame died with the Goodchild girl, or his dynasty faced ruination.

The magistrate moved alongside Louisa. In solemn tones, he addressed the crowd. "People, it is time to decide."

He grasped the sack over her head and whipped it off, displaying her face for the first time.

Gasps rent the air. People shouted all at once.

Grindrod rammed his cane. Waited for the noise to subside. He pointed his staff towards his right; where Kitty, Henry and the others stood.

"Let you have say," the magistrate commanded.

The majority, wooed by Louisa's beautiful looks, golden hair, and serene appearance yelled "Free her," "She is surely innocent," "Let the girl go."

A considerable number dissented, persuaded by Grindrod's rhetoric, but most voted in her favour. Kitty's heart skipped a beat. Henry jumped twice, a laugh gurgling from him.

Grindrod addressed the mass to the left. "What say you?"

They had no doubts.

"She bears the mark of the devil." "Satan has claimed her." "She has forsaken the lord and let the brand of the beast sit upon her."

"The test. The test – she must face the test!"

The heart which had skipped a beat only moments earlier now resided in Kitty's stomach. The mob had been exposed to Louisa's ruined aspect; her appearance the deciding factor.

Kitty now understood the Pendlebury's tactics. Tears filled her eyes. Louisa's destiny lay in the hands of a hundred or so folk in the centre of the crowd; folk who didn't know her kind heart, easy ways, or loving nature.

Folk who knew only what the Earl, through Grindrod, had told them.

At the rear of the platform, Mortimer Pendlebury screwed his eyes tight until only ragged folds showed. Felix held his breath and wobbled precariously as he struggled to maintain balance on the slick platform. Neither could bear the tension.

Centre stage, Silas Grindrod stepped from beneath the shelter of his umbrella. With a dramatic flourish, he pointed to the remainder of the crowd.

Rain pounding the river, hammering against trees and foliage, and the steady drip-drip of drops upon waterlogged turf, was the only sound.

Kitty prayed. Henry prayed.

Finally, a single voice emerged above the silence.

"She has two faces."

Another voice: "The devil creeps over her, inch by inch."

And another, louder. "A sure sign. The wench be a witch."

Cries of assent grew. "Let the water decide." "Test her."

Bedlam followed.

Guards grabbed Louisa. Dragged her to the stool. The crowd jostled for the best vantage point. Scuffles broke out. Men wrestled with each other. A couple tumbled into the river and were washed away, still fighting.

Kitty Cook sat in the mud and the filth and cried. Henry sat beside her, making what he intended to be noises of comfort amid his own tears. The other couple walked away, arm-in-arm, no desire to see more.

In the distance, Kitty saw men fasten Louisa to the stool. Four others clung to the rope as if their lives depended on it. Above the frenzy, she heard Grindrod's voice. "Wench, what say you?"

Louisa spoke to the crowd, head aloft. "I am not afraid of death, as you are the truth. Every night, the spider eats its own web and spins anew the following day. That is all death is to me. I devour my old life and prepare to build a stronger, better one next time."

She turned to face the Pendlebury's. "But those who know not the ways shall forever be ensnared in their own web."

At that, Grindrod gave a signal. "Release the ropes."

Kitty Cook, ashen-faced, hauled Henry away, back towards their waiting carriage, as Louisa entered the water.

By the riverbank, the Earl and Viscount watched the distorted outline of Louisa struggle beneath the waters. She tossed back and forth in her tethers. Her hair fanned outwards, golden reeds afloat in the river's ebb. After a few moments, Louisa's struggles ceased. The raging waters flowed by, undisturbed by air bubbles.

Grindrod looked at the Earl. He shook his head and displayed the palm of his hand. "A few moments more," he said through clenched lips. "To provide surety."

The crowd stilled. Wondered how long before the Earl released her. Just as they became uncomfortable, he nodded.

"Bring her up," Grindrod ordered. Four men hauled on the rope. The stool broke the surface, Louisa still shackled to it.

The girl emerged, her pallor more greyish blue than deathly white. Louisa's head hung forward onto her chest. River water streamed from her hair and clothing. A patch of green moss clung to her forehead.

Unease settled over the crowd. A witch should survive the test. Water would renounce her in the way she'd renounce Holy Water. Had they killed an innocent? Women sniffled into handkerchiefs, their menfolk hid their guilt.

The Pendlebury's exchanged smiles. It was over. They'd preserved their dynasty, gained retribution, and silenced Goodchild forever.

They offered their hands to Silas Grindrod, who gave a reverential bow in return. The crowd began to disperse. One of the Earl's men stepped forward. He cut the first of Louisa's bonds.

And screamed like a stuck hog.

Her one eye had shot open, blood red, madness within.

The crowd swivelled at the commotion. They turned in time to see the dead girl toss back her head. Water streamed from her hair, the droplets freeze-framed in a strobe-light flash of lightning.

Her blood-curdling shriek filled the air. "May the devil have his day. Let him touch them from afar. Take them all, and ne'er cease 'til the Pendlebury line be no more. So it be!"

The crowd rushed in all directions, some in panic, others to better see what had happened, still more to escape the witchery.

Shouts echoed around the village. A powdered-faced woman broke away from the stranger she'd accosted, just in time to see a surge of villagers force her four-year old son towards a smouldering pyre.

Someone made a grab for him. The hands pushed him away. The boy slithered on waterlogged mud, did the splits. The child struggled to his feet. Slipped once more and, with arms windmilling, tumbled from the riverbank into the raging foment.

The woman prepared to scream, but only swallowed dirt as she was pushed to the ground and trampled in the stampede.

Not five minutes after the Doom Brae Witch had spoken, the river's currents sucked Josias Pendlebury-Shanks from view.

Mortimer cowered at the rear of the platform. A tremulous wave of fear shook his voice. "She IS a witch. It is proven. Dunk her again. Commit her to the water. Now!"

Many of his men had fled but the strongest remained. He levered the stool, and the words of the Lord's Prayer caught in Louisa's throat as she entered the foaming river waters.

"Leave her overnight. Guard her. Do not raise her from the river 'til morning. Then, burn the witch," Felix bellowed.

Beneath the ferment, Louisa Goodchild remained still. After she'd unleashed her curse upon the Pendlebury family, all of nature had whispered its secrets to her. She wasn't afraid. Today was her beginning, not her end.

Those who remained by the bank witnessed a ghostly green glow, the shade of the Aurora Borealis, glimmer in the river's depths.

The phenomena rose to the surface, broke through, and hovered above. It pulsed to a heartbeat's rhythm then sunk back to the water, gradually fading to oblivion.

The river flowed dark and turbulent once more.

**

Hellfire reflected in the curved surface of the glass. As it gently rotated, a grotesque distortion of Mortimer Pendlebury's face appeared to float within the flames.

"Good health." The Earl raised the glass and sipped a generous measure of brandy. "Quite a day, my boy."

Felix remained silent as they chinked glasses.

Father and son sat in the drawing room of the manor's west wing. A roaring fire blazed in defiance of the wind and rain's fury outside. Lupo lay spread-eagled in front of the grate, a giant paw holding down the remnants of a gnawed bone. His tail thwacked in rhythm with the mantel clock's pendulum.

The men remained still as statues. At length, Mortimer stood and walked to the window. Rain smeared the leaded glass like Angel's tears. In the darkness, he watched the vague outline of trees bow and scrape in deference to the elements.

"Quite a day, indeed," he repeated. "But it is over. The fuss will soon depart. All that shall remain is the memory of how the Pendlebury family preserved the village from evil wickedness. Our family reputation is enriched, not besmirched."

The Earl looked at his silent son. "You remain troubled. Speak of it."

Felix swallowed the remains of his brandy and reached for the decanter. "What of Edwin? He must be told."

"Why?"

"You must ask 'why'? He will raise merry hell, that is why. Edwin won't be taken in by tales of witchery."

Mortimer snorted. "You still call them tales after what we beheld today? Nay, lad. They aren't tales. Besides, we have the good folk of Elderkirk to bear witness. Let him hear from them, not us."

Silence enveloped them once more save for the howl of the wind and the insistent rap of rain. Lightning's distant flare illuminated the room. Thunder followed, barely audible above the gale.

Lupo sat up, alert; bone ignored. He sniffed the air, circled, let out a brief, menacing growl, and settled again.

Mortimer retook his seat. "'Tis the heavens rejecting the sorceress, it is plain."

"Sir, we must get news to Edwin. He is not fly to the time of day. If he hears news from others, he will suspect deceit. We must keep him sweet. Doom Brae needs an heir beyond my inheritance The Earldom needs a line of succession." Felix rubbed at his stump of a leg. "And no-one shall wish to pair with a cripple like me."

One corner of the Earl's mouth curled upwards. "Felix, pray tell: do you think I am 'fly to the time of day', as you call it?"

"No, father."

"I see." Mortimer held the silence. "Then, you must know I am already aware you have an heir. Josias is his name, I believe."

The Viscount flushed. Cast his eyes downwards. "You know."

"Yes, I know."

"Edwin?"

"Who else?"

"The child doesn't know me. He is not worthy of the Pendlebury name. He can't be allowed to inherit the manor, which is why we need Edwin to spread seed and to remain part of our line."

Lupo pricked his ears again. They stood pointed and erect. A bass rumble emerged from the depths of his throat. The Earl admonished him, but the growl continued.

"You should have told me, Felix. I could have arranged for the boy to be..." he hesitated, "...removed."

Felix continued to inspect the rug at his feet. "I did remove the next one."

"The next one?" Mortimer roared. "How many side-slips of yours are out there, by heaven?"

"No more, sir. I swear there's only Josias. The other is not yet born. But you shall not hear of him, or her. A few florins and a word in Captain Woodcott's ear saw the wench sail far from these shores as soon as I discovered she was with child."

"Ye Gods, man. I'm beginning to think I exiled the wrong son."

Outside, the wind howled like a dervish. A freak gust drove down the chimney, carrying spirals of smoke into the room. Lupo leapt up, tail trembling between his hind legs. The hound yelped pitifully and bolted towards the closed door. It cowered there, whimpering to be let out.

The smoke cloud drifted towards the window where it hovered in the shadows, an amorphous olive-green mass, before its poisons snuffed out the candle's flame. The Earl of Pendlebury tisked as he walked to the window to reignite the tallow.

A blaze of incandescent lightning, so bright it blinded the Earl, projected his silhouette across the canvasses of family ancestors. Thunder roared like a voracious predator.

More lightning. Simultaneous thunder. Again, and again.

Felix shivered. "Father, I need my bed. My limb pains me and the day has been long."

"Nonsense, Felix. You need more brandy to warm your bones. I'll summon my man."

The Earl reached for the bell-pull as the manor creaked and groaned around them like an arthritic man rising to his feet. His fingers touched the velvet rope.

And the building lurched as if caught in an earthquake, throwing the Earl of Doom Brae to the floor. Mortimer found himself face down in Lupo's drool.

"No-one will sleep with this storm raging," the Earl said as he clambered to his feet. "A nightcap. Just one. Then we shall retire. Drink with me, Felix. Let us move on from today."

The door flew open. A footman entered as Lupo dashed out, sending the interloper head-over-heels. The man dragged himself to his feet, and then doubled-up, gasping for breath, hands on knees.

"What the Devil, Moncur? I shall have you flogged. Knock first, man."

Moncur looked up, his face florid, chest heaving. The bows of his wig lay unfastened around his shoulders. His shirt-tails hung over his breeches like a nightgown. He opened his mouth to speak but hadn't the strength. Waved his hand instead.

Mortimer and Felix exchanged perplexed glances. The sound of thunder rumbled in the distance. The sound came closer. Advanced towards them.

Not thunder.

Finally, Moncur found his words. "Sires, you must leave. At once. Lightning has struck. It has penetrated the eaves of the West Wing. The timber is alight. Sir, the manor – it's ablaze."

Mortimer set towards the door. Realised his infirm son wouldn't make it. He turned back to help him.

The roar intensified, and the ball of flame which rumbled up the corridor came to a dead halt in the doorway.

Intense heat filled the drawing room. Fingers of flame probed the walls and furnishings, reaching out for the Earl and Viscount.

The sound of breaking glass, the screams of servants, the roar of fire, the vitriol of the storm - all combined to baffle the senses and served to cause panic.

Mortimer spun round, trapped, frantically searching for an exit. The smell of thick, acrid smoke choked the Earl. Wood splintered in the distance, walls crumbled and tumbled, came crashing down at the far end of the corridor.

Priceless oil paintings singed in the heat. Tapestries curled in on themselves, soon spitting flames onto rug and carpet which flared in sympathy.

"Felix. Take my hand. Come."

Felix hobbled towards his father. He reached out, their fingers almost touching, before the ceiling split asunder. A blazing roof beam hung between them. Flames licked upwards; up towards the inferno bearing down from the floor above.

A curtain of fire lay between father and son.

"Felix. I shall return. I shan't desert you."

The younger man stood, paralysed by fear, wide-eyed and helpless. Mortimer shared a long gaze with him before the sound of breaking glass spurred the Earl onwards.

The ground floor window had shattered, showering the table with glass. Oxygen fed the flames, the fireball hungrily licking its way towards the source. It was now or never, Mortimer knew.

He dashed across the room. Vaulted atop the table. He ripped off his wig as he smelt it burn. Heat singed his eyebrows. He levered himself into the frame. Glass shredded his fingers, arms and stomach as he struggled to squeeze through the narrow exit.

Felix barely heard the words, "I will be back, I promise. Trust me, son" before he found himself alone in hell.

Outside the window, Mortimer rolled himself in mud. His clothing cooled so it no longer scalded the flesh beneath. For a moment, he luxuriated in the sweetness of driving rain before he dashed off into a wind that bit and snapped at him like a rabid dog.

Inside what was left of the drawing room, Felix prayed. He recited every prayer he'd ever heard and made a few of his own. He thought of his father, of Edwin, of Josias and the boy's harlot of a mother. Last of all, he thought of Louisa Goodchild.

He looked down to pray again. And froze at what he saw. Now, his thoughts weren't of Louisa. They were of the Doom Brae witch.

The Earl of Doom Brae emerged from the outbuilding and stood stock-still. He faced the manor. Its stonework glowed red with the heat of the firestorm within. Part of the West Wing was little more than rubble, a mix of black char and glowing redness; lava from a volcano.

He thought of the priceless antiquities within, the loss of his legacy, and the ruination of his reputation. Most of all, he thought of Felix, imprisoned within what was left of its walls.

Members of the household stood at a safe distance, staring at the remnants of the manor as the Earl slithered and slipped his way across a field of mud, a thick rope trailing behind him like a serpent.

He stood beneath the same window he'd squeezed through. It was too high. He couldn't reach it. He looked at it in desperation.

Part of the frame remained. The Earl fashioned a noose and tossed it at the frame. Three times he tried, three times he fell short.

"I'm back," he screamed towards the wall. "I said I wouldn't leave you. Have patience."

At the fourth attempt, the rope snagged. Mortimer scrambled up. The top of his head appeared in view. Swiftly, he unknotted the rope with his teeth and one hand as he clung to the frame with the other.

"Felix – I have a rope. I shall throw it to you." He ducked as a chunk of masonry plummeted downwards. "Hold fast and I shall haul you out."

He grasped the frame so he could heave himself up. His skin blistered with the intense heat of the stone. Gritting his teeth, he hauled himself into the frame. It was a ground floor window; a tight, narrow space. Could he manoeuvre himself sufficiently to cast the rope?

"Here I am," he shouted triumphantly, barely concealing a laugh. "I am back for you, son."

Mortimer looked through the window for the first time. Despite the raging heat, he was chilled to the bone.

The walls were blackened. Thick smoke filled the air, but crimson flames provided sufficient light for Mortimer to see.

Viscount Felix Pendlebury lay on his back surrounded by the fallen portraits of his ancestors, his eyes wild. But their gaze wasn't on his father. They were fixated on his peg leg.

The peg-leg which burned brightly. Flames consumed it, ravenously making their inexorable way towards the rest of his body.
Mortimer watched, aghast. He couldn't bear to look, yet he couldn't turn away.

A roar filled his ears. Not thunder. Not fire. He knew what it was.

He looked upwards. Saw the crack appear in the wall. Watched it widen as if fingers prized it apart. Stone crumbled, small and pebble-like at first, before larger chunks rained down.

Finally, the entire wall of the West Wing collapsed upon him.

All that remained of the Earl were his legs, protruding from the rubble of Doom Brae Manor.

The curse of the Doom Brae Witch had begun, and time would not see it beaten.

******
*****
***

BOOK THREE

The Third Telling.

A weave of the contemporary strands of The Doom Brae Witch to present a supernatural mystery as current as it is thought-provoking.

The air-brakes spat out a wheeze and a hiss as the coach crunched to a halt at the end of the winding gravel drive. The tour company representative stood, slightly hunched, at the front of the coach and blew into the microphone twice.

"Welcome to Doom Brae Manor and Gardens, the historic home of the Pendlebury family." She turned to gaze at the turreted home. "We are currently outside the main entrance of the manor. As you will see, the building left and right of the centre portico are a mirror image. As we look at the manor, the west wing is to our right. Once ruined by fire, the wing stood dormant for two-hundred years. It was restored to its former glory in 1976 using timber from a nearby forest and stone hewn from the very same quarry as the original material. Quite splendid, I'm sure you'll agree."

A murmur of agreement ran through the party of tourists as they craned their necks to take in the majesty of the building. The entrance to the manor was reached by a flight of thirteen stone stairs, worn smooth in places by three-hundred years of footfall. From either side, a ramp sloped gently to ground level. A small convoy of shire horses, carriages and liverymen lined one ramp, readying themselves to ferry the elderly and infirm around the grounds.

An ornate semi-circular portico, help upright by intricately carved pillars, sheltered the entrance from the elements. Marble statues guarded the door, one portraying a Roman handmaiden carrying a jug of wine, the other a Grecian Olympian. He was missing a hand and the discus it once held.

Once the initial hubbub subsided, the guide continued the speech she'd delivered dozens of times. "Doom Brae Manor is unique amongst the stately homes and castles of the United Kingdom in that it provides a hands-on, interactive experience of life in the 18th and early 19th century. Not only do you get to see what life was like, you get to live it."

The rep paused whilst her words registered with the party. She held the mic away from her and whispered to the driver, "Quiet lot we've got today. Need to milk them for all we've got to get a tip out of 'em."

The guide returned the microphone to her lips and painted a smile on her face. "Please bear with me whilst I collect your tickets and passes. I'll be with you as quickly as I can."

She hopped down the stairs and walked towards a posse of reception staff gathered around the manor's entrance. They all wore Georgian costume, authentic in every detail.

"Gee, honey. Look at the costumery. We got the real deal going on here," an excited client said.

"Uh-huh." His wife sounded bored already. "Must we go into the house, Hank? It's a real fine day and I'd like to explore the grounds. Weather been as wet as Ol' Man River all the time we been over here. Seems wrong to spend a day like today indoors when we could be outside enjoyin' it."

"Relax, Mae. We got plenty a' time for both. Look, here they come." He pointed towards the rep and the manor staff making their way towards the coach.

A chap in a long purple tunic and lime-green leggings clambered into the coach. He wore a voluminous white wig, almost triangular in shape, curled in on itself at the edges.

"What devilment do we have here?" he asked as he took the mic. He shook it. Sniffed it. The tour party laughed as he licked it as if it were an ice-cream. The coach's speakers echoed with a rasping sound as the man's tongue rubbed against it. He feigned surprise at the noise and stumbled backwards, hand on heart. The party sniggered again, Hank and Mae laughing louder than their fellow-passengers.

"Good morning, my friends, and welcome to Doom Brae Manor."

A muttered chorus of 'thank yous' and 'mornings' came back at him.

The man cupped a hand to his ear. "Hark - did I hear a mouse squeak? I said, 'Good Morning'. "

"Good morning," the tour party responded with forced enthusiasm.

"Aha. Our guests awake. My good lords, ladies, and little ones. Welcome to Doom Brae. My name is Wilberforce Long and I'm a footman on this glorious estate. Today, you shall meet the lords and ladies of the manor, all the while in the company of the good folk who work their fingers to the bone to keep them in their accustomed manner. I believe you would refer to it as life Upstairs and Downstairs."

The man turned towards the entrance of the building. "In honour of your visit today, our courtiers have arranged a special welcome for you."

The tourists craned their necks, some half stood to see, as the manor doors swung open and a group of instrumentalists stepped out. Flautists led the way, followed by a stooped gentleman in dark wig plucking a lyre. A mandolin player somehow succeeded in doffing his top hat to the coach without interrupting his tune. At the end of the procession, three maidens shook and rattled timbral in accompaniment.

The minstrels wandered to where a line of stiff-backed, bewigged men stood, one hand tucked behind their backs. Facing them, a row of women wore voluminous skirts in various shades of blue, scarlet and primrose.

Mae took Hank's hand. "I think they're gonna' dance for us."

The band struck up a new tune. The women curtsied, demure smiles hid behind colourful fans, as their menfolk stepped towards them. The men bowed, took their partners fingertips at shoulder-height, and proceeded to perform an elegant processional dance.

"Waddya know. It's a line-dance. Hee-haw," Hank brayed, waving an imaginary Stetson.

The man who had introduced himself as Wilberforce Long spoke into the microphone again. "Today, we shall split you into three groups. Families: please alight your carriage now. You shall be travelling with Megan and her band who will teach you the music, dance and song of our age."

A blonde-haired lady waved towards the coach, waggling her timbrel above her head. The children aboard waved back.

"Once finished with Megan, a member of our kitchen staff will help you prepare your own picnic from the foods of our day, before you complete your time with us by playing the games our children play, while learning the origins of some of the nursery rhymes you know so well."

Megan stood by the coach door as Wilberforce Long concluded his mantra. "So, young ones, are you ready?"

Excited shouts deafened the coach's occupants as the children scrambled out, their parents trailing behind.

Once left with only adults, Wilberforce Long's tone changed. "Now, we shall send some of you to explore the grounds and the woods first. Mr Fairbody will accompany you." A young man in a gamekeeper's costume stepped forward. "For the rest, you shall go indoors with Miss Lambert." A woman in a cook's pinafore curtsied.

The man in the peculiar wig addressed the group again. "If I can be of service to you, or if you wish to ask me any questions, please do so before I leave you to your travels."

The company put their heads down, turned to look out the window, none prepared to speak first.

None but Hank. "Hey, bud," he asked. "Why you got a slice of stuffed crust pizza on your head?" He guffawed loudly. The others tutted. Even Mae looked away.

"I know not of what you speak," the Wilberforce Long character shot back. "Nor the strange tongue in which you express it." The others smiled at the gentle putdown. Hank flushed.

Long's voice took on a serious timbre. "There is a reason your young ones have been sent afore you. My lords and ladies; be warned that not all in Doom Brae is as it seems. Darkness lurks within our grounds and halls. Sinister goings-on fill our history, a history of despots and wickedness, witches and curses."

Long moved to the steps of the coach. Turned back to face the passengers for a final time. "As I take my leave, I beseech you to take great care, my friends, for you are about to discover what puts the Doom into Doom Brae."

Strident organ tones belted out from speakers hidden around the manor's entrance, accompanied by an amplified wicked laugh straight out of a Christopher Lee B-movie.

Hank's eyes lightened. "This is gonna be sweet, Mae. I feel it."

Mae looked less than convinced.

**

The young man who went by the name of Erasmus Fairbody led the party up a meandering country-stream of a path. He brought the group to a halt here and there, indicating wild flowers and singling out the tracks of deer, cattle and smaller creatures which, he explained, roamed free throughout the estate.

At the top of the hill, the Fairbody character asked his audience to turn and look back to the manor house. An audible gasp of admiration escaped the group. They looked over gently rolling land which led down to twenty-five acres of formal gardens.

A couple of Canadians joined Hank and Mae. They muttered their admiration at colourful flower beds, rockeries transformed into shapely inkblots by lavender and heather, and orangeries which reflected sunlight like diamond ear-rings.

Fountains sent a glittering cascade of silver water high into the clear air from a pair of kidney-shaped lakes either side of the manor house. Immaculately tended lawns, a cluster of privets and hedges moulded into elaborate creatures, and a large aviary to the south of the manor completed the chocolate-box picture.

Hank raised a camera the size of a bazooka and began clicking away. Others with more modest equipment joined him while still more simply committed the scene to memory, during which time Fairbody outlined the history of the gardens in eloquent terms.

After a few moments, the gamekeeper herded his party together. He marched them to the periphery of the estate. "Ladies and gentlemen, we are now overlooking public land; land owned by the parish of Doom Brae and not the Pendlebury family. Yet, it is here where the Earl of Doom Brae spent much of his time with his two sons. It is in the land beyond the estate where he taught his sons the skills of huntsmanship."

Erasmus Fairbody halted his speech and invited a question from a man in waxed jacket and tartan cap. "Excuse me, I was wondering why the Earl hunted off-estate when he has so much land available?"

"You ask a good question, sir. The Earl, despite his wealth, is a prudent man. He has no desire to damage his own land or deplete his stock of deer."

An elderly woman raised her hand. "You mention the Earl and his sons. Did the womenfolk join the hunt?"

The gamekeeper looked unhappy. "Alas, madam, they did not. Sadly, by the time the Viscount and Lord Edwin were of an age to hunt, the Countess, Lady Elizabeth, had fallen foul of smallpox. The Earl and his boys hunted alone."

Mae piped up. "Did the Earl remarry?" she asked.

"No, madam. His father, the second Earl, raised his son to believe a wife's role was to provide a man with son and heir. The Earl never did remarry. He had no need. In the eyes of his Lordship, Lady Elizabeth had fulfilled the requirement of any woman."

Mae and the other women shook their heads at the stark reminder of their gender's history.

As they'd been talking, Fairbody had led the tourists back into the estate. They reached the fringe of Bluebell Woods where they rested from the heat under the shade of an oak tree.

Fairbody's mood changed, evident by the tone of his voice. "My good folk, we are now about to enter Bluebell Wood. Stay close to me, I beseech you, lest our woods reveal their secrets to you; secrets best kept hidden."

The party closed ranks as Fairbody led them into the woods. He stopped at various junctures. Conveniently, a pair of red squirrels scaled a sycamore tree in front of their eyes. In his haste to snap them, Hank clattered his elongated camera lens into the head of the lady alongside him. She rubbed the side of her face and moved away with a scowl.

At the next stop, by a bubbling brook, Fairbody pointed out flora and fauna. In a clearing, they came across a wild hog snuffling for fungi. A majestic stag emerged from a patch of brambles and turned to watch them, its movement almost robotic. It was only when a badger crossed their path in dappled sunlight, and Fairbody explained the nocturnal nature of the long-snouted creature, the party realised the truth.

The woodland creatures were animatronic.

"Gee, and we thought Disneyland had it good. I hate to say it, Mae, but the Brits have gotten one over us here." For once, Mae had to agree with her husband. The effects were stunning.

Fairbody gave a furtive glance around. Beckoned the tourists to him. He lowered his voice. "I ask you to be on your guard. Some of you may have heard of the witches of Pendle." Some nodded, others shook their heads. Hank nodded but didn't have a clue. "What is less well known," Fairbody continued, "Is that we have our own tale to tell, the tale of the Pendlebury witch." The party laughed at the obvious play on words. "And I urge caution, for she is oft seen around these parts when she senses strangers about."

Fairbody led them deeper into the woods. Stopped suddenly. "What is that I smell?" A device secreted in the roots of an oak tree puffed out a foul aroma, much the way a bakery circulates the smell of warm bread to entice customers.

The party began to gag. Pulled their jackets up over their face. Fairbody explained, "Aha. The scent of the stinkhorn mushroom. I fear the witch may be close. We must hurry. Come, this way."

He ducked under a bush. The tourists followed, but there was no sign of him. The Fairbody character had slipped into a hide disguised as a grassy mound. They looked around them, puzzled.

Suddenly, a speaker crackled to life. It emitted a cackling laugh at the same time as a hologram appeared in front of the party. A couple of women closest to the projected image jumped in fright, shying from it and clutching hands to their hearts before they dissolved into fits of nervous and embarrassed laughter, much to the amusement of their fellow tourists.

The hologram wasn't particularly convincing. The wart-faced, sharp-chinned image could've been lifted from the Wizard of Oz, but that only added to the humour.

Fairbody leapt from the hide, startling the company once more. "'Tis the Pendlebury witch; or the witch of Doom Brae as she is better known," he cried. "We shall hear more of her anon but, for now, we must hasten from her before she casts an evil curse upon us. Quickly, this way. Through the hedgerow and far away from the ugly crone."

The party followed Erasmus Fairbody onto the next stage of the adventure. All, that is, except Hank. He hung back, staring avidly at the hologram.

"Ugly?" he said in reverential tones. "You're the most beautiful creature I've ever seen."

The witch turned directly towards him and fixed him with a smile. Sky-blue eyes glowed from a flawless face fringed by long flaxen hair.

"Beautiful," Hank whispered again.

**

The party stood in a meadow part-way back to the manor waiting for Hank to catch up. The guide gave him a harsh look for his tardiness. Hank raised his hands and nodded an apology in response.

Erasmus Fairbody acknowledged Hank's regret with a curt nod and was soon regaling the party with vivid descriptions of the flora of the period, and how it changed and evolved over the millennia.

Hank quickly recovered his breath after his exertions but just as quickly lost interest in Fairbody's words. Not for him lectures and talks. He responded to visual stimuli, to mechanics and motion, not speech. He turned his back on the group and found himself staring uphill, back towards Bluebell Wood.

Raised as a country boy, Hank was always at home outdoors. But there was something special about those woods, something mesmeric, which pulled at his heartstrings. He set aside the special effects and the electronic wizardry which brought to life the woodland creatures: he just knew he'd felt at home in its sunlit glades and shaded bowers.

It reminded him of his childhood. He'd been lonely as a child yet, paradoxically, felt comfortable in the wildernesses of his home State. The grounds of the Doom Brae Estate bore little resemblance to the territories he explored in his youth, yet he'd found instant peace here.

Hank was aware Erasmus Fairbody continued his well-versed presentation, but the words drifted by him.

"…and we see today how much a visionary Capability Brown was. The immature saplings he planted at irregular intervals on the approach to the manor have blossomed into the splendid orchards we see spreading all the way to the main highway."

The company murmured in appreciation as a girl in a maid's costume began doling out fruit from a handcart wheeled up to them. Behind her, a trailer with built-in brazier offered roasted chestnuts.

"Sir," Erasmus said. "Sir?" He had to raise his voice for the man to hear him. "Would you return to the party, please?"

The man kept walking away from him, slowly, methodically, almost like a sleep-walker.

Mae looked around. Hank wasn't at her side. "Hank. Where you goin'? Get your ass back here, honey. We're all done up there. You holdin' everyone up. Again."

Hank took another couple of paces. Stopped. Turned 180-degrees to face the party, a blank expression in his eyes, face a mask. He completed the circle and set off once more, back towards the dark mass of Bluebell Wood.

After a few shuffling steps, Hank stopped abruptly. He hung his head, fell to his knees, and sobbed.

Mae broke from the party at a trot. She called his name. Once. Twice. Three times. Hank didn't respond. Not to her, he didn't. Instead, he responded to something else; something unseen. He raised his hands above his head, fingers extended skywards, and muttered something unintelligible.

Three other tourists broke rank and hurried towards Hank. Erasmus shouted to him. "Sir, are you all right? Do you need help?"

Hank let out a deep moan, an otherworldly sound which raised gooseflesh on those close enough to hear. Slowly, he raised his head.

"Hmm? You guys talking to me? Yeah, sure, I'm fine. Guess I'm a little tired, that's all."

The guide and Mae exchanged glances. "Has this happened before?" Erasmus asked, all pretence of Georgian-speak gone.

Mae shook her head.

"No history of epilepsy or seizures? Perhaps the hologram triggered something?"

Mae's head moved left and right again. "No. Nothing."

Erasmus handed Hank a bottle of water. "Here, take a drink. A few sips." Fellow-tourists took an arm each and helped him to his feet. "Steady, now," Erasmus urged. "Take your time. You've a long day ahead if you wish to carry on. Or we could leave you to rest in the coach if you prefer, after our nurse has checked you over."

Something shifted behind Hank's eyes before he fixed Erasmus with a cold stare. "No quack's gonna' be cupping and blood-lettin' me, boy."

Erasmus breathed a sigh of relief. The man was compos mentis enough to recognise the day's theme. "Good. That's better. We could get a wheelchair for you if it helps, though."

"You kiddin' me, man. I'm fine. Real fine. Let's get this show on the road." He straightened himself as if nothing had happened.

As they set off towards Doom Brae manor, Mae raised an eyebrow. She took Hank's arm in the crook of hers. "What was all that about?" she whispered. "You sure you're ok?"

"What was all what about? Nuthin' happened, cutie. Just real taken aback by the forest and the animatronics and the hologram. Don't know how they did it, that's all"

"But that's your thing, Hank. You love stuff like that. You sure never acted that way on the Tower of Terror."

Hank expelled air, horse-like. "Tower of Terror ain't nothing like the purdy witch girl."

Mae opened her mouth to correct him, but her response was drowned out by Hank's voice calling across to another group of tourists heading towards the wood guided by their own 'Erasmus Fairbody' character.

"Hey, buddies," Hank shouted. "You got a real treat lined up for you up there."

The original Erasmus asked him to remain quiet. "Please, don't spoil the surprise for them. Keep it to yourself, if you would."

Hank put his finger to his lips. "Sorry, sorry. Not another word, I promise."

"Good. Thank you."

As they returned to the rest of their party, Hank broke into a strident song directed towards the other party.

"Marie, Marie La Voodoo Veay
She's the Witch-Queen Of…
Of New Orleans.

"You know," Mae said to Erasmus, "I think I preferred him when he was odd."

**

He sat with arms folded high against his chest. A scowl darkened his face as he glowered down at a tiny pewter plate littered with gingerbread crumbs. Alongside it, a coffee cup lay curdling, an oily film across the surface.

"Oh, for goodness sake. Cheer up, Hank. You said you liked authentic and it don't come more authentic than this."

"But I want a chilli dog."

From the tone in the voice, Mae expected it to be accompanied by a stamp of feet and juvenile bawl. "Honey, I don't think chilli dogs are popular amongst Brits even in this day and age, let alone nearly three hundred years ago."

"And the coffee's undrinkable. Tastes like swamp water."

Mae rolled her eyes at the couple sharing their table. She forced the last of her game pie into her mouth and made a tumbleweed motion with her hand to indicate she'd speak once her mouth was empty.

"Should have gone for the pie. It's awesome." She dabbed flakes of pastry from the corner of her mouth with her little finger. "And it says here on the menu the coffee's from what is now Yemen. It's where the family imported it from in them there days."

"Well, it still tastes like mud."

"It's probably ground," the man opposite Hank offered, earning a sneer in return.

Hank's stomach let out the rumble of a flatulent hippopotamus. He snatched the menu from Mae, signalled to a waitress and ordered a slice of apple pie, "And a Pepsi."

The maid pushed back her frilled linen bonnet. "Sorry, sir. We have fruit juice, freshly pressed lemonade, or water. Unless you'd care to partake in a flagon of ale. Or perhaps a gin, or mead?"

"So, you got no Pepsi. What sort of place is this? Water. Just water."

He shooed away a pair of sparrows who pecked at a few discarded crumbs at his feet while the maid offered a slight curtsy which didn't extend to a smile.

While he waited at the courtyard table, Hank studied the splendour of the manor house, and the thought he'd soon be striding the ancient corridors lightened his mood.

By the time the maid returned with his sweet dish, Hank was deep in conversation with his table companions. "Say, waddya make of it so far?"

The man, Clint Reubens, shielded his eyes from the sun as he replied, "Cool. I expected a boring mausoleum, but the trip's been more than that. I love the fact we experience what the Pendlebury's did back in the day. Not just get talked at, know what I mean?"

Hank nodded. "I sure do. Never come across anything like this place before. Kinda like a theme park but the way it's all set up is real neat. And we haven't even started inside the ol' place yet."

The man's wife, Althea, a tiny mouse-like woman with staring eyes, snickered. "I hope it's better than the witch in the woods. I thought it was a cheap effect. It let the place down, I reckon."

Hank gave her a stern look. "Hey, I thought it was awesome. Felt I could almost touch her."

The woman shrugged and slid her eyes to her husband. "Each to his own, I guess."

But Hank didn't hear her. The sparrows at his feet fluttered away as a shadow darkened the table. A huge magpie landed with the beat of heavy wings. Its splendid black and white plumage and oil-blue wing feathers belied its scavenging habits which earned it the title the Thief of Birds.

Mae recoiled from it, but Hank watched, enraptured. He felt compelled to meet its cold stare, even while he sensed its coal-black eyes search for something deep within him.

In the unfathomable depths of the bird's gaze, Hank saw a faint colour rise in its eyes, no more than a pin-prick of light; a luminous green light. And a voice chilled him to the bone. A voice he felt, rather than heard, whisper, "I shall steal your soul."

An intense surge, as if he were inside a car which crested a rise too fast, dragged his stomach downwards. Only it didn't stop. It kept going, hauling him further and further with it.

His field of vision swam. Images on the periphery swirled and drew inwards like water down a plughole until only the magpie remained visible. Whilst everything else moved downwards, it spread its wings and rose like a phoenix but, to Hank, it seemed to have merged with him; become part of him.

He closed his eyelids until everything around him disappeared into a black hole of emptiness.

When he opened them, he was alone at the table. The others had left him. Something else was different, too. Maids in bonnets and puffed-out skirts still fussed around the courtyard but there were no other customers. There wasn't, he realised, any other tables.

Hank had been sat opposite the aviary, the orchard behind it. Now, he realised, he was looking over open fields. No birdcages, no fruit trees. Just rugged fallow land on which cattle grazed; land interspersed with hawthorn bushes and a few feeble saplings.

A chubby woman with rosy red cheeks broke off her business and offered him a benevolent smile. The woman bustled over to him and, to Hank's open-mouthed astonishment, ruffled his hair.

He heard the woman speak. "Are you alright, H…"

"…ank? Hank? Are you still with us?"

Hank blinked several times at the sound of Mae's voice.

"Huuh?"

Mae's tone was etched with concern. "You sure you're ok, honey? I mean, really sure?"

Hank tutted. "Yeah. Course I am. What makes you think otherwise?"

Mae exchanged glances with her table companions. It was the mousey woman who spoke. She gave Hank a curious look. "You drifted off from us there."

"And you weren't too good out in the fields earlier," Clint added.

Hank wanted to ask how they hadn't seen the illusion, too, but decided against it given the tone of the conversation. Instead, he gave a dismissive wave. "I'm good. Just pondering how these guys do the FX, that's all. Some technology they must have."

"I'm pretty sure they'll never tell us," Clint said. "Now, you sure you're ok?"

"Sure, I'm sure." He wrinkled his nose. "Hey, what's that goddamn awful smell?"

The others sniffed the air. "Nope. Can't catch it," the man said.

"You're kidding me, right? It's rank."

Althea gave a Mona Lisa-like smile, but the conversation was interrupted by the waitress taking their plates, asking if everything had been to their satisfaction.

Mae kicked Hank under the table to elicit a "Yeah, all good, thanks."

The waitress-cum-maid reached across Hank for Mae's plate. As she raised it, Hank caught the acrid scent again.

"There - that's it. It's coming from your plate. What've you had again?"

"Game pie. But there's none left. I ate it all so it can't be that. Just left a sprinkling of the garnish. Some greens, a little tomato and some mushroom."

Hank clicked his fingers. "That's it. The smell. It's those damn stinkhorn from the wood. You trying' to poison your customers?", he accused the waitress.

She frowned and smiled at the same time. "I assure you, sir, you are mistaken. We only use the finest field mushrooms. All freshly picked and perfectly edible."

Mae kicked Hank again. "It's totally fine. THEY were totally fine. Hank, you gone crazy today, boy."

The maid curtsied one last time before leaving Hank and Mae to their disagreement; a disagreement cut short by the arrival of the Wilberforce Long character and his harlequin-coloured garb.

"My Lords and Ladies", he bowed and scraped. "I trust you enjoyed our delicacies. You shall now be escorted into the house where, amongst many things, you shall witness how and where our meals are prepared."

After a beat, he continued. "It will, of course, have the Doom Brae twist. All may not be as it seems. Why, you may ask? Then I shall tell you. The kitchen is where the Doom Brae Witch worked."

Hank's face brightened at the news. As Wilberforce used a brass-headed cane to direct various groups to their respective guides, Hank and Mae stood to leave. Hank extended his hand across the table. "Been good talkin' to you guys. Hey, you never said where you folk from."

It was Althea who answered. "We're from Danvers, Massachusetts."

"All-righty. Can't say I know it."

"You will, but probably by its former name."

"Which is?"

"Salem Village"

**

The woman with white hair so big it swirled above her head like a tub of frozen yogurt introduced the party of twelve guests to an elegant man dressed in a green waistcoat and cherry-coloured breeches. Despite his attire, his face shouted 21st Century. Probably because it was.

The man doffed his hat. "Thank you, Miss Batkins. Before I return you to Mary," he gave Miss Batkins an imperceptible bow, "It is my duty to give you some information about the majestic building before us." He offered the manor a flamboyant hand gesture.

The party before him shuffled their feet, keen to continue the tour.

"Doom Brae Manor was one of the first buildings to be constructed in the Palladian style. Note east and west wing are exact replicas of one another; a perfect mirror image."

The tourists raised their eyes over the man's head and nodded their understanding. Hank stifled a yawn.

"Also, we have Greek and Roman influences," he signalled to the marble statues either side of the entrance door, "as well as the typically artistic stonemasonry of our age." Another effete gesture towards the portico awning, edged as it was with ornate swirls and waves of white plaster so thick it resembled icing on a wedding cake.

"Do you notice anything else unusual about the manor? Something that hints at its age and the period of its construction?"

The man in the waistcoat filled the silence himself. "Look at the windows. Note how those of the ground floor are small, the first floor larger and those of the uppermost floor larger still. This is to bear the weight of the building; to ensure it has fewer weaknesses at the points where most weight sits."

He paused long enough to draw his audience's attention back to him. "This feature was to play a significant part in the history of the manor, and one which makes its story such a momentous one."

Hank's attention wandered. His gaze flitted between the horse-and-carriage convoy, up the hill towards Bluebell Wood, and to the Greco-Roman statues. A puzzled frown crossed his features. He couldn't quell the feeling that something wasn't right; something had changed. He shook his head to clear his mind and refocused on the prepared speech.

"Finally, before you continue the tour of the manor with Miss Batkins, there are two more features I must point out." His voice adopted a serious timbre. "Features which make Doom Brae THE most appropriate of name for our manor."

The tourists hushed. They sensed the boring part had come to an end.

"If you look towards the roof of the manor, you will see it's lined with crenulations."

"Excuse me, sir. What are 'crenulations'?"

"My apologies. I should use the word 'battlement'. Notice how the roof wall is interspersed with gaps through which an archer releases his volley of arrows before taking shelter behind the raised elements. It is a mediaeval feature; a period in history which fascinated the third Earl of Doom Brae, and one which required Royal Assent during peace time."

The group looked at the feature anew. Tried to imagine it lined with bowmen.

"Legend has it, when the sky is clear and the moon is full, an apparition visits the manor gable and can be seen peering from between the crenulation."

Twelve pairs of eyes instantly homed in on the rooftop.

"It is said to be the ghost of Lord Edwin Pendlebury, youngest son of the third Earl of Doom Brae, returning to search Bluebell Wood for a sight of his long-lost love. A lover believed by some to be the Doom Brae witch."

A noise drew the group's attention and they saw the outline of a crouched figure dash across their line of vision. Hank drew his camera but was too late. The fake Lord Pendlebury was already descending the fire escape at the back of the manor. Hank tutted his disappointment and lowered his lens.

The guide addressed Hank. "Fear not, sir. You and your companions may yet get the shot you desire, for I said there were two features of the manor I wished to speak of. Please, if you look at the centre of the portico, just above the feature which resembles a semi-quaver."

Fingers pointed and cameras rose to the place the guide had indicated.

"You will see a statuette. This is a gargoyle; the only one you will see on the entire Manor."

Hank sensed something was about to happen. He trained his lens on the feature.

"It is in the form of a gryphon; a mythical beast, half-lion, half-eagle, which represents the guardian of the divine. Please, feel free to take photographs."

Hank readied his camera as he leaned into Mae. "Dollar to a dime that old bird is going to move," he whispered.

Sure enough, no sooner had he spoken than the head of the gryphon rotated from westward-facing to look directly at the group. Cameras clicked, phones captured the movement on video.

A puff of smoke masked the gryphon for an instant, accompanied by the sound of nails drawing down a blackboard. Or of a stone slab, like the cover of Dracula's tomb, dragging aside.

When the smoke cleared, the gryphon stood with eyes wide and wings spread. To a chorus of 'No way' 'Will you look at that' and a few 'Jeezus', the gryphon launched itself from the portico and circled the group several times, the animatronic mouth opening as its tongue lapped at air like a lizard.

Birds nesting in the manor's eaves fled for their lives while cameras attempted to track the animatronic beast's movement against the backdrop of stonework and sky as it soared and dipped above the crowds.

"JK Rowling, eat your heart out", Hank yelled as he set his camera on Continuous Shoot mode.

After four circuits, the gryphon settled on the Olympian figurine and posed for photographs before it returned to its rightful place above the portico. Another puff of smoke and, when it cleared, the gryphon was once more motionless as death.

Green-and-cherry-red man basked in the applause of the group while Mary Batkins and her ice-cream hair moved into place to lead them into the manor.

Hank saw an opportunity to review his footage while the handover took place. He flicked through the images, nudging Mae whenever he came to a particularly aesthetic shot.

Mary Batkins finished her introduction and ushered the party forward. They headed towards the manor entrance where the refrains of Bach-composed organ music greeted them.

Once again, Hank was left in their wake. He was staring at the image review screen of his camera. Amidst the series of shots of the gryphon in flight, towards the end, there was a series of blank images. Hank estimated there to be around sixteen frames of nothingness before the images reappeared.

He did a double-take between statue and screen.

He couldn't comprehend how he had a photograph depicting a gryphon perched on a discus held in the right hand of a statue.

Hank checked again. A shiver convulsed him.

The sculpture was shorn of right arm and hand. There was no discus on which a gryphon could alight.

**

Hank ran to join Mae and the rest of the party just as they exited the Grand Hall.

His camera swung from his shoulder like a wrecking ball, narrowly missing a priceless blue and gold vase. His footsteps reverberated in the opulent surroundings - until Batkins half-turned and offered him a glare.

He slowed his gait to a feverish walk, finally close enough to grab Mae by the elbow as the group entered the smoking room, first stop on the interior tour.

"What are you doing?" Mae's words came out hushed but there was no denying the frustration in her voice.

"You gotta see this. There's something going on here and I can't work it out, for the life of me."

"What do you mean?"

"Here, look at this." He twisted his shoulder-strap and held the camera, awkwardly, while Mae squinted at the screen.

"Is that it? You hold me back to look at a photograph? We can look at them back in the hotel, or on the coach." She glanced over her shoulder at the muffled voices behind the smoking-room doors. "We're missing the tour. Come on; let's go."

Hank held her still. "Tell me what you see."

"The front door, the Greek statue, the gargoyle-thing. What exactly am I looking for, Hank?"

"The gryphon. Where is it?"

"Like I said: it's on the statue. On the stump where its arm was. Now, can we go before I miss any more of this?"

She pushed open the door, drawing glances from the tourists, and joined them while Hank studied the image.

The gryphon was indeed nestled on what had once been the elbow of the ancient sculpture. Nestled on the stump, not the discus. Because there was no discus; nor any arm.

"Double-you-tee-eff?"

The next half-hour bypassed Hank. While the others gawped at the lavish royal suite, the spacious chambers and dressing rooms of the Pendlebury family, and the decorous corridors linking them, Hank tried to come to terms with his state of mind.

They toured the staff quarters, comparing and contrasting the dark, squalid rooms, rock-hard beds and bare furnishings, all while Hank's brain did its best to process the earlier events.

Batkins pointed paintings by Hogarth, put names to the faces of the Pendlebury's captured in oil, and explained how the Earl removed all images of Lady Elizabeth as they bore no resemblance to her appearance after her features were ravaged by smallpox.

While she did this, Hank settled on the only explanation possible: the electro-magnetism involved in the special effects somehow, and in some way, had interfered with his digital photographic equipment.

The more he thought about it, the more convinced he became. It was the one thing that made any sense. By the time they reached the library, Hank was once more at Mae's side, taking in Miss Batkin's litany with relish.

The company sat on rows of hardwood chez-longes, cushioned by plump fabric and gaudy upholstery. Like church pews front onto an altar, each bench faced the vast bookcase stacked with an array of hard-bound books, gold lettering on the spines. The collection adorned the entirety of the southern wall, from floor to ceiling.

At its centre, above the lectern where Miss Batkins had taken up position, Hank noticed a large sign advising pregnant women, those prone to seizures or anyone with a heart complaint or pacemaker, to make themselves known to a member of staff. 'NOW'. A woman did so and was led through a side-door.

From behind the bookcase, a series of dull thuds, muted laughter, and muffled shrieks emerged. Hank nudged Mae. "There's more fun in the next room, just you watch."

Miss Batkins gave an exaggerated cough in order to capture attention. When that failed, she clapped her hands in the brusque manner befitting her Head of Household status.

"Lords, ladies and gentlemen, I crave your attention. We are about to visit the hub of this wondrous estate. It is, of course, the kitchen. Before we enter, I must forewarn you that this is no ordinary kitchen, nor you ordinary visitors. You shall be privileged to witness scenes denied even the Earl of Doom Brae himself and, I assure you, your senses shall reel from what you will experience."

The audience gazed around the library as she spoke. They marvelled at the ornate ceiling, the lavish candelabra suspended from it, and the battery of torches pinned to the wall by solid gold fixings.

Miss Batkins addressed the tourists again. "Pray tell me, what sights do you expect to behold within? What delicacies will our staff be preparing for the Earl and his guests this evening?"

"Pheasant? Partridge? Grouse?" proposed one.

"Venison," said another.

A third, "How about pastries and fruit pies?"

"Lots of vegetables, I would imagine."

Miss Batkins nodded at each offering. "And what scents and aromas will greet you?"

A hand shot up. "The scent of warm, baking bread," a heavy-set woman offered.

Batkins' big hair wobbled like gelatine as she nodded her agreement. "Yes, you could expect to notice such an aroma. Anything else?"

"Steaks searing, or hogs being roasted over a fire," the man from the café, Clint Reubens, suggested.

"The smell of pan-fried dumplings," another observed.

Mae threw up her hand. "Spices."

"Ah yes. All sensible suggestions. But, alas, not."

She produced a handkerchief from the hidden depths of her skirts, depressed a bulbous swelling attached to a small bottle, and sprayed liquid onto her kerchief.

"Our age is very different to yours. Ingredients differ. Cooking methods do not resemble yours." She cast her eyes downwards. "And, I regret to say, hygiene is an issue for our ladies. We do not engage in the filthy habit of bathing and, with the heat, well...I'm sure you can imagine."

The party laughed as she dabbed her nose with the perfumed handkerchief. Miss Batkins glanced around like a spy in Red Square. She beckoned the audience to her. Her voice dropped to a stage whisper.

"You may have heard of a creature known as The Doom Brae Witch. Be forewarned. She has employ within our kitchen. You may observe some signs of her presence. Look for them. If you spot them, it may, just may, mean she's at work somewhere within."

She raised her voice once more. "Do not be afraid." The audience jumped at the resonance, then giggled at their reaction. "Our best alchemists have been hard at work. Attached to the rear of the seats before you, you shall find the results of their labours. They will offer you protection from her spells and curses. "

Hank stretched out a hand. Withdrew an object from a pocket. A pair of spectacles. "It's like Disney's Muppet 3-D, Mae."

He slipped them on as the bookcase slid open and the floor, complete with rows of chez-longes and anticipatory tourists, glided forward.

The bookcase closed behind them. They were in the kitchen.

And Batkins hadn't been wrong.

A device buried in the arms and supports of their seats assailed the party with a volley of stenches. Hank, Mae and their group gagged as the sour smell of sweat, spoiled and rotting vegetables, and mutton fat rained down on them like the blows of a heavyweight boxer.

A mix of live actors, holograms and animatronic cooks and maids crowded into the kitchen space. Above the heat and squalor, the scents gradually changed.

From the weighty reek of foul breath and fetid cheese, more pleasant smells emerged. Rich gravies, sweetmeats and the fresh citrus smell from platters overflowing with fresh fruit lightened the air and cleared the senses sufficient for the party to appreciate their surroundings.

In a corner, a dark object with luminous eyes seemed to survey the events. It lowered its head and lapped at a bowl at its feet. "A black cat," Hank observed. "I betcha the witch is gonna make a showing. That'll be her familiar."

His eyes scanned the actors, slid across to the work surfaces, over to the giant range on which a selection of meats turned on a spit, and upwards. Strung from the wall above the range, fowl and game hung awaiting maturity.

Alongside them, Hank spotted a leathery-creature, a lizard-like object and long-tailed vermin. He nudged Mae and pointed them out. "What did I tell you? 'Wing of bat, eye of newt, tail of rat'; all that nonsense. She's here."

He made the whoo-woo noise of a child imitating a ghost. Mae shrugged him off.

On stage, actors whizzed back and forth. Some carried plates laden with food, an elderly animatronic man in tailed coat leaned over a hologram of a rotund woman, in ubiquitous linen bonnet and apron, as she carved a joint.

Hank found it almost impossible to determine real from imagined. Towards the centre rear, another woman – hologram, actress or mannequin - stirred a steaming pan of broth with a huge ladle.

Then the lights failed.

Women jumped as the auditorium was plunged into darkness. Mae let out a nervous cry.

"Relax, honey. All part of the show."

A mighty crack, like a thunderclap, rent the air. The tour party jumped again. An electronic sizzle followed and the audience, man and woman, screamed as a burst of static lifted them from their seats. Nervous laughter ensued.

Slowly, a faint glow appeared. It grew in brightness, projecting a greenish light downwards from the ceiling until the pan of broth glowed under a phosphorous cone.

Except it wasn't a pan of broth any longer. It was a cauldron. An ugly, scarred crone sat alongside it. She stirred the bubbling, steaming contents as she turned her head towards the audience and extended a bony finger towards them.

The hologram was much more realistic than the one they'd seen in the woods, and they stiffened with fright as the crone rose from the kitchen floor and moved out and over until it levitated above them.

The tour party swivelled their heads to watch as, in a burst of fireworks, the hologram fragmented into crystals and appeared to shower down upon them.

They flinched away from the 3-D effects before bursting into laughter and applause.

All except Hank. He hadn't seen any of it. His eyes were fixed on stage where three characters remained side-by-side.

A chubby red-faced woman, who seemed vaguely familiar, laid a protective hand on the shoulder of a young boy. On his other side stood a beautiful blue-eyed, flaxen-haired girl.

Hank knew instantly who she was. She tossed her head, hair cascading down her back like a shower of gold, and crooked a finger towards Hank, inviting him forward.

Hank rested his hands on his seat, pushed himself upwards, and glanced towards Mae.

By the time he looked back, the stage was bare.

**

The party remained abuzz with the drama and sensory-overload of the kitchen escapade.

Mary Batkins had handed the baton back to Wilberforce Long as the tour built towards its climax. He still looked as though he'd been colour-coordinated by a blind man.

Long ramped up the tension with stories of mysterious goings-on through the ages, interwoven with snippets of historical detail. Wilberforce Long led the group to the rear of the servants' quarters and stood outside a low, windowless access door while the group gathered around him.

"We stand outside the only access and egress point our house staff are permitted to use. Not for them the grandeur of the main staircase, the magnificence of the entrance hall, or the Palladian splendour of Doom Brae Manor's exterior. No, our servants, maids and kitchen staff all use what I believe you good folk would name 'the tradesmen's entrance.'

He rapped on the door with his staff. "Behind this door, you will find a stairwell. It leads us to the lower reaches of the manor, to the eastern corridor. At its foot, directly across the corridor, another door awaits us."

Wilberforce held a silence. He straightened his wig. Pulled at an earlobe. Pretended to wonder whether to say more. "The door of which I speak leads downwards. Some say it leads to hell. In a trice, you shall discover the truth."

A blast of icy air expelled itself over Hank and his group. They all shivered, most laughed.

"One-by-one, you are about to learn how difficult even the simplest of tasks is for our hardworking people. Their rations are meagre. The Earl gives prominence to his personal staff." He sniffed haughtily. "I am fortunate to count myself amongst the lucky souls."

An image projected itself above Long's head. He feigned shock before reading out the words projected against the wall. It warned those with mobility problems, fear of confined spaces or poor eyesight to excuse themselves from the attraction.

"It is most important you do as the magical words forewarn. I wish you to experience what the people of our house go through each and every night. Contrary to what you may imagine, candles are not freely available in the quarters. Cost is one reason, the risk of fire another. One candle per week is as all we are granted. And its flame is soon extinguished. So, ladies and gentlemen, one-by-one, please step into the dark, forbidding world of Doom Brae Manor."

Wilberforce Long disappeared into a service lift disguised behind a colourful three-tiered dressing screen. A mysterious voice issued the guests with instructions from a speaker in the ceiling. 'Take great care,' 'Enter one-by-one,' 'Do not enter until called', and 'Follow the light'.

The door creaked open unaided and the first tourist stepped into the darkness, giggling nervously as she did so.

Hank passed the wait exchanging small talk with folk nearby. Baroque music filtered around, the strident organ and harpsichord tones periodically interrupted by an electronic voice declaring 'Will the next guest please enter the unknown.'

After Mae disappeared through the door, Hank quickly flicked through some of the pictures on his camera until the door opened. He . knew the drill. He stepped inside even as the voice invited him through.

Inside, it was darker than anything he'd ever experienced. Hank reached out until he felt rough stone beneath his fingertips. He extended his other arm. His hand rasped against the wall even before he needed to flex his elbow.

Hank waited for the light. None came. He felt for the edge of the step with his foot. Gingerly, he stepped down. Once one foot was planted, the other followed.

Still no light.

He clung to the handrail. Took another step. Then another. The silence clawed at him. Hank whistled a tune. It echoed around the well-like staircase as if a runaway train approached.

He stopped whistling. Waited for the light.

Still nothing.

He began to sweat. Felt his pulse rate increase. Not knowing who or what may wait on the next step disoriented him. The walls closed in. He spread his arms. No, they were the same distance away.

Hank took another step. Increased his pace. Began taking two at a time. He stumbled. Grabbed at the handrail. Was the rail closer to him? Was he about to be squashed between stone?

Blood pounded his temples. He sat on the cold, bare stair. Held his head. Flicked sweat away. How much further? And, where was the damn light?

Hank stood once more. His head swam. He steadied himself, took another step and, around the next turn, saw the light. A faint green glow, little more than a pin-prick, but something to focus on.

He made his way toward the light, almost running now, his footsteps echoing so it sounded like half a dozen men raced downward.

Without warning, he rushed headlong into a door. Relief flooded through him. He reached for the handle. Opened the door. Only to find yet more blackness beyond.

Hank almost cried, then he remembered Wilberforce Long's instructions. Another door lay opposite. He reached out. Touched it. And heard the comforting sound of voices beyond.

He heard something else, too; an indistinct tapping from somewhere nearby. He listened. Yes, someone was drumming on a window. Yet, how could they? It was daytime. If there was a window, there'd be light.

Then, what?

His hands touched the wall. He ran his fingers up it until they rested on something solid. The rapping came more insistent, and closer by. He folded his fingers around the object. It felt familiar. He touched something else. Glass. Glass within a frame. Yet, not a window.

With creeping certainty, Hank realised someone was knocking not on a window, but on a mirror.

Worse, they were knocking from INSIDE the mirror!

The door behind him flung open. Light bathed the corridor. Hank turned, wide-eyed.

"That was boring, wasn't it?" the last of the tourists said as he emerged.

**

Across the corridor from the darkened staircase, the tour party sat cross-legged in front of Wilberforce Long; schoolkids at story time.

They were in a bare chamber scarcely large enough to contain them. To their left, the door through which they'd entered. To the right, a set of ancient stone steps led down into blackness.

Long stood in a spot where a single beam of light shone upwards, directed at his chin so his face showed as a patchwork of light and shade. Water from a concealed tap slicked the rough pebbled wall behind him. Hidden from view, engineers twiddled consuls which steered radio-controlled rats around the party.

Wilberforce recounted the legend of the Doom Brae witch trial in his quaint Georgian cant. His version wasn't historically accurate, but it still engaged and enthralled his audience.

Applause reverberated around the chamber as Long took his bow. When the echoes faded away, he announced a change in the schedule.

"Good folk, at this point, I am expected to escort you, at your own peril, down to the Doom Brae Manor dungeon. The dark exhibits it contains betray our Earl's love for malevolent days of yore."

Wilberforce noticed some of the tourists face drop. "Fear not, for see them you shall. However, before you do, we have some special visitors amongst us today. I have recounted the tale of the Doom Brae witch. Now, I have the pleasure to introduce you to Mrs Althea Reubens."

"Hey, that's our friend," Hank whispered to Mae.

"Althea lives in a village known to us all, and she has kindly agreed to share the story of her home with us. Ladies and gentlemen, please welcome Mrs Reubens."

Wilberforce led the applause as Althea rose nervously. Long manoeuvred her into position above the light. Althea cleared her throat and slid her eyes downwards.

"Thank you, Mr Long. I know you're all eager to move on, and so am I. But our host thought you'd be interested in what I have to say. Why? Because I come from Salem Village, that's why."

Ears pricked up and backs straightened at the mention of the name.

Althea Reubens snickered. "Thought that would grab your attention. It was interesting to learn the background to Miss Goodchild's trial, because there are many parallels with events in Salem. Back in the late seventeenth century, Salem was, shall we say, a difficult place to live."

She looked at her husband. "Clint would say it still it has its problems. Nowadays, it's black against white, rich versus poor."

Sage nods of empathy greeted her words.

She continued. "Back then in Massachusetts, neighbour battled neighbour over real estate, family set itself against family over petty jealousies and rivalries, much like the Pendlebury family Mr Long has just told us about. And it was family strife, in a home as far removed from Doom Brae Manor as you can imagine, which precipitated events in Salem."

Althea's voice grew stronger as she gained in confidence. She even raised her eyes to meet her audience.

"A young girl, Betty Parris, was accused by her older cousin, Abigail Williams, of having 'powers beyond nature'. Betty, so it is said, bore marks on her body of 'unnatural origin'. What is more, her cousin accused her of 'moving objects without physical force'.

Wilberforce Long interrupted. "Indeed, dear lady. Just as the Doom Brae witch forced the mirror from the wall."

"Yes; except in Salem, things didn't stop there. Others claimed they'd witnessed similar events elsewhere, in both young and old, male as well as female. Rumour and mistrust spread like wildfire. Folk saw an opportunity to incriminate their neighbour. By the end of May 1692, no fewer than sixty-two people were under arrest."

Heads shook within the group, low whistles coming from some. Hank spoke up. "You know us Yanks; always bigger and better." The group laughed.

"Are there any other similarities between Doom Brae and Salem?" Long asked, keen to move things along.

Althea flushed. "Yes, there is. While Louisa Goodchild had her dalliance with Lord Edwin, and the Viscount is said to have used the girl to his advantage, many of the Salem accused were brought to account for a lack of Puritanical values. Girls and women were accused of attracting men by Malleus Maleficaram."

"Kindly explain, dear lady."

"Of course. My apologies all. Malleus Maleficaram is an ancient log which documents tales and legends of men having…," she hesitated, " 'Encounters' of the flesh with demons. it details incidents of men having their minds swayed, and of the prophecy of evil events. In short, Mr Long, of behaving exactly as Miss Goodchild was accused."

A member of the group raised her hand. "Sorry to interrupt, but you did say sixty-two were arrested, didn't you? I did hear you correctly?"

Althea nodded.

"And were all found guilty?"

"Actually, no. Twenty were executed. Fewer than most imagine but, of course, far too many."

The temperature in the chamber had plummeted. Breath came in clouds from those who spoke. Shivers convulsed the few who still wore their summer garb.

Even Wilberforce Long, in his heavy apparel and triangular wig, looked pasty. He folded his arms and rubbed the palms of his hands against them. "Tell us, Mrs Reubens, why were the unfortunate score found guilty whilst others walked free?"

"Much of the testimony was verbal from those who claimed to witness the events. Of course, many of these weren't neutral or unbiased accounts. In fact, they rarely were. So, in the majority of cases, the magistrate demanded corroborating evidence."

"Such as?"

"They were asked to recite the Lord's Prayer in the belief that those who did the devil's work were unable to speak the Lord's words."

Most the group stood, now; stamping their feet for warmth.

Hank buried his hands deep in his pockets. His nose shone red against pale, cold flesh. "Surely they all passed this test, though. What made the twenty stand out from the others?" he asked.

"Simple. When entering a pact with the Devil, it's claimed he uses a claw or a branding iron to mark the witch as his own. Quite simply, all sixty-two were checked for such marks."

Frost clung to the chamber's walls. Water no longer trickled down them. Instead, it froze in a glassy pool.

"And, the twenty all bore ugly moles, skin blemishes, fleshy folds, or vivid scars." Althea's words to the group were solemn.

"In short, they bore Satan's mark."

**

A disembodied voice crackled in the ear of the man charged with playing the Wilberforce Long character. Long pressed a finger against the hidden earpiece and gave a thumbs-up to the CCTV camera disguised within a bowl of fruit.

"Ladies and Gentlemen: may I have your attention for a moment? At this stage of your tour, we would normally take you straight through to the dungeons before concluding your visit with a carriage tour of the grounds. If I could pray your forbearance, we have a change to our schedule."

The group shuffled their feet to keep warm in the frigid air.

"We owe thanks to our friend for her interesting tales from Salem. They were, I'm sure you'll agree, well-worth hearing. However, as a result, we have caused quite a tailback behind us. We will, therefore, come back to the horrors of the Doom Brae dungeon in a short while and take our trip round the grounds first. Our carriages await, so I shall escort you to your coachmen and, when you return, we shall conclude your visit with the nightmarish cellar dungeons. Should your nerves permit, that is."

The dungeon was always the highlight of the tour and Wilberforce feared the announcement wouldn't go down well. On this occasion, he needn't worry. The party were more than happy to escape into the warmth of late afternoon.

Hands shot to foreheads to shield their eyes as they stepped into brightness after hours inside the manor. A line of coachmen in brown breeches and long brown frieze coats trimmed with extravagant gold brocade, aided passengers into their carriage and quickly set off in convoy.

By chance, Hank and Mae found themselves sharing a coach with the Reubens. Hank sat back and watched livestock graze in the fields whilst Mae engaged in chat-chit with the couple.

Hank learned the Reubens had family in New Port Ritchie, Florida. Clint's brother worked for the Port Charlotte Fire and Rescue Service, where Mae's cousin Alwyn spent some time.

Hank stifled a yawn. In the warmth of the sun, and with the gentle rocking motion of the carriage, he felt his eyelids droop.

His eyes opened as the carriage lurched and jolted. He looked around while he regained his senses, before smiling at Althea who sat opposite. She fixed him with her beady eyes and smirked back.

They were alone.

"Where are the others?" Hank asked.

"They wanted a look around the stables. Our driver will pick them up on our way back."

"When was this?"

"Five minutes ago, I guess."

Hank furrowed his brow. "Gee. Thought I'd just rested my eyes." Althea laughed, a curious high-pitched sound. "You've been out almost quarter of an hour now. Been a long day, has it?"

"It sure has. Enjoyed it, though."

He tried to get his bearings. The fields to the left were overgrown, no sign of cattle. A copse of saplings lay to his right; ahead, a brooding mass of woodland. "Where are we?"

"Doom Brae."

"I know that." He felt guilty for snapping at Althea. "I thought your stories of Salem were darn interesting, Althea," he offered by way of apology.

Althea sat with hands folded in her lap while she continued to fix him with her stare. "Thank you. But they weren't stories. It's fact."

Hank nodded. "I guess."

"No guessing about it." The coach lurched left and right as it left the track and crossed open grassland, but her head barely rocked. "It's all fact."

"Real sad. Twenty innocent people executed over a load of bull. Can't imagine it, can you?"

"I certainly can. But it wasn't a load of bull, Hank. Sure, some were innocent. But, not all."

Hank poo-pooed. "What? You trying to tell me they were witches? You need get a job here, Althea, if you think that."

"I didn't say they were all witches." Althea didn't blink; just penetrated Hank with her stare. "Only some of them were."

"You serious?" Hank's voice wavered. He put it down to the coach's motion but wasn't entirely sure. "You don't believe all that old smoky, do you?"

Althea's voice remained calm, quiet, and emotionless. "As a matter of fact, I do."

Hank spat out a laugh. "Witches and wizards? Gryffindor and Slytherin? Why would you think any of that was real?"

"Because I'm one of them."

Hank waited for the punchline. She remained silent. He waited for her odd high-pitched laugh. None came.

"Come on, lady. You're trying to tell me you're a witch? Get real, man."

Althea shrugged. "Whatever."

"I bet you a hundred bucks. Make it a thousand bucks. Put a spell on me."

Althea's laugh came this time. "Then, you'd better show me the colour of your money. I already have."

"What?"

"Cast a spell. Why do you think you fell asleep? Why do you think Clint and Mae explored the stables? Because I made 'em."

Hank shook his head. "Lady, I thought you were a bit strange, but never imagined you were this deluded. Why would you want to do that?"

Althea just smiled and stared right through him. "Driver. Stop the coach, please."

The coachman pulled back the reins. The horse gave a whinny and tossed his mane.

"Wait. What are you doing?"

"Get out the coach, Hank. We're going for a little stroll."

He didn't know why, but he clambered out. Althea followed. They stood at the fringe of Bluebell Wood.

Hank fidgeted with his hands. "Are we supposed to be here without a guide? I mean, isn't this the part where the T-Rex bursts outta the trees?"

"No need to worry, Hank. I don't communicate with the beasts. Not often, anyway. I can't move inanimate objects. And, I'm a bit old in the tooth for the seduction spell, don't you think?

"Then, you're not a witch. Come on, let's get back for Clint and Mae."

Althea was already inside the wood. Against his better judgement, he followed. He found her in a clearing beside an ancient, fallen tree. He watched Althea, her hands still clasped together, eyes closed.

Her nostrils flared as she breathed through her nose. She snapped her eyes open and spoke.

"You sense her too, don't you, Hank? That's why I brought you here. You can sense the Doom Brae witch."

He laughed, but it was a nervous one. "Yeah, I sure do. Gandalf's here, too. And look, there's Tinkerbell hiding in the tree."

"I know you feel her presence. You saw her here, in the woods. And in the courtyard café. The manor, too. You've sensed her in so many places." She fixed him with her icy stare. "Don't deny it, Hank. I know you have."

He hesitated. Shrugged. "Maybe. Say, does that make me Professor Dumbledore?"

Althea stood in the shadows, almost invisible. When she spoke, it was as if her voice came from a wizened oak. "Don't jest, Hank. I may not do all those things Wilberforce Long said of the Doom Brae witch, but 'witch' is a very broad term. Some of us are Sayers who foretell the future. Others are Seers. They see things from the past. Things they can't possibly know."

She fixed Hank with her cold eyes. "You're neither of those. So, what are you? A transmigrant?"

"Whoa. I'll have you know I'm a happily married man and…"

"A transmigrant is a soul shifter. He, or she, moves from host-to-host. Half-believers explain it away as reincarnation."

Hank shivered. Violently. He felt neither cold nor warm; just unnerved. He knew the woman from Salem was talking nonsense, yet she scared the hell out of him.

"Well, Althea. It's been real interesting talking to you, but can we go back to our carriage now? I'd like to finish this tour before the manor closes."

The mouse-like woman gave a half-smile and led him by the hand to the coach. As they clambered in, she spoke.

"You can deny it all you like. But, same as you, I feel things. Sense them. What I can't figure is why you can sense her. You haven't got other powers. You intrigue me, Hank; you really do. I've never come across a non-believer with a gift."

He opened his mouth to speak but, instead of words, all that came out was a yawn.

His eyelids fluttered. Mae sat alongside him, Clint and Althea opposite. All three were engaged in a discussion about the impact of cutbacks on Port Charlotte fire and rescue emergency services.

Try as he might, Hank couldn't harvest the vague recollections of a hazy dream.

✳✳

The slow, doom-laden beat of timpani heralded the convoy's return to the manor.

Bass rhythms grew louder while the company clambered from their carriages, until the battery became painful. They felt the beat throb and pulse within them as the volume increased even more.

Suddenly, they were plunged into silence.

Hank's ears sang as if he'd left a rock concert. He rubbed them until they reddened. Some of his fellow-tourists plugged fingers in their own. Others shook their heads to exorcise the ghostly echoes.

So pre-possessed were they that they failed to notice their three principal guides, Wilberforce Long, Erasmus Fairbody and Mary Batkins, emerge from the manor.

Long stepped forward. Hank saw Wilberforce's lips move but it was a while before his words seeped through the residual buzz in his ears.

"… conclude your visit," were the first words to register. "The dungeons await you. So, too, does none other than the Earl of Doom Brae himself, Mortimer Pendlebury. Ladies and gentlemen, I beseech you to show his lordship respect. The Earl does not suffer fools gladly. You will be wise not to incur his wrath."

Mary Batkins and the gamekeeper, Fairbody, moved to join Wilberforce Long.

The man in the stuffed crust pizza wig concluded his speech. "Ladies and Gentlemen, it has been our pleasure to escort you around our wondrous home. But now, we must leave you. The dungeon is not a place to trifle with. We dare not enter. Good luck, dear friends. I fear you shall need it."

The party filed past the three guides, the late-afternoon sun casting their long-legged spidery shadows over the Roman and Grecian guardians and across the manor walls.

Some of the trippers thrust coins and notes into the hands of the Georgian characters as they snaked past. Mae fumbled in her purse and handed the proceeds to Hank to pass on.

He shook Long by the hand. "Hope I didn't embarrass you earlier. About the wig, I mean."

Long smiled. "No sir. I've heard a lot worse dressed like this, I assure you."

Mary curtsied in appreciation as Hank handed over a few dollars.

"I'm pleased you managed to see all the tour," the Erasmus character said. "You had me worried at one point."

Hank laughed. "Gee, seems a long time ago now. Thanks for your concern. Honestly, I feel right at home here. This is my kinda' place," he said, taking a good look round. "And I'm swell. Real fine."

He watched the backs of Clint and Mae disappear down a flight of steps. Althea walked a few paces behind.

"At least, I think I am," Hank concluded.

He caught up with them outside a heavy wooden door adorned by rusted metal fittings. A tall haughty-looking man stood in front of the party. Two muscular men holding axes guarded the entrance.

None spoke.

When the last of the stragglers joined them at the foot of the stairs, the gentleman pushed at the door. It swung open with an exaggerated groan. The party of twelve stepped inside, into cold and darkness.

They jumped when the door clanged shut behind them, the noise deliberately amplified to provoke a startled action.

The drum beat began again, much softer and all the more menacing because of it. A single torch flared. The group blinked at the sudden light.

They were in a large cellar, dank and musty. Stone columns held up the ceiling. In contrast to the manor's opulence, there was nothing ornate about the pillars. No carvings, decorations. Just plain, bare stone.

The guards led them forward, into the middle of the chamber. More torches flared, flooding the space with light and shade.

A platform sat against one wall. Above it, three oil-paintings; the Earl of Doom Brae, Viscount Felix Pendlebury, and his younger brother, Lord Edwin. Left and right of the platform stood two suits of armour; a nod to the Earl's fascination with all things mediaeval.

A tall, high-backed chair, an ermine throw tossed over it, sat centre-stage. A smaller chair, less-intricately carved, remained empty next to it.

The party whispered to one another as they studied the artefacts. A burst of trumpets made them jump. A door opened. Two bewigged gentlemen emerged. One walked regally to the centre chair. The other hobbled behind, supported by crutches.

The men mounted the platform. Hank's eyes slid between the portraits on the wall and the seated men. The Earl and Viscount.

The Earl had a long, hawkish nose and looked like he sported eyebrow wigs. Hank nodded. The actor bore a passing resemblance to the gent depicted in the portrait. The man portraying the Viscount was less of a lookalike.

A huge dog, a Great Dane, perhaps, lumbered on stage and plonked itself at the Earl's feet with a groan.

Mae nudged Hank. "I feel I'm on a Game of Thrones set," she whispered.

Hank looked at the armour, the portraits and the hound. "I was thinking more Scooby-Doo."

"Silence!" the Earl of Doom Brae roared. "I shall not have peasants speak in my presence. My name is Mortimer Pendlebury. I am the third Earl of Doom Brae. This is my son and heir, Viscount Felix. My other son, Lord Edwin," he smirked, "Is indisposed."

Each member of the party sensed he was talking directly to them. "I gather you folk have born witness to my estate. What say you?"

Caught in the moment, lost in the virtual world of the setting, no-one spoke.

The Earl smiled. "Good. You remain silent. You learn your lessons well." The man stood. "My informants tell me you know of this place. So, it will come as no surprise to you to discover that I call this my playroom." He rubbed his hands together and laughed like a pantomime Abanazer.

"Come. Follow me. I wish to show you a few of my toys."

A trapdoor opened beneath the Earl and he slid from view in a puff of dry ice. The guards solemnly ushered the tour party down a short flight of steps until they stood at the lowest point of the manor. Mortimer Pendlebury emerged in front of a floor-to-ceiling red velvet curtain. "I take pleasure in the history of our land. But my pleasure comes not from our conquests, our heraldry, or our status in the world. It comes from our inventions and our ingenuity. It comes, my citizens, from things like this."

The velvet curtain swished aside. The audience drew breath. They now stood in an even larger antechamber. It held an array of equipment the like of which they'd never before seen.

Clint sidled up to Hank. "No wonder they don't let kids see this place. It gives me the creeps."

Hank was about to speak when he observed the Earl's eyes upon him. He contented himself with a nod.

Mortimer Pendlebury walked the length of the dungeon. In a far corner, a see-saw like object towered above them all. A mannequin, trussed like a chicken, sat upside down on a wooden chair.

The actor playing the role of Pendlebury tenderly ran a finger over a wooden support. "This is my favourite toy. Pray, do your eyes recognise it?"

No-one spoke.

"You have permission. You may speak when I address you."

Althea Reubens broke the silence. "It's a ducking stool."

The Earl applauded; a slow clap which echoed in the stone cellar. "Very well done, my friend. You observe well. Tell me, dear, what be it used for?"

"The test. It's used to determine the guilt or innocence of a witch." Althea fixed the Earl with her bird-like stare. "Of course, it doesn't work."

Clint groaned. He knew this was a charade, yet the act was so mesmeric he felt sure Althea had sealed her fate.

"Oh, but it does work, my dear. I assure you."

"Not every time."

Despite everything, Clint grabbed Althea by the arm. Dragged him to her.

"Your man is very wise, madam. He knows when you should hush. You are fortunate the stool is already occupied, or I would have you sit upon it. But, as you see, occupied it is. This is the very stool", the word 'REPLICA' flashed onto the wall, prompting laughter, "On which the guilt of the Doom Brae Witch herself was proven. And here she is – Miss Louisa Goodchild."

The stool lowered into a well built into the floor. An effect threw up a swell of water as the Louisa mannequin disappeared from view.

The Earl took a dozen paces to his left. The guards ensured the party followed his every move. A table with attachments and bindings, pulleys and rollers, lay in front of Mortimer. In the cool of the chamber, an audience member at the front of the group shivered. He yawned involuntary as his body craved extra oxygen to warm him.

The gesture didn't go unnoticed by the Earl. He walked up close to the man, so close their noses touched. "Do I bore you?"

The man shook his head and shivered once more.

"You deny it. I see. Then, I must know the truth. Guards, take him."

Hank spoke through gritted teeth. "This guy plays a real good part, Mae."

His wife nodded. She, too, wasn't prepared to be caught speaking out of turn.

The guards feigned brutality as they led the man to the table and laid him upon it. When the tethers were fastened, they stepped aside for Mortimer Pendlebury.

"This, of course, is not a British invention. It was first used by Emperor Nero. But we became masters in its use. This, my friends, is the infamous rack."

The Earl moved to one end of the bench and grasped a handle. He wrenched it towards him. The machinery creaked and groaned. A recorded scream shrieked from beneath the table.

The audience laughed, but the sniggers stopped. Abruptly. The man really was being stretched. His fingers inched towards the edge of the table. The screams grew louder.

Hank watched, open-mouthed. He snapped his fingers. "I got it, Mae. I know how it works. He's not being stretched. The table's being made shorter. How cool does it look, though?"

Mortimer Pendlebury left the rack, tutting as he did so. He confronted Hank. "Well, well, well. I can't decide if you are six-bottled or a nincompoop. Either way, you shall pay for your insolence." The Earl stage-whispered to the tourists. "Methinks I have just found my next exhibit."

Hank's face creased in smiles. "Yes! Hey, Mae, hold this for me, will you?" He passed her the camera. "Make sure you get some good shots, yeah? Now, where do you want me, guys?"

The guards stepped forward. Took an arm each and frog-marched Hank to a Russian Doll-like creation. Mae fiddled with the camera and hoped she was getting the shots Hank wanted.

The guards opened the door. The inner door was lined with sharpened nails, knifes and blades. They pointed in every direction.

The Earl of Doom Brae addressed the audience in sinister tones. "The time is late. My table shall soon be set, and I need garner an appetite for it. This, my good friends, is the last of my playthings. I grant you leave to speak of it without impunity."

A young woman in skinny jeans and cropped T-shirt raised a hand. "Speak, girl."

She said nothing. Instead, she stood in front of the Earl and tugged at her T-shirt. The Earl laughed. The girl turned to face the audience.

The T-shirt bore the name of a rock group.

Iron Maiden.

The party nodded, familiar with the device.

"It is," Mortimer Pendlebury concurred. "And we have an occupant. Our friend – our RUDE friend – is about to experience it. Note there can be no escape for the blackguard. The blades point every which way. Once the door closes, his end is assured."

Hank couldn't wait to step into the sarcophagus, but he hesitated. "Hey, wait. Can I have a photograph? Mae, come here. Clint," he signalled the man forward. "C'mon Althea." He looked around. "Where's Althea?" He thought he saw her leave the cellar. "Oh, never mind. Let's get the show on the road. Smile, peeps."

The character playing the Earl stepped in, aware the coaches waited outside, engines running. "We shall have no such wizardry here. Guards? The maiden awaits."

Hank felt the Earl's men push him inside. One leant close to him. "Don't worry, sir. Look." The actor pressed the palm of his hand against a patch of nails. They immediately retracted into the shell of the maiden. He moved his hand higher. Did the same thing. "And again, see?"

Hank winked at him. "Thanks, but I already guessed the trick."

The guards stepped aside. The Earl walked to the casket. Laid a hand against it. "Goodbye, my friend," he smiled.

He gave the door a shove. It swung shut, slowly. Mae clicked away, capturing Hank's smiling face.

The device clicked shut with a satisfying thunk. There were no phony screams, no amplified music, nothing. Nothing except a pool of blood flowing from the base of the casket.

The lights came on. The party applauded and bent to gather their belongings, ready to leave.

They saw the Earl and his men exchange glances. One of the guards ran a finger through the fake blood. Held it to his lips. Only when he staggered back, and the other actors dashed towards the cabinet did they begin to suspect something was wrong.

Mae missed the signs. She was engrossed in getting the best shots for Hank. She hoped he'd be proud. She was still snapping away when the sarcophagus door swung open.

Mae stopped clicking.

Hank was impaled to the inner door, run through by dozens of sharpened spikes.

The onlookers screamed, wept, cried out.

Hank hadn't cried out. He couldn't.

The first spike penetrated his throat and rendered him silent.

**

A shroud of silence blanketed the darkened room. Tawdry gifts and tat hid in alcoves, their crassness discretely veiled from view.

Near the gift shop exit door, four chairs, arranged in a semi-circle, sat beneath a single dimmed uplighter. Two were occupied: one by a uniformed policewoman, the other by Hank's wife.

Hank's widow.

A handkerchief lay crumpled in Mae's lap. The WPC held the distraught woman's hand while a medic in green coveralls crouched in front of Mae. She handed her a flimsy plastic cup and a handful of sedatives. Once she was sure Mae had swallowed them, the medic moved to one side.

A door creaked open in the distance. A blast of sound entered the room, alien and discordant. DI Cotton closed the door behind him and silence returned, save for Mae's snuffles and the squeak of Cotton's shoes.

He took a seat alongside Mae. "How are we now?" He cringed at his words. He hated this part of the job. Wasn't comfortable with the grieving relative thing. Although he directed his words at Mae, he looked at the WPC.

Sandra Senior patted the woman's hand and rolled her eyes. Cotton shrugged his shoulders; a 'what am I supposed to say' gesture.

"I'm… I don't know what I am." Mae raised the handkerchief and blew her nose.

Cotton left his seat and squatted in front of her, knees cracking like popping candy. He raised the woman's chin with the tips of his fingers and looked into bleary eyes. "I'm truly sorry for your loss."

He tilted his head, a signal for Senior to follow him to the far side of the room. As she did so, the medic slipped into the vacated seat.

The detective and Sandra walked through the gift-shop, his shoes squeaking like a church mouse, where they waited outside the door which signified the dungeon's exit.

"We're just about done here," DI Cotton said to her. "Witness statements taken. All give a consistent story. Forensics checked the equipment in there. It's all working as it should."

"So, we're no further forward? There's no gadgetry involved? No-one meant to trigger something but didn't, either deliberately or by accident?"

Cotton gave Sandra a look. "Senior, I do believe you're questioning my competence."

"No, sir. Sorry, sir…"

"Relax, Sandra. I'm not being serious. No, the spikes are inlaid on a series of panels. They're designed to automatically retract under pressure. They've always done it before – thankfully – and they're doing it again now. Every time. They just didn't work when it mattered."

They heard laughter from inside the dungeon. Cotton stuck his head around the door. "Shut up, you lot. We've got a widow in here. I don't think she'll find much to laugh at, do you?"

Cotton and Senior looked towards Mae. She hadn't heard anything. She was lost in her own world.

"And before you ask," he continued to Senior, "Harris has run checks on all staff working here. Nothing on any of them. No links to the victim. Mo Khalif's done the belt-and-braces check on the tour party. He's drawn a blank, too."

Sandra sighed. "Where do we go from here, sir?"

"We go home, that's where. There's no crime here. It was an accident, that's all. A mysterious one, but an accident all-the-same. It's for the Health and Safety Executive to solve the mystery. I'll wait for the Family Liaison crew to arrive but you're free to go, Sandra."

The door behind Mae and the medic opened. The cool of night entered alongside a woman wearing a leather jacket, silk-scarf and mid-length skirt. The woman shook Mae's hand, held it for a few moments, and took a seat next to her.

"Speak of the devil," the DI said. "I need a word with the wife before the FLO takes over. You get yourself home. It's late. I'll be right after you."

Cotton took a deep breath and headed for Mae and the FLO. He shared a grim smile with the Liaison Officer. He knew her. She'd make sure the widow got whatever help she needed. Still, he knew he was compelled to offer more condolences.

Cotton knelt again, not too close, not too far, from the tearful Mae.

"I have to go now. This has been a terrible day for you. It'll be no consolation for you, but I'm satisfied this has been a dreadful accident. There's no more for me to do here. I'll leave you with Teresa. She'll support you in any way she can, right up until the time you're ready to fly home."

Mae nodded. "Thank you, officer. You've been very kind."

Cotton felt a knot tighten in his throat. He coughed before continuing.

"Now, I know you've only just met Teresa so, before I go, are you sure there's no-one I can get to help you; anyone back home you want me to inform?"

The woman released a fresh flood of tears. Cotton rubbed the stubble on his chin. He wished he'd never spoken.

Mae shook her head. "No. There's no-one. Absolutely no-one. We're both only children of only children, Hank and me. Our parents are long gone. No brothers. Sisters. Aunts or Uncles, nieces or nephews."

She sat silent for a moment as the realisation struck her. "It's the end of a generation."

Cotton stood. Shook Mae by the hand. He felt more doleful than usual. Her words – the end of a generation – hit him hard.

The DI realised he'd witnessed not only the end of a life, but the end of a family line.

Cotton stepped outside into darkness, case file tucked under his arm. The cover contained only the most basic information; date and location.

And the name of the victim.

Hank Pendlebury.

**

DI Cotton removed the file from beneath his arm. He stood in night air that was warm, silent and peaceful. The rhythmic pulse of blue light from the vehicles guarding Doom Brae Manor's drive cast a sub-aquatic glow across the estate.

Cotton sauntered across to the patrolmen. After a quick exchange, the lights were extinguished. One car crunched away from the manor towards the highway. The other pulled in front of the house, waiting for Mae Pendlebury.

A single coach stood in the moonlight. Cotton made his way to it, clambered up the steps, and spoke to its occupants.

"I've spoken to most of you already, but for those I haven't met personally I am DI Cotton of Southern Borders police. I'd like to thank you for your co-operation today. I appreciate it's been a long and difficult day for you. I've no wish to delay you any longer than necessary, so I'm pleased to say you're free to go now. Thanks again, folks. Driver, it's all yours."

Cotton stepped from the coach. It spluttered to life, sides shuddering like the awakening of a beast. From outside, Cotton heard the driver speak into the microphone, his tone subdued.

"Because there's no public transport out here this late, I've agreed to drop off some of the manor staff in town. I'm sure you'll appreciate they've had a rough day, too, and they also had to stay behind to talk to the police. I promise I'll get you back to your hotel as soon as I can."

The driver took silence as approval. He released the handbrake and pulled away into the night.

The interior of the coach remained ghostly quiet. No-one spoke. Some of the occupants looked down at the floor. A couple sent text messages to worried relatives. Many more looked out the window, seeing only their haggard reflections gaze back at them in the nocturnal black mirror of night.

A woman dressed in maid's costume yawned. Alongside her, a man dressed as a farm hand wondered how long it would be before the manor opened for business again.

Clint and Althea Reubens had taken it worse than most. Clint sat upright, pale, drawn and red-eyed. Althea sat still as stone, hands clasped in her lap, trying to remain stoic.

The coach came to a halt at the junction with the highway. The click-click of its indicators sounded like a mantel clock counting out time. Subconsciously, a woman checked her watch.

Ten minutes to midnight.

Wilberforce Long glanced out the window. He allowed himself a melancholic smile at what he saw. For the first time, he could see what the man meant. Hank had been right. His wig did look like a stuffed crust pizza slice. Long removed it and bounced it on his lap.

Behind him, an elderly traveller rummaged in his pocket for a mint. He watched the reflection of his friend sat next to him as he donned a pair of glasses and opened the glossy Doom Brae Manor brochure.

Further back, the final Georgian couple sat in silence, hand-in-hand. The woman looked towards the man for support and comfort. He tried to reassure her with his eyes.

The girl turned back to the window. Her reflection showed a serene smile below ice-blue eyes and long, flaxen hair. At least, that's what it would have displayed. But the window revealed no reflection.

There wasn't one.

Louisa Goodchild laid her head on Edwin's shoulder and fell into a peaceful slumber.

****

Author's note:

This is a work of fiction. Any similarity to any person, living or dead, or to any events, other than those quoted as historical fact, are purely coincidental.

Thank you for taking the time to read *The Doom Brae Witch* – it means a lot to me.

If you did enjoy it, it'd be great if you could keep an eye out for my next work, which will be available soon. Oh, and please, PLEASE leave a review on Amazon so I get your feedback.

You can follow me on:

Twitter - @seewhy59

Facebook - @colin.youngman.author

Thanks again.

Colin

About the author:

Colin had his first written work published at the age of 9 when a contribution to children's comic *Sparky* brought him the rich rewards of a 10/- Postal Order and a transistor radio.

He was smitten by the writing bug and has gone on to have his work feature in publications for young adults, sports magazines, national newspapers and travel guides before he moved to his first love: fiction.

Colin previously worked as a senior executive in the public sector. He lives in Northumberland, north-east England, and is an avid supporter of Newcastle United (don't laugh), a keen follower of Durham County Cricket Club and has a family interest in the City of Newcastle Gymnastics Academy.

Coming Next

from

Colin Youngman:

DEAD Heat

The Conclusion to the DEAD Trilogy

Printed in Great Britain
by Amazon

15974529R00109